QUENTIN & Toi

A Legendary Hood Tale

2

A NOVEL BY
MOLLYSHA JOHNSON

© 2019 Royalty Publishing House

Published by Royalty Publishing House
www.royaltypublishinghouse.com

ALL RIGHTS RESERVED
Any unauthorized reprint or use of the material is prohibited. No part of this book may be reproduced or transmitted in any form or by any means, electronic or mechanical, including photocopying, recording, or by any information storage without express permission by the author or publisher. This is an original work of fiction. Names, characters, places and incidents are either products of the author's imagination or are used fictitiously and any resemblance to actual persons, living or dead, is entirely coincidental.
Contains explicit language & adult themes suitable for ages 16+ only.

Royalty Publishing House is now accepting manuscripts from aspiring or experienced urban romance authors!

WHAT MAY PLACE YOU ABOVE THE REST:

Heroes who are the ultimate book bae: strong-willed, maybe a little rough around the edges but willing to risk it all for the woman he loves.

Heroines who are the ultimate match: the girl next door type, not perfect - has her faults but is still a decent person. One who is willing to risk it all for the man she loves.

The rest is up to you! Just be creative, think out of the box, keep it sexy and intriguing!

If you'd like to join the Royal family, send us the first 15K words (60 pages) of your completed manuscript to submissions@royaltypublishing-house.com

SYNOPSIS

After finding out Toi & Mickey's true occupations Legend and Tone have to figure out if they can get past the lifestyle choices they don't approve of. In the midst, destroyed friendships, old family connections and petty rivalries set out to end any chance these couples have to reconcile.

NOTE FROM THE AUTHOR

To everybody that supported my first series *Let a Real Boss Treat You Right*, thank you I appreciate it. I hope you guys continue to enjoy and support me with my future projects. If you have any questions or concerns pertaining to me, feel free to hit me up on social media.

QUENTIN "LEGEND" SANTANA

"You know you were fucked up for missing her grandmother's funeral," Tone shook his head at me as he drove.

"That shit wasn't on purpose. The service started at 9, I had my shit set for 6 so I could get up, get dressed, pick up some breakfast, then take it to them. I wanted to be there when she walked in the church; I knew she was going to need that support. My shit didn't go off; I didn't wake up until damn near noon."

"How the fuck did that happen?"

"Isyss' stupid ass did it. I don't know how that sneaky bitch broke into my damn phone but she turned my shit off."

"Nigga, why was she even around you? The fuck was you doing?"

"I was at my mother's house, and she came to pick Diamond up. I dozed off while she was helping baby girl get her stuff together and she took that as a fuckin' opportunity. Mia must've told her I was going because I was talking to my mother about it and the bitch was in the room."

"Your sister forever on that bullshit."

"I know," I shook my head.

I know it's fucked up to say, but I'm really at the point where I'm about to hate my own baby sister. Since she was little she's made it a point to be up in my shit. I know siblings are supposed to meddle or whatever, but Mia takes that shit to the next level. She's spoiled, sneaky, and selfish.

Growing up without our father around made her possessive over every man in her life. When it comes to my uncle she can only do so much, but me? If she sees a bitch getting too close, she figures out a way to fuck it up.

The only reason she sticks close to Isyss is because she can easily get her dumb ass to do whatever. Like going in my damn phone and fucking with my alarm. That had Mia all over it. She's not dumb enough to do it herself, so she uses somebody else to do her dirty work; that dummy is Isyss.

This shit with Toi has her ten times worse because of the past they have. She's jealous of the girl and now she's fucking up our shit.

"So what are you going to do? Did you tell her what happened?"

"With the space we're in, I am not about to tell her Isyss was fuckin' with my phone. I'll let her calm down some. It doesn't even matter right now, she aint even trying to fuck with me."

"Are you really taking yourself away from her spa?"

"I'm not tied into shit. Yeah, I wrote the checks, but everything is in her name. I have no say so in it at all, well not enough to do something. I'm not even worried about that, I knew what it was when I bought it for her."

As far as Toi and anybody else knew, I was a silent partner in her spa but I'm really not. I never had any intentions on pocketing money from her business; it was always going to be 100% hers. I didn't bother telling her because I didn't see the point, and I still don't.

Whether I'm with Toi or not, I know she's a smart girl and destined to be great. I'm not about to fuck her shit up when she's working her ass off to get it done. Just to make sure she didn't have any issues, I paid the contractors off. I don't know how much she has in her savings account, and I don't care, but I wanted to make sure she wouldn't have any issues with the building while taking care of her family.

"I think you need to try and work that shit out once she calms down. Toi is a good girl; she was just hustling for her family. You should respect that shit, especially knowing she was financially responsible for everybody in that house," Tone shrugged.

"I know that, and honestly I wasn't even mad about what she used to do. It was the thought of her still doing it or doing it to me that pissed me off. With you telling me Mickey was with that nigga I figured she knew about it." The whole situation with Toi and what she used to do had my mind fucked up for a few days.

When Tone told me about Mickey robbing Tip, my first thought was Toi had to know something and she was probably there. I didn't know what she and Mickey were up to as far as getting money was concerned, but I came to the conclusion that whatever it was, they were doing it together. I instantly started to get paranoid; overthinking shit. Wondering *is this bitch trying to set me up?* So, I went to confront her about it.

That was a bad idea because shit got all fucked up. I went over there on some angry shit, when I should've sat the fuck down and thought about it. I never gave her the opportunity to explain the situation, I just went straight at her neck. Toi aint no punk, so of course it didn't go over well, and missing her grandmother's funeral just fucked shit up even more.

"I know how you feel nigga, trust me."

"What's the deal with you and Mickey now anyway?" Here he was talking about me and Toi but I don't think he's forgiving Mick any time soon.

"I don't trust shorty, and I'm not saying I think she's going to try me or some shit. I just don't trust what comes out her mouth now. She lies too damn good and I don't fuck with that shit, especially when I'm not doing it to her."

"So you think she's going to keep doing it and not tell you?"

"Basically, and I don't have time for that sneaky shit. You know how close to these niggas she has to be to take the shit she gets? Before he got is shit blown off Tip let it slip that she got away with a couple hundred thousand in jewelry and she got cash too."

"Damn, well she really on her shit huh?" I laughed. I mean, the job aint nothing to brag about but shorty good at it if she's getting niggas like that.

"Man that's not the point," he shook his head.

"Look I was pissed about that shit too and I get why you're mad. As far as I'm concerned she was borderline cheating on yo ass but I think you need to ask yourself a few questions."

"Questions like what?"

"Do you think she fucked that nigga? Why she needed that much money and are you willing to just walk away from her? Mickey is a lot to handle but it's not like she's a fucked up person. Didn't you tell me, her mother is always on her back about money."

"Yeah but she could've just came to me for that shit."

"Mickey wasn't about to come to you for no damn money," I had to laugh at that thought. Mickey is too heavy on her independent women shit to come to this nigga and ask for money. Even I knew she wasn't about to do that shit and she aint even my girl.

"She gotta get over that prideful shit and start asking for help if she needs it. I'm not beat for the bullshit so it's whatever. You spoke to Yung?" Tone asked, changing the subject.

"Yeah, nigga got baby number two on the way."

"It's too bad Taj aint fuckin' with him like that. I told that nigga he was a dummy for even fucking that up."

"I'm not surprised he fucked it up, he's 21 and stupid. I'm just mad it was with KeKe's bird ass. Out of all the bitches in the world, he runs to that one." Yung is like a little brother to me but damnit if the nigga don't live up to his name.

He's young minded as hell, and it's not really difficult to understand. He's still in his early twenties with money pouring in and a lot of eyes on him. I just think that fucking with KeKe again was dumb. She's the definition of a bird. He had to know she was going to do some bird shit like telling his girl he was fucking around. I know he regrets that shit; he lost his girl and almost lost his life.

"This relationship shit is a fuckin' headache man," Tone shook his head. "I'm cool on that shit for now. I'm keeping my mind on the business."

"Yeah alright, we'll see." Tone could talk all the shit he wants to but I know him and I know for a fact he's going to start missing Mickey pretty soon. He'll be right back with her at some point; I'm just waiting to see the shit for myself.

ANTONIO "TONE" MONTEGA

"Aye ma, what I tell you about leaving the door unlocked?" I shouted for my mother when I walked in her house. "Where you at?"

"I'm in the living room, quit screaming!" I heard her shout back. I went into the living room where she was sitting on the couch watching television.

"What's up ma?" I greeted her when I sat down next to her. She kissed my cheek and smiled earning a smile right back.

Like my dad, my mother is full blooded Dominican but because of their complexions people didn't realize they were more than just black until they went bilingual on your ass. With a clear Mahogany complexion, long black hair, and a picture-perfect smile, a lot of people often thought she was my older sister instead of my mother.

"Nothing, I was supposed to go out with your aunt but she wanted to switch up plans at the last minute. What are you doing here? You're not one for pop ups."

"I just came to check you out. Where's pops?"

"He's down in that damn basement as usual. I don't know why I agreed to him having his own room, he's always down there."

"Would you rather him being on your ass all the time?"

"No but that's not the point," she said and I laughed.

"Yeah alright ma," I stood up. "I'm about to go talk to pops real quick," I let her know before I left the room and went downstairs.

"I thought I heard your voice upstairs," my father said once I hit the bottom step. He stood up from his chair and we hugged briefly. Looking at my pops was like looking at an older version of my-self. He was basically a clone of me with some grey hairs thrown in the mix.

"What you down here doing? Ma doesn't like this room too much."

"Your mother doesn't like anything, I'm used to it. What's up with you? You don't make pop-ups over here, what's on your mind?"

I wanted to say the same thing I told my mother but he was going to be able to tell my ass is lying. I might as well tell him what's bothering me. Shit, he might end up giving me some good advice.

"Me and Mickey broke up," I told him. He and my mother haven't met Mickey yet but I damn sure talk about her enough to them.

"Damn before we could even meet her ass? What happened?"

"She was lying to me and you know I don't like that shit."

"Lying about what?"

"How she get her money. Come to find out, she was out here robbing niggas."

"What you mean robbing?"

"Robbing niggas pops. Getting close to the muthafuckas then hit their shit when they don't expect it. She did it to somebody I knew and he came at her in the club. We get back to the crib and she told me what it was. The crazy thing is I'm not even mad at what she did. I'm mad that she was still doing it while we were together and she lied about it."

"Was she sleeping with them?"

"She said she wasn't. I believe her as far as that, she aint about to lie on her pussy but I still can't trust her ass."

"Well if you can't trust her you did the right thing by letting her go. Not just for you but for her too. Did you talk to her about why she does that stealing shit and what can happen if she runs into the wrong nigga?"

"All she said was she needed the money. I don't doubt that she did but she could've come to me for that shit."

"That would make sense if she was the type of woman to openly take help from somebody. From what you told me about her, she's stubborn, independent, and hard headed. Do you really think she would come to you about some money?"

"I get what you're saying but still."

Knowing Mickey the way I do, I know she's not about to come and ask me for money. She doesn't even like taking money from me when I offer it to her ass. She's head strong and she doesn't trust men but God damn. I would rather her just say that then go and lie in my face about some bullshit.

Lying is the ultimate deal breaker for me. I'm a patient nigga, I can look past a lot of things but lying isn't one of them. Especially if you're lying about something that could easily be worked out.

"Still what? I'm not saying let whatever she did slide. If you don't trust her it wouldn't be fair to neither one of you to be with her. But I know you care about her because she's all you talk about when you come here."

"What's your point pops?"

"My point is you need to figure out if what she did is deep enough to walk away. So she did some bullshit, everybody does once in a while. I don't think it's a big deal. I robbed a few niggas in my day."

"So of course you cool with it," I chuckled. Pops is crazy.

"I'm just saying I've heard you go on and on about this girl. You haven't been this stuck on somebody since that last girl."

"I know, and they both lied to me."

"One doesn't really compare to the other. I don't think you need to let her go so quick. Besides that one fuck up, you describe her as a good woman."

"She is a good woman.'

"So what the hell is the problem?"

"The problem is I don't trust her pops. I'm not about to commit to somebody I don't trust. I won't say we'll never be together again but I'm not fucking with shorty like that right now. I don't think I'll ever fuck with her unless she makes some serious changes."

"Well if you want to let a good woman go, then fine go ahead and do that. Don't com crying to me if she moves on to the next nigga."

I sat back shaking my head. Of course he would be on the opposite end of the spectrum. He usually is. I can count on my hands how many times I've went to my dad about something and he actually told me I was right.

* * *

"Hey Tone," a group of chicks shouted me out when I walked into Foot Locker. I threw them a head nod then went to the wall of sneakers. I had no idea what I wanted but I felt like spending money so I came in here.

"Antonio Montega?" Hearing my government name being said on the side of me, I turned around coming face to face with someone I never thought I would see again.

"Cassie?" With a smooth almond complexion, slender but slightly curvy body, long jet black hair and green chinky eyes, Cassie looked just as good as she did years ago. As good as she looked I wasn't happy or excited to see her ass.

"Yeah, it's me. Wow, you really grew up huh?" she chuckled showing off that perfect smile. "The last time I saw you, you were long and bony."

"That's what happens when people grow up."

"You're right. I've heard good things about you. I'm working at medical center; I finally got my nursing degree."

"Word? That's what's up. I know you always wanted to do that shit. I wish I could say I'm proud of you but I'm not. I really don't even want you talking to me right now."

"Come on it's been too long. I haven't seen you since-"

"Since I found out you lied saying you had a miscarriage when you really aborted my baby?" I cut her off then let out a bitter chuckle.

"Really Tone? After five years you're still mad at my ass?"

"Yup so you need to get the fuck back.'

"You could at least let me explain myself. You never let me say anything; all you did was go off."

"There was nothing for you to explain shorty. I was a good man to you, I did everything for you. You killed my seed then lied about it, bitch fuck you. You need to be on your knees thanking God your stupid ass is still breathing."

At that point I was over being in the mall period so I just left while she stood there looking stupid.

Cassie was my first love. We met freshmen year in high school and we dated until we were 25 years old. As far as I was concerned Cassie was going to be my wife. I loved her with everything in me. She was there before I had anything and I thought we had the perfect relationship.

When she told me she was pregnant I was ecstatic. We were about to have a baby and shit was going to be perfect, but I was wrong. Two months into her pregnancy Cassie had me thinking she had a miscarriage. I was sympathizing with this bitch, held her while she cried for our baby but then I found a bottle of pills in her bathroom.

I didn't know what the fuck Misoprostal was so I took pills to my doctor so he could tell me. Nothing he explained stuck in my brain until I heard him say it could cause a miscarriage. I thought I was about to fall the fuck out when he said that.

Apparently misoprostal is used by people who have ulcers. I know for a fact Cassie never had that problem so there was no logical reason to have those pills.

It took me all of 30 seconds to figure out what was going on. She took the pills on purpose and faked a miscarriage for sympathy. I don't give a fuck about her reasoning, her excuses or anything else. If she didn't want a kid, she could've talked to me like an adult instead of doing some grimy shit.

By the end of the night I had all her shit out of the apartment we lived in and I had the locks changed. The whole relationship was dead after that. I wanted to kill her ass but I let her live just because I didn't want her mother going through that. It isn't Ms.Tangie's fault her daughter is a sneaky, conniving bitch.

It's been five years since I've seen or spoken to Cassie and time is only going to keep passing by. I don't want anything to do with that bitch. If she loves her life she'll stay the fuck away from me.

LA'TOIA "TOI" HENDERSON

I sat in my bedroom at my grandmother's house going through email after email on my lap top. Besides going out to my spa location and anywhere else that involves business, I haven't left my house. Since my grandmother's funeral a few weeks ago I've been focused on business, family and nothing else.

My mother was still having a hard time and so were the twins. I used to tell them all the time they need to get their shit together when it came to our grandmother. Now, they understand what I meant. They didn't fully appreciate her while she was here and now that she's gone they feel like shit.

I haven't even been out with Mickey and Taj which I feel a little bad about. Taj is pregnant, Mickey is acting like she's okay but I know she's upset about her break up with Tone. Shit, we haven't even had the chance to discuss the fact that we're all broken up at this point.

It's crazy how shit works. We were all together and happy two months ago and now everything is all fucked up.

When I left Quentin's house the night he came in there beastin' I didn't think it would really be over. I felt like once he calmed down, used his brain and really thought about it he would make shit right. To me it wasn't even that deep.

We had a good night until the nigga Mickey robbed recognized her and they ended up in a damn fight. Mickey spilled the beans about her stealing from a few niggas to Tone and he told Que. That's when he decided to come to the condo he let me move into going off on me about what happened.

Que had to come to his own conclusion that I was involved because Mickey and Tone never mentioned my name, he just assumed. Instead of being a grown ass man and talking to his woman like he had sense, he went off. I was all types of bitches, and probably selling my pussy according to him.

Then he kicked me out of his place because I'm apparently trying to steal from him too. This man spent millions of dollars on a business for me and has basically been taking care of me since I met him. He knows everything about me, why would I steal from him? Que wasn't using his head he was reacting off pure emotion.

When my grandmother died I expected him to be there despite how he felt about that argument. I know he knew what happened because Tone called me to give his condolences. Tone tells Que everything so there was no way he didn't let that man know about her death.

Not coming to her funeral really fucked me up and put him on my shit list. If you know me you know my grandmother was my world. Everything I am is because of what she instilled in me. I loved both my grandparents and my pop pop was a great man and father figure but my grandmother was my heart.

Quentin knows this; he knows that it would've meant everything to have him there. Even if it wasn't to comfort me and just so he could pay his respects to someone he claimed he cared about, I would've respected him. That would've meant despite how angry he gets at me he still has my back and cares.

Instead he comes to my house after everything is done with some flowers and a weak ass apology. I don't know if he thought I was going to appreciate it but it actually pissed me off. I knew from there we wouldn't be getting back together so easily, if it all.

He kicked me out of his apartment after coming at my neck crazy all because he found out some old shit. Then he didn't even show up for me when I need all the support I could get. I can't respect a nigga like that, especially when he's far from perfect himself.

Besides the drama with him I was still trying to deal with my own emotions. My grandmother dying came out of nowhere. I was with her the night before and as far as I could see, she was fine.

Come to find out she was having heart problems but she never said anything. She kept that shit to herself and I was pissed at her for it a little bit. I understand she probably didn't want to scare us or maybe she was scared herself but I wish she would've said something. That would've been better than just having her here one minute and gone the next.

Now that she's gone I feel like my responsibilities leveled up times 100. I was already carrying the weight financially, now I have two teenage girls to look after. Since I was my grandmother's beneficiary the house belongs to me, and I have full custody of Jayla and Kayla. Thankfully I don't have to chase behind them since they aren't babies but they're some slick heifers so I have to keep an eye on them.

As far as business goes, I have everything moving on my spa. The remodeling is coming along great, the licensing and permits are about to come in so now I have to focus on my branding. When I cut off everything with Que, that meant I cut off his people too. Now, I know longer have Dutch helping me. She was getting me in contact with certain people but I wanted no parts of Legend Santana so she had to go.

I'm not broke by any means but I didn't have the money to hire somebody to help me so I had to do everything by myself. It's harder than I thought it would be but I'm getting it done. My spa will be up and running in a few months and I'm determined to make this business a success.

'Come in," I called out when I heard a knock on my door. When it opened my mother came in with a small smile. "Hey ma, what's up?" I looked up from my lap top.

"Hey, I'm just coming to check on you. I'm cooking are you hungry? You haven't been eating like you should be."

"Ma I eat, trust me," I let her know. If anything I eat too damn much. Uber Eats and Grub Hub have been my best friends these last few weeks.

"Not that stuff you keep ordering, I mean real food. You need to eat something with some substance."

"Pizza and hot wings have substance and I always get broccoli from the Chinese restaurant."

"You trying to be funny, haha that was hilarious. Listen, I'm cooking and when I'm done you're going to come downstairs and eat with us. I'll come up here and pull you out this room so don't try it."

"Fine ma," I shook my head. She could try to come up here if she wants to. She's going to be mad when she finds the door locked.

"Mhm, get up and come to the kitchen now. I don't trust you. You're going to lock the damn door or something," she closed my laptop then stood there with her hands on her hips.

"Really ma?" I had to laugh because she was right. I had every intention on locking her ass out my room.

"Yes really, come on. You need to come on and snap out of this funk. I thought I was doing bad, but you got me beat."

"I'm fine, I'm just trying to work and you're stopping that."

"Well take a break and come help me cook. Let's go, you know I won't leave you alone until you do."

"Okay," I said while running my hands through my hair. "I'll be down in a minute ma."

"Alright; don't play with me Toi. Come downstairs and don't lock this door."

"I'm not, I'll come down I promise."

"Okay," she gave me a side eye then walked out my room. I opened my laptop and finished the email then went down to the kitchen.

"I'm here. What do you want me to do?"

"Peel those potatoes for me," my mother said while pointing to the big bowl of large potatoes.

I grabbed a knife then took a seat at the table and got to work.

"So Toi," my mother started. "How have you been doing?"

"I'm fine," I quickly answered.

"That was a lie if I ever heard one," ma said then turned to face me. "Toi I'm worried about you."

"Why?"

"You're walking around here like a zombie. All you do is work and stay locked up in that room. That is not like you."

"Ma I'm fine I just have a lot going on. Going out somewhere doesn't do anything for me. I have too much to do."

"Toi you can work and have a social life, you've done it before. I know you're hurting because of mama's death and breaking up with Quentin didn't help." She came over and gently grabbed my chin making me look up at her. "Stop playing tough girl and be in your feelings every once in a while. Working over your hurt isn't going to make it go away."

I moved my head from her hand letting out a sigh. "Ma I am fine. Yes I'm hurt about grandma and Que but I can't focus on that. What do you want me to do, go crying every five minutes?"

"If that's what it takes for you to relieve yourself of that weight you're carrying on your shoulders. If I'm an addition to whatever stress you're harboring I'm sorry. I am your mother; I should've been the one comforting you. Instead I had you worrying about me and the double mint twins."

"It's okay."

"No it's not. Toi you've had to take care of too many people at too young of an age. I want you to take some time for you, even outside of your spa."

"What do you suggest I do ma? I can't be away from here too long because those two heifers upstairs will think they can do whatever they want and I'm not for that."

"I have Kayla and Jayla under control. I want you to focus on you and do something that will put a smile on your face."

"I hear you and I'll try to get back to myself," I assured her. I could understand where my mother was coming from. I've been like a hermit crab these past few weeks but it's because I wasn't in the mood. Maybe she's right about being cooped up in my room consuming myself with work.

Lord knows I need to get out of the house and see something different. Starting tomorrow I'm going to attempt to get back in the swing of things. I have some changes to make first.

* * *

"Hey mi amigas," I greeted Mickey and Taj when I got to their table. They looked up at me and their mouths dropped.

"Bitch that better be a weave," Taj was the first one to speak up. "I've been asking you if I could cut your hair for years and you always said no. Now you walk your ass in here with half of it chopped off?"

I had to laugh at the look on Taj's face. She really looked upset while Mickey was sitting there with her mouth open in shock. It was understandable. The last time they saw me my hair was black and flowing down my back. Now I was rocking a feathered, auburn brown shoulder length bob.

Honestly I felt like a whole new person. Besides getting a trim sometimes to get rid of split ends, I've never cut or colored my hair before. I've had my hair the same way my whole damn life, I think a change was needed.

"No it's not a weave," I answered Taj when I sat down. "I had Beautii do it and that was a tough one because I don't want shit to do with anybody in cahoots with Quentin."

"She did a damn good job, you look good but bitch I wanted to do it," Taj said back then laughed "What do you think Mickey?"

"I mean I like it but I'm stuck. Girl, I've never seen your hair short," Mickey said after her initial shock wore off.

"It's never been short," I chuckled. "I wanted something different so I figured why not chop this shit off."

"Well it looks good but I feel a way about you not letting me do it. I'll let this shit slide though."

"Thank you for letting me slide Taj, I appreciate it. Enough about my hair, how is the little munchkin coming along?"

"Fine, even though I'm tired 80% of the time. If I'm not tired I'm stuffing food in my mouth." Taj shook her head.

"Are you still ignoring your baby daddy?"

"When it comes to our child, no. If it's not about the baby we don't have shit to talk about."

"I thought you weren't mad anymore."

"I'm not but that doesn't mean I like his ass any better. I was good to that nigga for the short amount of time we were together and he fucked up with a bird. That was his bad, and his wrongdoings. I'm not about to be in my feelings over it but fuck him." She shrugged. "It is what it is."

"How far along are you?"

"I'm just hitting five months. It's a boy," Taj said with a big smile.

"Yass, little honey bun has a wiener," I joked making us all laugh. "You got what you wanted."

"Lord knows I don't have time for a little girl."

"We're throwing you a baby shower. A bomb ass baby shower," Mickey told her. "It's going to be huge and perfect."

"I don't want a baby shower."

'What do you mean you don't want a baby shower?"

"Who's coming? The only family members I have are some distant cousins I don't talk to. I have associates but I'm not cool enough with them to invite them somewhere. Anthony has a lot of family but I'm not having a party to meet those niggas. Just bring whatever y'all want my baby to have to my house and I'm good."

"Fine, but you better make room because I'm buying that baby mad shit."

"So, I take it you're doing well after your break up," I said to Mickey.

"I'm fine, break ups happen oh well." Mickey was putting on a good front like she doesn't care but I could see past that. I know her like the back of my hand. She was hurt by Tone dumping her; she just doesn't want to admit that shit. Usually I would press her but I'm going to let Mickey be the big girl she is and deal with her emotions the way she wants to.

After we ate and caught up with each other we all walked outside so we could leave.

"See you bitches later," Taj said to us before getting in her car.

"Later preggo," I waved at her. When she pulled off I looked at Mickey. "What are you about to do?"

"Go home and get my stuff together. I'm going down to North Carolina to see Myles and my mother in two days."

"Really? Aww, I miss his little big head self. How are you getting there?"

"Flying, I'm not driving down there, fuck that shit."

"Well before you go let's go have some drinks. I don't want to go in the house yet. Come on now, you're dressed for a few drinks. We both are."

I was wearing a white Self-Portrait one shoulder frill top, dark skinnies, with a pair of Gianvito Rossi *Gianvito* alligator pumps on my feet. A gold and green Franck Muller Snake bracelet watch sat on my wrist while diamond and emerald Halo earrings decorated my ears.

Mickey had on light blue skin tight jeans with a white long sleeve body suit under. On her feet was a pair of Aquazzura suede ankle boots that matched her red Tommy W Natural fur bomber jacket. She dyed her hair blonde and pulled it up into a high genie ponytail that went down her back and swayed when she walked. The bitch looked good as shit, she was beyond dressed for drinks.

"Fine let's go. But I'm not trying to have a bunch of niggas in my face nor do I feel like slapping a bitch, so you better pick a chill spot."

"It will be, just follow me." We both got in our cars and she followed out to this place called BJ's. I only know of them because Que bought me there a few times. It's really laid back and the place is filled with niggas who have too much money to be in somebody's face on some thirsty shit.

When we got there Mickey and I took a seat at the bar and ordered our first round of drinks after getting comfortable.

"So Mickey, how are you really doing?" I asked. Her nonchalant attitude was cute earlier but I know it was bullshit.

"What?" She looked at me confused.

"You heard me. How are you doing for real? Don't try to sit there and act like you're perfectly fine because I know for a fact that you're not. It's okay for you to admit that you're hurt about you and Tone."

"I'm not hurt Toi, I'm pissed off. I understand why he was upset. I get it but the fact that he ended our whole relationship over that shit blows me. Talking about he can't trust me like I was cheating on his ass or something," she shook her head letting out a bitter chuckle. "I told him everything about me. I opened up to that nigga about my life, my son and everything I went through. What did he do after that? Walk away because I was getting money in a way he didn't approve of. That's bullshit to me."

When I saw tears starting to well up in her eyes I knew she was seriously upset. Mickey is not a crier so if she goes there something is really affecting her.

She grabbed a napkin then dabbed the corner of her eyes.

"Aww, Mick."

Laughing she waved me off. "Don't aww me Toi. I'll be fine. Break ups happen. I'll get over this one like I did the last one. Mean time in between time, I'm using my money from Tip to open a store?"

"What kind of store?"

"I want to open an online store. Most of my comments and DM's on Instagram is people asking me about my clothes and makeup. They ask about my jewelry, my hair and nails. I thought about it and then it hit me. I can start my own clothing line with my own ideas and use it that way."

"Yasss, that's a really good idea," I boasted. I never thought about Mickey getting into fashion but she's actually a great fit for that industry. She's bold, creative and very business minded. My girl knows how to get that money and she will work her hands to the bone to get it.

"Thank you," she smiled. "I'm going to call it Pride Killa. I'm going to start off with clothes first, but I eventually want to go into makeup, and hair. I already found some manufactures to get some things made. I'm getting my website started, by the way I heard about this graphic design company. Supposedly they're a big deal, you want to come with me when I go next week?"

"Yeah I'll go. I need start on my branding so that's a good idea. I'm proud of you friend."

"And I'm proud of you," we both laughed. "We're growing up girl."

"I know, cheers to that." We held up our glasses like we were toasting. Once all the serious stuff was out the way we started those drinks back. I don't know if I was trying to drink my stress away or what, but I know I was on my third Mojito while Mickey was on her fourth Whiskey sour.

I wasn't drunk but I felt good. Too good to drive home and Mickey was just as buzzed as I was. We were still sitting at the bar cracking up talking about our high school days.

"Remember the day you met Bless," Mickey said and I sucked my teeth. "Be salty all you want, that shit was funny. Randal was mad as shit."

"Trying to be cute and make him mad I damn near threw myself on an idiot," I rolled my eyes. Bless was my first love if you want to be technical. I met him when I was 17 and I only talked to him to make my boyfriend at the time mad.

I gave him my number with no intention on talking to him. I planned to ignore all text messages and calls from him and I did. Then, he started popping up on me. I should've been annoyed and creeped out but my young ass was actually flattered. From there we started talking and it grew into a relationship. I was with him for four years before I finally decided to let that shit go.

Not only was he disrespectful, he was a liar and cheater. To top everything off his side bitch who turned out to be Quentin's sister, was stalking me. I fought her multiple times before my common sense kicked in.

I realized as long as I was dealing with Bless she was going to be a problem because he was clearly still fucking her. After the last time I fought Mia, I broke up with Bless and hadn't talked to him since. Last I heard he moved down to Atlanta and made a name for himself.

"He's the reason I know for certain niggas aint shit. He was the definition of a dog ass dude."

"Trust me girl, I know. I fell for the biggest dick head imaginable. Been there did that. I'm off niggas. The only person of the opposite sex I care about is my son. Fuck any other nigga,"

"Damn Mick, you still going hard on these niggas?" We heard from behind us. Mickey turned around but I didn't move. I know that voice, I remember it as clear as day even though it's been over a year since I've heard it. How the fuck did we speak this nigga up like that?

"Oh God, why are you here? I thought you were Atlanta's problem now," I heard Mickey respond.

"Still the same mean ass Mickey I remember. What's good Toi? You can't speak?"

Turning around I looked at Bless who still was handsome as ever. He was standing there looking like a six foot tall Hershey bar. His milk chocolate skin was just clear and beautiful as I remember, he still had his hair cut low and now he had a short beard. Bruh looked damn good but it's too bad I know he's an asshole.

"I don't like speaking to bitch niggas," I answered dryly.

"How do you have an attitude with me when you the one that dipped out of nowhere?"

"I wrote you a very detailed note so you know why I left."

"Alright I fucked up, but you were still fucked up for doing what you did. It's cool though, you'll make it up to me."

"I'm not making up a damn thing. You can get the fuck outta here with that shit," I said back, looking him straight in the face. I wanted him to know it wasn't shit happening over this way.

"I see that mouth didn't change for the better."

"Bless, get the fuck away me. Pretend I don't exist like you've been doing."

"Nah I'm good on that last thing. I'll leave you alone for now shorty. Aye Mick, my nigga Brick said he'll be seeing you real soon ma."

"Fuck you and Brick," Mickey snapped at him.

"I'll make sure to tell him you said that. Oh and Kareem wanted me to give you his condolences. Make sure you let your whole family know," Bless said with a smirk then started walking away.

I turned to Mickey and before I could stop her, he reached over the bar and snatched the bottle of liquor from the bartenders hand as he was pouring.

"MICKEY!" I screamed her name when she launched the liquor bottle in Bless' direction. If it wasn't for him moving at the right second she would've taken his head off with that damn bottle. She hopped off the stool and was about to charge at him but I blocked her.

"Fuck you bitch! Your pussy ass friend gon get his watch! Muthafucka!" Because she couldn't get past me, she grabbed her glass from the bar and threw it at Bless who was standing near the entrance laughing like shit was funny

By now we had the attention off everybody in BJ's. They were looking at us like they had front row seats to a movie.

"Mickey stop! Can y'all get him the fuck outta here please!" I shouted at the bar tender who signaled for security to remove Bless from the bar.

When they got him out Mickey snatched away from me and stormed towards the bathroom. "I swear I hate that nigga," I mumbled under my breath.

"Ma'am, I need you to come with me," a security guard said when he walked up.

"If we're getting put out don't worry about it. We'll be out as soon as she comes from the bathroom," I let him know.

"You're not getting put out. I need you to grab your things, get hers too and follow me. She'll be with you as soon as she comes out."

I looked at him like he was crazy because he had to be. I'm supposed to follow a man I don't know and never seen before? Hell no.

"Nah I'm good, I don't know you. I'm going to wait for my friend and we're going to leave."

"Nobody is going to do anything to you, my boss told me to come get you. I'm just following orders," he replied. I noticed Mickey coming over with a security guard walking behind her.

"What the hell is he talking about? His boss wants to see me?" Mickey asked when she got to me.

"I don't know, this one said the same thing. I'm not following these niggas. Let's go." Despite the drama I was still pretty buzzed but I was damn sure about to sit in the car with Mickey until I could get a Lyft.

Mickey gathered her things while I paid our tab. "Toi! Mickey!"

Hearing our names we both turned around to see Que and Tone's friend Barry coming toward us. "Y'all good?" He asked, giving both of us a quick hug. "Why you throwing bottles and shit in my place, what happened?"

"You shouldn't let bitch niggas in your place and bottles wouldn't need to be thrown," Mickey countered back.

"Wait, your place? You own this?" I polled.

"Yeah," Barry nodded.

"Figures." Of course, Que would bring me to his friend's place of business. Why am I not surprised?

"Y'all not driving home, I saw y'all tossing those drinks back."

"Saw?"

"Yeah, I can see everything in my office."

'Oh boy," Mickey said after sucking her teeth.

"Oh boy is right. Y'all know I have to tell them about that bottle throwing shit right?"

"You don't have to do anything. We're no longer their concern and I know you know that," I noted.

"I understand what you mean and that's real cute but you know better than that. The only way I could turn my head was if they were on some fuck you shit. I have yet to hear those niggas say that so I have to tell them. Just how things go, y'all get it."

"Whatever Barry," I waved him off.

"I knew you would understand. I'm taking y'all home; my boys will follow us in your cars. Let me get your keys."

Knowing he was not about to let it go, Mickey and I handed him our keys then followed him out the door. Between running into Bless and Barry having to tell Que about that run-in had me blown.

LEGEND

"What's been up with you?" Saint asked when Beautii walked out the living room with my mother and the rest of my aunts. They were probably on their way down to the wine cellar so they could drink and talk their shit. I was perfectly fine with it because now it was just me, my cousins and our uncle Saint in the room.

I came over here to get some free food since they have dinner at Saint and Beautii's house every Friday. I used to come on the weekly basis but once I got with Toi my visits dwindled down.

Not because she kept me away from the family, it was the other way around. I didn't want to bring her around because it would be some bullshit going on.

After my sister Mia and Toi got into it on Thanksgiving, every positive opinion my mother had about Toi went out the window. She doesn't care about what happened or who was really in the wrong. Mia has a problem with Toi so now my mother does too.

She and Mia are on the same level of petty so bringing Toi around wouldn't do anything but start an altercation. She's respectful but she's a grown ass woman. Shorty is not going to sit back and let my mother pop shit about her.

"What you mean?" I looked over at him.

"Nigga you've been walking around on some defensive shit lately. You good?"

"Hell no, Toi dumped his ass," my cousin Noel said and they all started laughing.

"How did you fuck that up? Toi was bad as hell man," Dante added in.

"Nah bad aint even the word, that girl is beautiful." Carnell gushed. "Do you know how rare it is to see a woman and just be like, yo she's beautiful. Beyond being sexy, or if she got a fat ass, like it's damn near scary and ridiculous how pretty she is? That's what this nigga had." He pointed at me.

"Man, shut the fuck up," I shook my head because he's right. Toi is literally the most beautiful woman I've ever seen in my life. Between her flawless brown skin, pretty brown eyes and that smile of hers. I have yet to see anybody that looks better than her. She's a stunning woman on top of being a bomb ass person and it got fucked up.

"Yup that's what's wrong with him," Saint laughed. "You still trippin' about that robbing shit she was doing?"

"Nah, but she doesn't know that. I haven't had the chance to talk to her about any of that shit."

"Well then maybe you need to."

"Man I'm not going to Toi right now. She's still pissed at me, I'm not about to have her snapping at me."

"Now he's scared of her unc," Noel laughed again. "Nah for real bruh, I think if you want her you better go get her. A chick like that doesn't stay single for long. You should know that better than anybody."

"For real, you were ready to wife her up quick as shit. Nigga only knew her for a week and was bragging about her and shit," Nate pointed out.

"I hear y'all but I'll deal with that when it's time for me to. Besides, niggas already know not to go for that one. It aint public knowledge we're over."

"Fuck outta here if it aint, she deleted all the pictures of y'all off her Instagram. For girls, that means a lot. Go ahead and wait if you want to, when the next nigga trying to get at her don't be salty."

"Despite these niggas clowning you, they're right. I told you when you got with Toi that she was a special girl. It's not too many 22 year olds selfless enough to be financially responsible for their whole family," Saint recalled. "I understand you being upset about what she was doing. Shit, I was upset when Beautii told me about it because I know she's better than that. She and Mickey both but they felt like that was their only option at the time. Toi stopped doing it though and that's what you didn't let her explain. You fucked up on that then missing Ms. Henderson's funeral made it ten times worse."

"You and Beautii missed it too."

"Nigga we weren't in town and we still reached out to her when we found out. The situation is different."

"Well I don't know what to do about it. She's not trying to talk to me right now and I can't force her ass to be with me…I can't, right?"

"No nigga you can't," he laughed. "I understand giving her time but nigga it's been how long now?"

"She's not trying to hear shit I got to say unc," I told him.

"Did she give you the Porsche back?" He asked about the car I bought Toi for Christmas.

"Nah, but it's in her name she doesn't have to."

"Man listen, I know Toi. I've known her since she was a teenager and the girl has a lot of pride. So much pride that if she was done with you, trust me she would've given the car back. Even with it being in her name she would've returned that shit. The fact that she didn't tells me she's not 100% done with you. She might not admit that shit but that's what it is. It's not like she didn't already have a decent working car before you got her a new one so she has another option."

"I hear you," I nodded. I get what he meant but I didn't agree with that shit. I gave shorty a brand new Porsche. Nobody is about to give that shit up, I don't care how much pride you have.

After choppin' it up with everybody for a little while longer I left to go to a meeting I had with my team. Nothing special just making sure everything is still on track and in place like it's supposed to be.

"Aye Legend; Tone hold up." Barry came over to us once we dismissed the meeting. "Last night your girls came to my spot and got lit." he told us.

"Are you talking Toi and Mickey?" I asked just for clarification.

"Yeah."

MOLLYSHA JOHNSON

"Okay and?" Tone shrugged. "Is there a point to this story?"

"Well shit was going fine until that nigga Bless came in there. I don't know what they were talking about but he and Toi looked familiar. Then shit went left and ended with Mickey throwing a bottle at that nigga."

"Fuck you mean they looked familiar?" I questioned.

"Exactly what I said. I'm not saying it's something but she knows that nigga. You can figure out the rest from there."

"How did Mickey get involved?" Tone asked him.

'I don't know, he must've said some shit to piss her off. He didn't touch either of them but Mickey almost took his damn head off with that bottle."

"Shit, she needs to work on her aim," Tone chuckled. "Thanks for telling me man."

"No problem. I'll hit y'all up tomorrow I'm out."

"That nigga is going to answer Chanel's calls then go creeping as usual," Yung joked.

"Man, get the fuck outta here," Barry laughed.

"Nah he's right, how you convinced your girl to move all the way down to Miami for ten years I will never know," I shook my head. Most people didn't know Barry was engaged with two kids. He's been with his girl for over a decade but she doesn't live in Jersey. Somehow he convinced her to move to Florida with their son while he stayed up here to make the money.

"Shit can be dangerous up here and I would rather her and my kids be away from the bullshit. Trust me it aint all it's cracked up to be. I'm down there every two damn weeks and that's about to stop because she's trying to come back."

"Chanel is coming back up here?" I asked before I busted out laughing. I know Chanel very well; we all went to high school together. Shorty is crazy as shit so if she's moving back up here this nigga is about to have a time on his hands. He's been far from innocent since she's been gone.

"I'm trying to get her to stay down there but she aint having it so she might be back up here sometime soon. We'll see. Y'all niggas pray for me because," he shook his head like he was stressed.

"I got you. Fucking with Chanel, your life is in danger so I'll ask God to spare your ass."

"Thank you because I really need everything I can get. Later y'all," he said before walking out.

"What you think Bless was talking to Toi about?" Tone asked as we walked outside.

"I don't know but I hope it's no bullshit involved. I don't have time to be worried about that nigga and what the fuck he's doing."

"Are you going to ask her about it?

"I want to but I've learned my lesson about flying off the handle with her about shit. I'm going to talk to her about it but it's not a priority. I need to get us all the way straight before I even get to that point."

If my drama with Toi has taught me anything it's to calm my ass down an actually speak to her. Toi doesn't respond well to yelling and screaming so I know not to come at her like that again. I will be asking her about that Bless shit as soon as I could without coming off like I'm at her neck. I don't need our makeup turning into another breakup. I'm good on that.

"Fuck what y'all talking about. Y'all remember that bitch Tasia?" Yung blurted out of nowhere.

"The one you used to fuck with?" Tone polled.

"Yeah, she's having a party tomorrow night. I think we need to go see what's up with that."

"Nah I'm good. Tasia don't do shit but throw parties at her house, I'm not for that bullshit. A nigga needs a section and some real bottles. Not somebody's dusty ass living room surrounded by little ass girls," I said.

I'm not really one for house parties; they always end in some bullshit. They don't monitor who comes in so it's full of high school kids. You think you're talking to a grown ass woman and it's somebody's child, I don't like that shit. Yung can get that off because he's practically still a baby himself but it aint my thing.

"I told the bitch I was coming so let's go. Y'all not wanting to stay in there would be perfect for me. I can pop in real quick then be out. If she knows I'm with y'all, she won't get on my fuckin' nerves."

"Are you fuckin' with her again? I thought you were trying to fix shit with the girl you have pregnant right now."

"Man Taj aint fuckin' with me at all. She has made it more than clear so I'm stepping back and doing me. We're going to co-parent then leave it at that."

"Say that now, let's see how you feel once she has that baby. All that shit is going to change. Since we're all catching up ad shit," Tone chuckled. "I ran into Cassie."

"Oh shit, where did you hide the body?" I asked and he started laughing. I don't know what was funny because I was dead ass serious. This nigga vowed to blow her damn head off if she even spoke to him again.

"I didn't kill that bitch, I wanted break her fucking neck though. She was on the same 'let me explain' bullshit."

Are you going to let her?"

"Hell no, there's nothing she could say that would make me feel different. What logical reason would she have to not only have an abortion but lie and say it was a miscarriage? If I didn't find those pills I never would've known. Fuck her, she better stay the fuck away from me."

"Damn calm down you turning red and shit," Yung joked.

"I hate that bitch man," he shook his head.

"You have every reason to but he's right calm yo ass down. You know how you get."

"Whatever man, can we go?"

"Yeah let's go so your hostile ass can relax," I grabbed my keys off the table and we headed out. "Yung we'll roll through there for a second but we aint staying. I'm not even walking in that muthafucka."

KAYLA HENDERSON

I was sitting on my bed going through my phone when Jayla came in our room and sat on her bed. Usually I wouldn't say anything but the look on her face had me wondering what the hell was wrong with her. She didn't look upset per say, but she wasn't happy either. To the average person she looked fine but I know better.

"What's the matter with you?" I asked.

"Jamal is so damn annoying bruh," Jayla groaned. As soon as I heard his name I rolled my eyes. "Don't even do that Kayla, I saw you roll your eyes."

"I don't know why you chase after that nigga, he ain't shit," I shrugged my shoulders.

"How would you know that? You barely know him."

"I know enough. He pulls you in every direction and you just go for it. He's not all that, what do you see?"

"He's fine as hell so stop it. Lucas isn't too much better."

"The difference between Lucas and Jamal is I know Lucas is mine. I'm texting him right now. He doesn't diss my ass like Jamal does you. You can do way better Jayla, that's all I'm saying."

"Whatever, I don't want to talk about him anymore. Malaysia said her sister is having a party tonight," she said, changing the subject.

"Tasia is always throwing parties. So?"

"So we should go."

"Toi is not about to let us go to that party, it's going to be a bunch of grown ass people there. I wanted to ask but I figured what's the point in wasting my breath. I know she's going to say no."

"Who said she has to know? You know how Toi is. She's going to come in the house, take a shower and go to sleep. We just have to leave after she pokes her head in here. Come on, I heard Lucas was going to be there."

"I know he's going to be there, don't try and bring him up to get me to go. You just want to go because Jamal's big turtle head ass is going. I'll go though, you lucky I feel like having fun."

"Good I really wasn't trying to go by my damn self. What are you wearing?"

"Clothes, we're not matching tonight. That's way too much."

"I'm right there with you, we already have the same face our clothes don't have to look alike."

"Exactly," we both laughed.

My sister and I were close, and I love her to death but that whole dressing alike because we're twins shit was never our thing. The only time we've ever dressed alike is when my grandmother forced us to. Besides, our styles were completely different.

Jayla is the more, I guess you can say, conservative as in she likes to cover up more, I like to show some skin. Our personal styles are so different; it makes it easier for people to tell us apart. Plus we wear our hair in two totally different colors. When we turned 16 in January, Jayla opted out of her usual black and Toi let her dye it dark red. I decided to go up a couple shades lighter so my hair was honey blonde. We both had extensions and wore them bone straight with a side part.

"Wait, what about aunt Geneva?" Jayla asked me.

"She goes to bed early and if she is in the living room, we'll just go out the back door," I told her.

If my aunt isn't in the kitchen cooking, she's either in the living room or her bedroom. She doesn't really bother us at night because Toi is usually the one that checks in. During the day she's on us like a hawk, it's like her and Toi have shifts when it comes to us.

"Right, okay. What are you wearing Kay?"

"You'll see when I get dressed," I said back with a chuckle.

"It's going to be your usual hoochie get up. Just remember it's March, it's still cold outside."

"Shut up," we both laughed.

JAYLA HENDERSON

"You look like a damn hoochie. I hope you don't plan on taking no pictures for the gram because Toi will flip. That is a shirt not a damn dress," I told Kayla when she came out of the bathroom fully dressed, if you can call it that.

This girl had on a black long sleeve tunic top, that she bought in a size small knowing damn well we wear a medium. Now I know why she did it, she wanted it to fit like a mini dress and she was right. On her feet were some flat over the knee black suede boots. When she grabbed a black leather jacket off her bed and put it on, I raised my eyebrow.

"No, you don't," I went behind Kayla and pulled the jacket back so I could see the tag. "You really lost your damn mind, that's Toi's jacket."

"So? It's just a damn jacket."

"Bitch that's Saint Laurent, she probably paid thousands of dollars for that. You better take that off."

"Jayla quit being scary, alright? I don't look like a hoochie I look damn good. And don't worry about Toi's jacket or her, we're good. This was your idea anyway remember."

"Yes I remember but I didn't say show your ass or steal Toi's clothes. Besides the jacket that shirt is too damn short."

"It's not too short for me."

"Sad, you need to take a lesson or two from me," I said while looking at myself in the mirror.

I was wearing a pair of ripped skinny jeans, a fitted white t-shirt, with a red flight jacket and my red and white Air Max 95's. My hair was pulled back into a ponytail and I was ready to go. We were only going to a house party; all that dressy shit was unnecessary in my opinion.

"Yeah no I'm good on that, let's just go before she wakes up or something. Our Uber is outside." We both grabbed our phones and keys then quietly went downstairs. Thankfully aunt Geneva wasn't in the living room so we were able to get out the door with no problems.

"You think somebody in here will tell her they saw us?" I asked Kayla once we were in our Uber.

"Nah I doubt it. If you see somebody you think will tell just stay away from them," I nodded my head then sat back in my seat while going through Instagram on my phone.

When we finally got to Malaysia's house we got out of the car and walked right inside of the party. As soon as we walked inside it wasn't even two minutes before Kayla saw Lucas and went to be up under his funny looking ass all night.

I knew I shouldn't have told her to come with me with that nigga being here. I would've been better off coming here by my damn self; it would've felt the same anyway. A part of me wanted to tell her ass off but I didn't feel like arguing with her so I just went into the kitchen where liquor bottles covered the counter.

I picked up a couple of bottles and looked at them until I found an unopened one. I don't know if they dropped a pill or two into these bottles I'll be damned if I'm about to be in here losing my mind.

After fixing myself I drink I went back out into the living room and sat down in one of the few empty chairs. I'm surprised I found a seat with how crowded this house was.

"JAYLA!" Hearing my name I looked up and saw Malaysia walking in my direction. She came over to me and pulled a chair next to mine then sat in it.

"What's up? You having fun?" she asked in my ear.

I shrugged. "It's cool so far. Me and Kayla just got here not too long ago."

"Well you know Jamal is up in here right?"

"He is? Where?"

"I saw him go upstairs with that bitch Leah, you better go handle that. You already know what they're doing up there."

I shook my head and downed the rest of my drink. "I'm not about to sweat his. If he wants to be on that bitch it's his business. I'm about to go fill my cup and I'm turnin' up fuck him," I went and got myself another drink and quickly drank it down. I made another one then went back out to the living room. I was about to try and find my seat when I felt somebody bump into me. To my surprise it was Jamal.

"Jayla, what's up ma?" He said with a smirk on his face.

"Nothing, move," I went to walk past him, but he grabbed my arm and pulled me back.

"What's wrong with you?"

"Why don't you go ask Leah what's wrong with me. Don't go fucking bitches then come to me like you aint did shit."

"Whoa wait a minute, you're not my girl so I don't even know why the fuck you mad. You already know what this is and you know I don't want a girlfriend."

"I don't care if I'm not your girlfriend. Don't talk to me when you just finished fucking a bitch five minutes ago," I pushed him out of the way and walked to where everybody was dancing. If he could do him I can do me too.

When *Bartier Cardi* came on I started dancing by myself up until I felt somebody come up behind me. Usually I would turn around but this time I chose to say fuck it. I didn't feel like seeing who it was I just felt like having fun. I danced with this person for three songs straight. I finally turned to see who I was dancing with, our mouths dropped in shock.

"Twin!?" Yung shouted when he saw my face. He always called Jayla and I both twin because he can't tell us apart. "THE FUCK IS YOU DOING IN HERE!"

"Um," I tried to say something to explain myself but I came up empty.

"Let's go." He grabbed my arm and pulled me towards the front door. I was wondering where he was pulling me until I saw Que and Tone sitting on the steps smoking. *Aww shit, I'm dead.* "Look who the fuck was in there thinking she grown!" Yung shouted getting both of their attention.

When they looked up at me the smiles they just had on their faces dropped.

"What the fuck?" Tone hopped up first.

"Jayla?" Que looked at me with his eyes squinted. I guess he was trying to figure out if he said the right name. "You're sixteen what the fuck you doing in there? It's grown ass men in that bitch!" Que yelled at me.

This isn't good; why the fuck did I have to get caught by these three niggas? They treated me and Kayla like little sisters since they met us. It was cool when we wanted something because they would give it to us with no hesitation, but shit like this made it not so fun.

"Where the fuck is Kayla at? I know she came with you," Tone said to me. Now, I know I could straight snitch on her and I should since she ditched me but I wasn't going to do that.

"No, I came by myself," I lied and they all saw straight through it.

"She a damn lie, they don't shit separately." Yung said and I rolled my eyes.

"I know, that's why we're about to go look for her. Let's go." Que grabbed my arm and pulled me back into the party with Yung and Tone behind him. He went over to where the stereo system was plugged up and took the cord out the wall making everybody look over at us.

"Yo, what the fuck Legend? Why you turn the music off?" Somebody in the crowd yelled.

"Y'all see this girl right here," Que pointed at me. "She's 16 years old and it's another one in this bitch that looks just like her. Y'all can either point her out or I'm tearing this place the fuck up!"

Nobody said anything they just looked around. It was quiet for a couple of seconds until we heard shouting and shit breaking coming from upstairs. When it stopped Yung came down with Kayla thrown over his shoulder.

"I got her bruh let's get the fuck outta here!" he yelled while walking out the door.

"Alright, y'all can keep going now. Bring yo little ass on bruh." Que pulled me outside and towards his car. "Kayla what the fuck was you doing up those fucking stairs?"

"I wasn't doing anything damn. Mind your business," Kayla snapped back.

"WHO THE FUCK YOU TALKING TO?!" All three of them yelled at the same time."

"She was upstairs with some pretty boy ass nigga, being on some hoe shit," Yung said, and Kayla glared at him.

"I'm not a hoe so don't call me one."

"If a nigga got you upstairs during a party with a house full of people, that's hoe shit lil mama. You wasn't about to talk in that muthafucka. You're too fucking beautiful, smart and young for that shit."

"I don't give a fuck what y'all was doing, you two shouldn't even be here. Get in the fucking car man." Que snapped at us.

We both climbed into the back seat of his car with attitudes all over our faces, hers more than mine. I already know what's about to happen. He's going to take us home and tell Toi everything.

If my grandmother was still alive, there was a chance we could get away with this. The most she would do is yell at us because she was too old to really whoop our asses. Toi on the other hand is young, and full of energy. She's about to kill our asses.

TOI

Leaving from the twins' room I saw my mother peeking out of hers. "What the hell was all that yelling?" She asked then her eyes fell on the belt in my hand. "You beat them? What happened?"

"They snuck out then had the nerve to be at a party full of grown ass men. Quentin and his friends saw them there and brought them home," I answered her.

"Those sneaky little heifers; I hope you got them good."

"Oh I did," I opened my room door and threw the belt I used on my bed.

"Is Que still here?"

"Yeah he's downstairs."

"You're about to go down there?"

"Yeah so?"

"Girl take that damn scarf off," she snatched my scarf off my head then combed my hair down with her hands. "I'm still mad you cut your damn hair off."

"It's not all gone, it'll grow back. Stop ma," I moved my head away from her hands and went in my room to look in the mirror. I grabbed the brush off the dresser and brushed my hair down. "What did you pull my scarf off for?"

"Because that man is clearly here to talk to you, so go look like something while you do that."

"Ma, Que and I are over. I don't care about how I look in front of him."

"You care about him and he cares about you. Why are you broken up again?"

"Because he kicked me out then skipped grandma's funeral, that's why."

"Okay both hurtful things, I get it. I still think you need to at least talk to him and see what happened. I don't think Quentin would just not show up for mama's funeral."

"He did though,"

"And I think it's a reason for it. Look Toi, you were happy with Quentin. The both of you were happy for each other. I don't think you should just toss it away so easily."

"I hear you ma, I do and you make a good point but Que and I have a lot of things to hash out. It's not going to be fixed in one sitting especially not right now."

"Okay, I'll let you do what you want to do with your relationship. I'm going back to bed, we'll talk about thing one and two's punishment tomorrow. Good night."

"Good night ma." She went to her room while I went down to the living room where Que was sitting on the couch going through his phone.

When I plopped down on the couch next to him he looked up at me, then at his phone then back at me with a confused expression on his face.

"Alright I was smoking like shit tonight so am I trippin' or is your hair short and colored different," he asked, and I started laughing at him.

"No you're not trippin'. I cut my hair, what do you think?"

"I think it looks good on you. What made you cut it? You love your hair?"

"I know," I chuckled. "I just wanted something different. Thank you for bringing them home. You didn't have to look out like that."

"Toi you know me better than that. I'm always going to look out for you and your family."

"I thought I knew you but some of the shit you did showed me a different side."

"I know and I was hoping we could talk."

"Talk about what Que?"

"About us."

"There is no us. That came to an end weeks ago."

"I know but I don't think it should've."

"Qu-"

"Just listen to me, alright?"

"Alright fine, go ahead," I sat back against the couch and gave him my full attention.

"The whole thing at the apartment was my fault. I should've let you tell me what the deal was instead of coming at you like I did. I was disrespectful, too damn disrespectful and I apologize for that. You can't be mad about me trippin' over that shit though."

"I'm not, I understand why you were questioning my motives with you. I just didn't like how you were coming at me. You didn't give me a chance to tell you anything."

"I know, it's just that when Tone told me what Mickey was doing I convinced myself that you didn't tell me because you were going to do the same shit to me."

"I wouldn't do that to you. You're a big part of the reason I stopped, you helped me realize and achieve other options. You know me, I'm not going to cross you like that Que and the fact that you actually thought I could is what hurt me."

"I know and I'm sorry. As far as your grandmother goes, I should've been over here as soon as I heard about it. That was another fuck up but I didn't just skip her funeral on some fuck you type shit."

"So what happened? Why weren't you there?"

"The night before I was at my mother's house and Isyss had Diamond over there with her and Mia. My plan was to get up early the next morning, come here and with y'all to the funeral. I made the mistake of telling my mother this plan with Mia and Isyss in the room. When I fell asleep one of them got into my phone, turned my alarm and volume off. I didn't wake up until noon. I'm not telling you this as some sort of excuse because there isn't one, but I just want you to know, I wouldn't just skip her funeral like that."

At this point I know when Que is lying and he was sitting here telling me the truth. That's what was fucking with me though. The fact that his missing the funeral was unintentional made me feel better but his sister and baby mama being the reason irritated me.

"Thank you for explaining that to me, I appreciate it. I can forgive you for that, and the shit with my past but….Your sister and BM," I shook my head.

"I'll handle them okay."

"That's the thing Que, you say that all the time and they keep doing shit. If they could fuck with your phone knowing damn well you were going to a funeral, they won't stop. They don't want you with me."

"I don't give a damn about what they want Toi."

"Neither do I but I don't have time for the drama. That's your blood sister and your child's mother. They're not going anywhere."

"Neither are you. Listen, I'm going to get that shit straight and taken care of alright, Toi I'm not saying we have to be together right here right now, but I want to at least be on speaking terms with you. It's been too fucking long."

"Why should I even let you back in my life Que? You couldn't even be there for me when I needed you, how do I know it's going to be different?"

"I'm telling you it's going to be different; I know you probably think I'm full of shit and I don't blame you but just let me prove it to you, alright?"

I thought about it for a few seconds then sighed. "Fine, we're friends though and that's all. I'm not your girl right now."

"That's cool with me. Are you coming to my cookout?"

"What cook out? It's still cold outside, it isn't spring yet."

"I know that. It's in a few weeks. I throw a big cookout at The Mansion every May. I charge people admission to get in and we party all night. Food, liquor all that shit. Bring your girls if you want to; just make sure you're there."

"Okay, I'll see what it is and try to make it down there."

"Not going to give me a definite yes huh?" He chuckled.

"Nah it's not that easy for you."

"I got you ma." We both stood up and he hugged me. "I'll talk to you later,"

"Alright." Que kissed my cheek then left my house.

"God please don't let this turn into something I'll regret," I mumbled under my breath.

MICHELLE "MICKEY" WHITFIELD

"Yeah, I'm good. I just landed like 30 minutes ago I'm in the car to my mother's house now," I told Toi while we spoke on the phone.

"That's good; make sure you kiss my god baby for me. You need to bring his ass back up here with you when you come back."

"That might just happen. What are you doing?"

"Nothing, I just got back in the house from the spa. Checking in on things, now I'm about to go chill my ass out."

"Oh okay, well take your ass to sleep because I know that's what you're doing. I'll speak to you later after I get settled in down here and shit."

"Alright ma, talk to you later. Don't let your mother piss you off," I hung my phone up then looked out the window.

I don't see how people live here; it's too slow for me. I get that it's quiet and it's a good place to raise a family but it's not for me. I need some hustle and bustle in my life.

It was thirty minutes before we finally pulled up in front of my mother's house. I couldn't help but shake my damn head because she didn't need a place this big. My mother is living in a 5 bedroom 3 bathroom house which in my opinion is too damn much for two people. Maybe if I wasn't the one paying the mortgage and bills in this muthafucka I would feel different.

After getting my bags out the trunk I went up to the front door and rang the doorbell. A few seconds later the door opened and I squealed when I saw Myles standing there. He smiled and jumped into my arms.

"I missed you so much," I said in his ear while I hugged him. When I finally let him go he wiped the tears that were coming down my face then hugged me again.

"I missed you too." He said back. I kissed his cheek then stood up straight.

"Grab that bag for me," I pointed at the smaller bag while I grabbed the big one then closed the door. "Where is your grandma?"

"She went to the store," he answered me.

"So who are you here with?"

"Nobody, I just watch TV until she comes back. Mommy I got 2k15,"

"I know," I *bought the shit*. "Come show me to the guest room baby." We went upstairs and he showed me the room my mother told him to take me to. I walked in and dropped my suitcases on the floor then kicked my heels off. "Come sit down I want to talk to you."

"Okay." He hopped on the bed and sat next to me. Looking at him I beamed with pride.

My son is so handsome and thankfully he looks just like me. We have the same light complexion, same eyes, same smile; he pretty much has my whole face. He's going to be a tall boy, because I'm not short and his father is at least 6'5. Myles is only going on eight years old and he's almost at my shoulders.

"How do you like living down here?" I asked,

Myles shrugged. "I like it I guess. I wish you could move down here with us."

"I know you want me with you every day, and I wish I could be with you too. I'm working on that. I'm going to make that happen really soon but I don't think I'm coming down here. You'll probably come back to New Jersey with me."

"Can we go see the empire state building?"

"Yes we can. You've seen it before but you were really young. I'll take you to see it again and we'll bring Aunt Toi with us. Plus you know what else; I'm going to talk to your grandmother about you coming with me for the summer but you'll have to come back when school starts."

"Why?"

"You go to school down here; you have friends down here and stuff, right?"

"Yes, but I wanna live with you."

"What about your grandma? You have to keep her company."

"I don't want to keep her company. Grandma is mean."

I chuckled. "I know she has her mean days but I'm here now so you don't have to worry about it. So you and grandma live here by yourselves?"

"No, Maya and Bree live here too," he said talking about my older cousin and her six year old daughter.

I had no idea they were staying here. I don't have a problem with it because Maya and I are cool. But why the fuck is she taking all this money from me every month if she has another grown working person living here.

"Oh really? Okay." Before I could ask him another question I heard the front door along with people talking. "Your grandmother is here come on." We walked out of the guest room then went downstairs to the kitchen where Maya and my mother were putting groceries on the counter.

"Y'all can't announce yourselves when you walk in the house?" I said getting both of their attention.

Maya laughed then came over pulling me into a hug instantly. "Damn girl you look good, thick as ever still," she said while looking me over.

"Gotta keep it up, I'm not trying to lose all the shit God blessed me with. How are you though?"

"I'm doing alright. I'm just maintaining."

"That's good," I smiled at her again then went over to my mother and we hugged briefly.

My mother and I don't have the closest relationship and it's mostly because I keep my distance. If I don't vibe with people I don't see the point in being around them a lot and my mother is somebody I don't click with too much.

One would think we would be close as hell all that we've been through but to be honest it just made us drift apart. I didn't really respect the kind of woman my mother was. I felt like some of the shit she did was weak and selfish. I remember her telling people she stayed with my abusive father as long as she did because of me.

Supposedly she wanted a two parent home for me. I knew straight off the bat that was bullshit. I hated my father and she knew that so her staying with him was all for herself. I would bet any amount of money that she would still be with my father getting her ass beat if his heart attack didn't take him out.

"So Mickey, how are things going with you?" Maya asked me.

"I'm just getting my money, nothing too different."

"What about the guy I saw on your Instagram?"

I knew she was talking about Tone.

"We were together but we broke up. We weren't really seeing eye to eye; I don't feel like talking about him though."

"Alright, well since you're going to be here all week we have to go out before you leave."

"I'm cool with that, just give me some time with my little man and I'll be happy."

Maya smiled at me then went upstairs. When she was gone I looked at my mother.

"So do you leave Myles here by himself often?"

"What are you talking about?" She looked at me like she didn't understand my question.

"I'm talking about the fact that when I got here my son was by himself. He's only seven, why is he being left alone?"

"Myles knows what to do when I'm gone. It's not a big deal."

"To you it may not be but it is for me. Ma, you never answered my question. Is he here by himself often?"

Smiling wickedly she looked at me. "Michelle I don't have to explain myself to you. I'm a grown ass woman."

"He's my child."

"And you're mine. What is your point? Myles is fine. Instead of questioning me maybe you need to go spend some time with your son. You have a lot of catching up to do."

I was about to cuss her ass out but I remembered Myles was in the room and looking straight at me. I just grabbed his hand and walked to the living room. I can already tell this week with her was going to be trying, and I really had no time for her bullshit.

***

I was in North Carolina for four days, spending most of my time with Myles when he would get out of school. We went to the movies, out to eat, laser tag, and Skyzone. On my fifth day there, Maya volunteered to take me out to eat so we could have a few drinks and catch up.

I stirred my straw around my drink before taking a sip then turning my attention to Maya who was just putting her phone down.

"This is a cute place," I told Maya as I looked around the lounge she bought me to.

"Yeah it's nice. I'm glad you came out with me. I wanted to take you out to lunch before you head back up to Jersey. It would've been sooner but I've been working my damn ass off," she said and I nodded.

Maya worked at Wal-Mart, I think she was the manager or something important like that. I'm not going to lie and say I didn't want to bust out laughing when she first told me where she worked. Once I stopped being childish I realized that girl works her ass off in that damn store.

"How much do you make there?" I asked. I was genuinely interested in knowing.

"I make about eight hundred or so."

"Every two weeks?"

"Yeah,"

"Oh, hell nah, how the hell do you live off that? My shoes cost more than that Maya."

"I have to so I do, I'm not you Mickey. You hustle your ass off and make a lot of money but I couldn't be like that. I'm not built that way. I'm good though, I have a place to stay. Your mother charges me $800 a month but it's a home."

"She charges you what?" I looked at her a little shocked.

"$800 a month."

"What the fuck? Why is she charging you?"

"Why wouldn't she? I mean I do live there and she said you only send enough to take care of Myles which is understandable."

"Hold the fuck up, she told you I only send what?"

"She said you send money for Myles' clothes and stuff but other than that her checks from your father's estate pays the bills."

"She's a compulsive fucking liar. I send her ass at least five thousand dollars a month. I pay the mortgage, her bills and give her money for her pocket on top of doing everything financially for Myles. She's pocketing your money; she doesn't need your help."

"Are you serious?"

"Yes I'm serious. She got an insurance check when he first died and that's how she got this house but that's it."

"Wow, she's fucked up. She knows I need all the money I make and she charging me when she doesn't even fucking need it. Your mother is a trip."

"She definitely is." I shook my head.

That shit pissed me off. Not only did she take money from this girl when she didn't need to; she lied and said I'm not doing shit for her. Better believe my mother was going to hear my mouth when I got back to the house, I can promise that.

After Maya and I finished eating she drove us back to the house and we went inside. When we walked into the living room her daughter was sitting on the floor watching television.

"Hey baby, where's Myles?" I asked Bree.

"He's upstairs with auntie about to get a whoopin'." she answered.

"A whooping for what?"

"He dropped the picture frame by accident." As soon as she said that I heard my mother yelling then heard Myles scream like somebody was killing him. Immediately I kicked my shoes off then ran upstairs and busted in her room.

This bitch had my son lying across the bed with his shirt off and a thick ass leather belt in her hand. When I saw her standing there, I instantly had a flashback of my father beating me when I was Myles' age. The memory alone set me the fuck off.

"What the fuck are you doing?" I screamed making her jump and look at me. "I know you're not hitting him with that fucking belt!"

"He did something wrong now he has to pay for it." My mother answered in a calm tone like nothing was wrong.

"Pay for it? He's seven years old you psychotic bitch. Myles get up right now!"

"Lay your ass back down!" She screamed then hit him with the belt again. When I heard his scream that second time, I pushed her into the wall with all the strength I had in my body.

"What the fuck is wrong with you? You're not gone beat my son like he's a fucking slave," I went over to Myles and pulled him up off the bed. "Listen," I wiped the tears from his face. "Go in your room, get dressed and pack as much as you can. Put all of your things into a bag. Right now, go." He ran out of the room and I turned back to my mother who was now getting up off the floor.

"Michelle, I've been raising this boy for the last couple of years. I know what I'm doing!" My mom shouted at me.

"You don't if you're in here beating him like that. You used to cry your fucking eyes out when my father did it to me because you couldn't stop him. Why the fuck would you turn around and do that same demented shit to your grandson?"

"So what? He got a whooping, kids get their asses whooped all the time."

"There is a difference between disciplining him and beating on him. That belt is thick as shit; he's only seven years old," I shook my head. "You're so lucky you're my mother or I swear to God I would knock you the fuck out."

"Knock me out? You mean like your father used to do?" She walked over to me and got in my face.

"Move ma, don't walk up on me like that," I stepped back away from her because I really didn't want to put my hands on her. After getting my ass whooped by my father and baby daddy for years, I've become unable to deal with anybody getting in my personal space. When you get too close to me, I automatically go into defense mode and I will swing on you.

"No tell me, is that what you were going to do? Put hands on me

Michelle I've dealt with it before it's not new to me." My mother stepped in my face again.

"Get the fuck out of my face!" I pushed her away then out of nowhere she slapped the shit out of me. I closed my eyes and prayed that God forgave me because I was about to kill this bitch.

I don't know how I got the belt from her hand to mine because I blacked out but I started hitting her with it. I don't even know how long I was hitting her or how many times I did it but I was tearing her ass up. It wasn't until Maya came in the room and got me away from her, that I snapped back to reality.

My mother was on the ground balled up into the fetal position shaking and crying. I felt a little bad because I don't want to do anything to my mother but hell, she made it go there.

"Mickey, what the hell are you doing? That's your mother," Maya said with a worried expression on her face.

"Fuck her; she was in here beating my son like he's a damn slave. This belt is thick enough to make a grown man cry. Myles is seven years old!"

"I know Mickey but calm down, you beat her ass now just leave it alone."

"I'm doing better than that. I'm getting my son and we're getting the fuck out of here."

"What are you talking about?"

"I'm talking about going back to Jersey with my son. Myles! Are you ready?"

"Yes," Myles came out of his room pulling his suitcase. "My Xbox can't fit in my bag mommy."

"Leave it here; I'll buy you another one. Go downstairs and wait for me." Mickey went in the bedroom and looked at her mother who was getting up off the floor.

"You're cut off from me. I'm not going to stop paying the mortgage because Maya lives here and that would fuck them up but a soon as she saves up enough money to get her own place, I'm not doing shit else for you. You're not taking money from Maya anymore either. I'm taking pictures of my son's back and keeping them. So go ahead and call the cops like I kidnapped him or try and fight me on custody if you want to. Your ass will be getting locked up. Maya," I looked over at her, "can you take me to the airport please?"

"Yeah, are you leaving right now?"

"Yes, if I stay here any longer, I'm going to kill her ass," I walked past Maya and went down to the guest room so I could get my stuff together.

My flight wasn't for another two days but I'm leaving now. I don't care how much they charge me to change my flight arrangements but Myles and I are getting the fuck out of here today.

TONE

When I saw Mickey coming out of the airport holding hands with a little boy I raised my eyebrow in confusion. *She went down south and kidnapped somebody's kid?* I walked over and met her halfway.

"Thank you for coming to get me. I could've called a cab or something, but that shit would've been a pretty penny and Toi wasn't picking up the damn phone," Mickey said to me when I got over to her.

"It's not a problem," I looked at the boy she had with her then back at her. "Who is this?"

"Oh this is my son Myles, Myles this is Tone say hi."

"Hi," he waved at me.

"What's up little man? I see you got the new Jordan's. I like those where you get them from?"

"My grandma got them from a store." Myles answered a big smile on his face.

"Well your grandma knows how to shop." Looking at him I couldn't help but chuckle. Grandma my ass, Mickey must've been telling her where to go because this little boy had on too much name brand shit for her greedy ass mother to be picking out. "Come on," I grabbed Mickey's bags from her and we walked to my car. I put their stuff into the trunk then we all got in the car and I pulled off.

"So what's up? I heard you went down south but I didn't know you was bringing your son back with you," I asked Mickey.

"I wasn't planning on it at first but some shit went down with my mother so I had to get him out of there."

"Care to elaborate?"

"Nah, not really."

"Yeah alright," I chuckled. The drive to her house was pretty silent except for random questions Myles would ask as we drove. I wasn't surprised that she wasn't trying to talk to me. It's been like this since we broke up. I haven't really spoken to her since our break up anyway. The fact that she called actually shocked me but I did what she asked and came to pick her up.

It's obvious she was still pissed at me but I don't understand why. I'm not the one who did her wrong, she lied and did all that bullshit not me.

When I pulled up to her house I got out and helped her bring the bags inside. Just when I was about to leave I looked at her and grabbed her arm.

"Let me speak to you outside for a second Mickey."

"Myles, watch TV I'm going on the steps for a minute okay." She turned the TV on for him then gave him the remote before stepping outside with me. "What's up?"

"I was about to ask you the same thing. Why are you acting like a bitch?"

"How am I acting like a bitch?"

"You call me to come do you a favor and that was fine. I don't have a problem helping you with anything and you know that. But, you sat in that car quiet as hell when that is not even your style. Your mouth usually stays running."

"I didn't have anything to say, Tone we really don't have shit to talk about. You broke up with me remember."

"Yes I remember but that doesn't mean you got to act like a bitch especially when you calling me for a favor. Listen, we're going to see each other alright, Taj and Yung are about to have a baby. Toi and Que are talking again. I'm going to have to be around you and vice versa so you might as well take all that hate you have in your heart for me and throw that shit away. Act your age ma; you're too grown for the little kid shit," I kissed her on the cheek then went and got in my car so I could leave.

TONE

The sound of my phone ringing knocked me out of the good ass nap I was in the middle of. Irritated I reached over on my night stand, grabbed my phone then answered it, damn near still asleep.

"Yeah," I said in a groggy voice.

"Nigga, are you still asleep?" Legend's asked.

"Hell yeah I'm asleep, damn what you want?"

"Bruh it's mad people down here for this fuckin' party and you still knocked out?"

"Aww shit, I forgot about that," I groaned looking at the clock. It was damn near 7 at night which means I missed a few hours of the festivities. But these parties don't end until the wee hours of the night so I wasn't worried about missing the good shit.

Every year when the weather breaks and spring really starts to set in, Legend throws a huge pool party at his club The Mansion. We have endless amounts of liquor, special performances from local artist, barbecue and some more shit. The shit gets bigger every damn year; I don't even know how I forgot about it. It's all that nigga Legend has been talking about.

"That's a damn shame. Get yo ass up and get here man. Everybody else is here but you."

"Alright, alright I got you. I'll be on my way down there soon," I ended the call and got up off my bed. I'm not really in the damn mood for a party but it is what it is.

I got my ass up out of my comfortable bed went to the bathroom so I could shower and get dressed.

By the time I got to the mansion it was already packed with people. The valets were on duty and working hard for their tips. Legend had really good timing because this

When I got out of my car, I walked straight inside ignoring the females that were desperately trying to get my attention.

I walked around the first floor for a minute before finally heading out back to the where the pool was. Of course it was packed with people, partying in and outside of the pool. Food and liquor was on deck because damn near everybody has a plate and red solo cup in their hands.

Looking around I spotted the cabana Legend and the rest of the crew were seated at was surrounded by bitches. Since word got out that Legend was single bitches were throwing themselves at him harder than ever. I knew what he was feeling because the same shit was happening to me.

I guess there some females that figured they better shoot their shot before we got snatched up off the market again. There were always girls trying to get our attention but the shit has been times ten lately. It's annoying as shit but funny as hell at the same time so I don't mind it.

"Yo, y'all lit over here," I said to my niggas when I got to them.

"As usual," Legend laughed. "Nigga, how did you forget about the damn party? We do this shit every year."

"I know but I was knocked the fuck out. It's not like you needed me for some shit."

"That aint the point," he put a blunt between his lips then lit it. "You know shit is going to get crazy as shit right?"

"Doesn't it always though?" I laughed.

"Just making sure you ready," we both started laughing.

"God damn!" We heard some nigga shout.

"Yo Legend, you might want to get your girl," Barry hit Legend's shoulder then motioned towards the entrance to the house.

My mouth damn near dropped when I saw Mickey standing there next to Toi and Taj. Not because I was shocked to see her, she looked good as fuck. She was wearing some distressed jean shorts showing off her pretty long legs; a floral off-the-shoulder crop top, and some multicolor wedge sandals.

Knowing Mickey the way I do, everything from her shoes, to her bag and sunglasses were designer. Her blonde hair was wavy and cascading down her back. From what I could see she had nothing but lip gloss on; shorty was on point.

Once I got my eyes off of her I saw Taj looking pretty in her long black and white maxi dress. Then my eyes went to Toi who from my view was either giving a nigga her number or taking his. Before I could even catch what was going on, Legend was on his feet and walking towards them.

"Here this nigga go," I shook my head.

Legend got over to them and grabbed Toi's phone from her hand. She looked up at him like he was crazy then they started bickering back and forth. I didn't really think shit of it until he chucked his phone across the backyard then pulled her inside the house.

Mickey and Taj came over to where we were and took a seat. It was funny both of their mean asses spoke to everybody except me and Yung. They're petty as hell.

"What's up Mickey?" I said to her.

"Hey," she replied in a dry tone. I laughed, walking off so I could get myself a drink. She has a stank ass attitude, Legend is trippin' over Toi when they're not even together and Yung is going to be crying about Taj ignoring at by the end of the night. I already know how this night is about to go. I'm going to need a couple of drinks to deal with this shit.

LEGEND

A nigga was prepared to turn up a little bit and chill with Toi when she decided to show up. I knew when I invited her that she was going to come in here looking good as shit. She was wearing an oversized light denim shirt that hung off her shoulders and stopped mid-thigh. Electric blue ankle strap sandals were on her feet, and blue aviator shades rest on top of her head.

All of the good things I felt about seeing her disappeared when I saw the nigga in her face. I'm not psychotic so I don't care who she talks to but she looked like she was taking his number or giving out hers. Either way that shit is a violation in my eyes. No we're not together but she's not about to bag another nigga in my presence. Hell no.

As soon as I snatched her phone and she looked up at me like I was crazy, I knew she was going to throw a fit. I don't give a fuck either, she should've known not to do that shit while she was in my space.

"Yo, you are buggin' right now Que. Give me my damn phone," Toi snapped at me while trying to reach for her phone.

"Nah you're good. You taking niggas numbers now? That's what the fuck we on?" I questioned her.

"What I do isn't your business, we're not together nigga. Give me my phone or I swear to God."

"You swear to God what?"

"Don't play with me. You done went and scared the nigga off, give me my phone back!" She shouted. Had the music not been on blast, she would've been causing a damn scene with how loud she was.

It actually pissed me off because I didn't get why she was taking shit so damn personal. I got her phone in my hand, okay? And? She acts like I'm about to steal or her shit or something.

"What you want it back so you can go call that nigga?"

"If you don't get the fuck outta here with that shit, I want it back because it's mine. Give me my phone Que!"

"Fuck this phone," I said before tossing that shit somewhere. I already knew she was about to cut up so I pulled in her inside and upstairs. We went to the master bedroom I transformed into my own personal office.

As soon as I closed the door Toi snatched her hand out of my grip. "Why the fuck would you throw my phone? That shit probably broke now!"

"I don't give a fuck. You were trying to be funny so laugh at that shit."

"You a childish muthafucka I swear to God. This is why we're not together now, you do too much. We were doing good with the being cool shit but here you go with this extra shit again."

"It wasn't extra. You did some bullshit. Just being cool or not, don't sit here and act like you would be cool with me getting a bitch number while you right there."

"I wouldn't give a damn Que, we're not together," Toi said, trying her best to sound confident. I didn't believe shit that came out her mouth just now. I could tell she was lying, the way she diverted her eyes told it all.

"You lying like hell right now ma."

"Nobody is lying to you. I don't care about what you think I would've done, the point is you shouldn't have thrown my damn phone!"

"First of all watch who the fuck you yelling at. You're getting too damn comfortable with that shit, relax," I told her. I knew she was going to be mad but that she was doing too much yelling for me.

"Whatever," she waved me off but I noticed she calmed that ass down.

"Whatever my ass; I see you lowered your tone."

"Nah that was funny, I'll buy you a new phone. What else you want?

Just tell me so you can quit that pouting shit. You're getting on my nerves a little bit, big baby acting ass."

I walked over to her pulling her in my arms. "I'm sorry that you're pissed off. I'm not apologizing about breaking your phone though. I meant to do that shit. It would be fake of me to say sorry knowing damn well I'm not."

"You're such an asshole sometimes."

"You knew that from the jump," I kissed her forehead then took that opportunity to kiss her on the lips. I thought she was going to play hard with me but she kissed me back. Using my tongue to part her lips I deepened the kiss while my hands roamed her body.

"Mmm, we have to get back to your party," Toi mumbled against my lips.

"Fuck that party," I pulled my pants and boxers down to my knees, fully exposing my dick.

"What are you doing?" she asked.

"I gotta feel this pussy, it's been too damn long," I whispered then turned me around, I gripped the back of her neck, slightly bending her over, causing her ass to meet my hips. With my free hand lifted her dress, pulled her thong to the side then slid into her.

"Ughhh," she gasped, as I stretched her walls.

"Damn, you drippin' already," I grunted, as I pumped into her. "You missed me baby?"

"Oh, damn," she purred, as she threw it back at me.

Her round ass bounced against me, as we moved in sync. When I felt my nut building up, I pulled out then stripped both of us out of our clothes before lying her across my desk. Grabbing her legs, I propped them onto my shoulders locking my arms around them. With her balled up in that position, she was defenseless while I drilled into her spot.

"Ahhh uughh shit!" Toi screamed in pleasure, as I pounded into her. "Wait, Que! Wait!"

"Shut up," I gripped her throat. "Be the bad bitch you claim to be and take this dick," leaning down I bit her neck as my strokes intensified. "Ooh shit, you leaking on this shit. You missed me huh baby?"

"Fuck! Y-yes baby okay! Please, wait."

"You better stop fuckin' playing with me Toi," I gripped her throat tighter as I rolled my hips into her. When I felt her juices running down my legs I smirked going harder.

"Uhhh," she panted, as her pussy began to fart. Without pulling out, I picked her up and sat in my chair with my hands behind my head. "Work this shit," I slapped Toi's thigh lodging my bottom lip between my teeth.

Toi clutched the top of my chair and began to ride my shaft.

"Fuck girl!" I groaned watching her pretty titties bounce in my face.

Showing out, she was crotched her body, literally dancing on the dick all the while her nectar coated me signaling she was having another orgasm. Involuntarily, my mouth fell open.

"Oh shit, just like that ma, fuck ride this shit." Making her booty jump, she stopped working her hips, as she tightened her muscles around my dick. "Oh shit!" Grabbing her chin I pulled her in for a kiss while I erupted inside of her. I don't know what she was thinking but as far as I'm concerned that just being friends shit is dead.

TOI

"Uh huh, just nasty," Mickey clowned when I walked up to her and Taj.

After being cooped up in the office with Que, going at it like rabbits for an hour I was finally back down mingling with everybody else. We took a shower in his bathroom, got dressed and went back to the party like nothing happened.

"Shut up," I gave her arm a light tap then sat at the table next to her.

"Y'all were gone for a good minute. Keep that shit up and you'll be popping one out next."

"Fuck out of here plan B is a Walgreens stop away. Mickey text my mother and tell her if she needs anything to call your phone."

"Myles is with her and the twins; she'll know to call me if something happens. I couldn't find your phone; nigga got an arm because I don't know where that shit went."

"It's fine, he's going to buy me another one. Why are y'all over here? Y'all didn't want to be under the cabana?"

They were sitting at one 15 tables that circled the huge pool. The sun was down so it cooled down some and the party was still live. The pool and every table were occupied and there were people spread out all over. I didn't think they would be sitting at their own separate table; we usually sit with the guys any time we're around them.

"We were over there but they're smoking so we took this table as soon as some people got up. I'm cool right here. I don't need Anthony and his whores in my face," Taj said then took a swig from her water bottle. "I am so mad I can't drink."

"I'll drink enough for the both of us. I got you." Mickey took a sip from her red cup.

"What are you drinking?" I asked her. Her eyes were low and she had a lazy grin on her face. She was tipsy as hell.

"It's a jungle juice they have at the bar. It's sweet as shit so I'm going to be fucked up. You know how that shit works."

"Hell yeah, it's always the punch that doesn't taste strong that gets you fucked up. They need to call it sneak juice; it creeps up on you like a muthafucka."

"Yup and while she's over sipping so is Tone. That nigga has been drinking like he doesn't have a liver and doing the most with those bitches over there."

I looked over at the cabana and sure enough Tone had a bottle of Remy Martin in his and bitches in his face. One girl was on his lap, he had two more on each side of him. The nigga looked like he was living the high life.

"That's another reason I moved. He's doing a whole lot and if I put my hands on him I'll be wrong." By the look on Mickey's face, she was ready to break Tone's neck. I don't know if he's purposely doing it to get at her but I do know he was putting on.

I've been around him in social settings before he got with Mickey and he was never the type to have girls hanging all over him. Tone says he doesn't like the thirsty shit but for whatever reason, he's enjoying it.

"We can leave if you want to Mick. I want to get some food but we can stop at McDonalds if you're ready to go right now," I told her. Even though I hadn't had the chance to even really enjoy the party because I was in the house with Que. Now, Mickey is sitting next to me looking like she's ready to commit murder.

"Nah you can go ahead and eat. I can wait a little while longer. I didn't commit a felony yet, I can hold out on losing while you get some food. We already had ours."

"I figured you did. I'll be right back," I went over to where the food was and stacked my plate with some barbecue chicken, some ribs, potato salad, baked beans and coleslaw. When I got back to the table Taj and Mickey were huddled up like they were plotting.

"What's wrong with y'all?" I asked, getting their attention.

"I'm trying to talk the crazy out of her head. Guess who just walked in and went straight up to Tone." Taj answered since Mickey was using her hands to massage her temples. I looked over at the cabana again to see Kareem's cousin, Cassie talking to Tone.

"Aww shit," I mumbled.

Cassie and Mickey do not like each other at all, and they haven't for years. It all started because Cassie's nosey ass used to tell Kareem shit about Mickey's cousin Bia knowing how he was going to react. Before anybody else knew he was putting hands on Bia, Cassie knew, and she would instigate their fights.

If she saw Bia waving at a nigga or wearing something Kareem deemed as inappropriate and Cassie would snitch. Once Mickey found out about what she was doing, shit got real. We were at a basketball game just chillin' when Kareem came there spazzing out trying to fight Bia as usual. In the midst of his yelling he let it slip that Cassie told him we were all up in some niggas faces, which wasn't true at all. Mickey heard that and she literally beat Cassie's ass all over baby Rutgers park.

She beat the bitch from the basketball park, to the kiddie park, to the swings, and then dragged her out the park into the street. Cassie got that ass stomped and beat all up and down Whiton street.

Since then it's been beef between them and Mickey swore it always would be. Shit really went bad because after Kareem murdered Bia, Cassie had the nerve to go on Facebook and talk shit. The ill feelings and the fact that she was all in Tone's face was enough to have Mickey out here acting a fool.

"Okay we're leaving before she kills this bitch," I grabbed a rib from my plate. "Let me tell Que I'm leaving and we can go." All the while eating my rib I went over to the cabana to Que who was talking to Barry. "Que, I'm about to go."

He looked up at me confused. "Why are you leaving? Shit still live ma."

"I know but your boy is trippin' and I don't want my friend going to jail for killing somebody," I told him. He looked towards Tone and Cassie who was in a full-fledged kiss.

"What the fuck?" Que shook his head. "This nigga is drunk and trippin'. Call me when you get home, alright?"

"Okay, I will."

We shared a quick kiss then he got up and went over to Tone.

I took my eyes away from them and looked over at Mickey who was getting up from the table. "Oh shit." Tossing the half-eaten rib in the garbage I made my over to Mickey blocking her path.

"Mickey, don't go over there and do some crazy shit."

"He's kissing that bitch in front of me like I'm not sitting back here!" Mickey shouted.

"I know but just come on, not today, alright? Not today, fuck him," I grabbed Mickey's hand and pulled her in the opposite direction. Cassie deserved to get her ass beat and despite them not being together Tone was in violation. As much as I wanted her to fuck the both of them up, I'm not going to let her make an ass of herself.

We got to the table and grabbed our things. I literally had to pull Mickey in the house so we could make our way to the front door because she wouldn't stop glaring in Tone's direction. For right now, I'm going to let Cassie and Tone live and get Mickey the fuck out of here. But, God help them the next time they run into her.

GENEVA HENDERSON

I walked through the aisles of Shoprite picking up things I could cook for dinner tonight. Toi told me Quentin was coming and bringing his daughter with him so I wanted to make something special for everybody. I know Quentin doesn't eat pork so my initial idea of baked pork chops was dead. Switching it up I decided to make chicken Marsala, asparagus, and some red mashed potatoes. Just in case baby girl doesn't like mushrooms I was going to have a separate pan of barbecue baked chicken.

Since my talk with Toi she's been getting back to herself. She's not cooped up in her room all the time and she's cracking jokes and acting like the girl we know and love. I know my mother's death was a hard pill to swallow; it was for all of us.

When it comes to Toi and the twins I know it really hurt them because just like me, she raised them. She was more than just their grandmother; she was basically their parents when the real ones weren't.

Losing my mother would've been heartbreaking either way but the fact that we were just getting our relationship repaired is what hurt me the most. I was finally in a place where I wasn't disappointing her and she was snatched away from me before we could fully enjoy being with each other. I am happy I got to spend one more Thanksgiving and Christmas with her before she left us. I'm at least grateful for that much.

"Auntie, can I get this?" Kayla asked while holding up a box of cereal.

"Go ahead. Jayla if you want something grab it so we can go pay for this stuff," I responded. I went to turn down another isle when I accidentally hit another cart. When I looked at the person I wanted to roll my eyes. Why did I have to run into this bitch?

"Geneva?" Beautii questioned like she didn't recognize me. I was blessed enough to get clean before I could do any real damage to my appearance so I know she knows for a fact I'm me.

"Beautii," I said in a dry tone.

"Wow, you've cleaned yourself up pretty well."

"Mhm, why are you talking to me right now?"

"I'm just being nice Geneva."

"You and nice don't really go together. I'm surprised you're in here. The last I heard you and Saint were in a big mansion in New York somewhere."

"We're in Sands Point to be exact, but I choose to come here so I won't have to stop again. I didn't know you cared."

"Oh I don't sweetheart trust me."

"Auntie, I got these." Jayla put a pack of Oreo's in the cart when she and Kayla walked up. Beautii looked at them with her eyebrows raised.

"Auntie? These are your nieces?"

"Mhm."

"Hi Beautii," they both greeted her at the same time.

"Hey girls," she gave them an uneasy smile. "I didn't know they were related to you."

"Well they are. These are Grace's daughters," I replied with a satisfied smirk. I knew exactly why she was looking like she saw a ghost and it was funny to me.

"Grace is their mother?"

"Yup and they just turned 16. They're beautiful girls aren't they? Smart too, she would be proud of them."

"So, um...so you're related to Toi too then."

"That's my daughter. It's a small world huh?" I began to laugh. "You have a good day Beautii. Come on girls." When we walked off I was cackling on the inside. I already know she's mentally losing her shit. If she wasn't already on the phone with her husband, she was damn sure going to giving him a call soon.

The twins and I finished our shopping then went and paid for it. On our way home I replayed my exchange with Beautii in my head silently laughing.

My history with Beautii and her husband Saint isn't a peachy one. All because Saint was dealing with my sister Grace before she died. Everybody knew Beautii and Saint were together, they were what these kids call relationship goals back in the day. On the outside looking in, they had the perfect relationship but that was bullshit.

Saint was really heavy in the streets, and he was being a whore like most men. I don't know how he met Grace but they were damn near inseparable. He would down play their relationship for the sake of his girl and reputation since it was public knowledge that Grace was an addict; but he loved her.

He loved her enough that he told her multiple times if she kicked her habit and stayed clean that he would leave Beautii. Grace never bothered to stay clean, at least not for him anyway so they never had the chance to explore a real relationship.

She would never admit it but Beautii knows that she has Saint by default and I know it eats away at her. I know she has some bitter feelings towards Grace, even in death. Beef with my sister means beef with me so we don't like each other either. Knowing how petty she really is, I can almost bet money that had she known Toi was my daughter she would've avoided any type of interaction with her. That super close play niece shit she does with Toi would be nonexistent.

* * *

"AUNTIE WAS FUCKING that woman's man?" Toi asked while she shook her head. We were in the kitchen preparing dinner and I ran down the situation to Toi. If Beautii switched up on her out of nowhere I wanted her to know why.

"Yeah, she could've had him if she stayed clean. Saint wasn't trying to wife a drug addict, that wouldn't even make sense in the business he was in."

"Wow, that's crazy. I'm glad you told me. Now if she acts funny I won't be caught off guard."

"Is this going to make things awkward between you and Que? I know he's close with his family."

"He is but everything should be fine. Beautii having an issue with me won't make a difference; his mother doesn't like me either."

"That is some petty bullshit. How is she going to have an issue with you because her daughter was hoeing?"

"That's just how some people choose to be ma. I'm not bothered by it."

"Good, don't kiss his mama's ass. If she can't see that you're a good woman because her daughter has an issue then that's her bad."

"That's the same thing I was thinking. I'm not worried about Que's family right now. I have other shit on my brain."

"Like the spa right? How is that coming along?"

"Great actually; I went with Mickey to this graphic design company and they've started on that. They referred me to a web designer so the website is getting started. The contractors are almost done; I just have to get ready to look for my staff. In two and a half months Bella Melanine will be opened and ready for business." The whole time Toi spoke about her spa she had a big smile on her face. I could tell she was proud of herself and I was too. I know mama is smiling down on her too.

"I am so proud of you Toi."

"Thank you, mama," I kissed her cheek then went to the oven. "I've been meaning to ask you something."

"What's up?"

"How did you pay for everything after you and Que broke up?"

"Well while we together he kept putting money in my account that I didn't touch like that unless it was for bills so that's how we've been doing fine. He paid off my contractors but he doesn't know I know he did."

I chuckled shaking my head. "That boy loves your ass."

"Ma spending doesn't mean he loves me especially when he has it to spend."

"I understand why you think that way but I really want you to sit back and think about everything that man has done for you so far. You think he's doing that for every woman he meets? I highly doubt it."

"Well it doesn't matter right now."

"Like hell it doesn't, you talk to that man all day every day. You might not be back with him but he's definitely back with you."

"How does that even make sense," she began to laugh.

"Okay you can think it's funny if you want to. That boy loves you; I'm leaving it at that," I shrugged my shoulders.

When the doorbell rang I looked over at Toi who was looking at the watch on her wrist. "That's probably Que. He's early as shit."

"He probably smelled the food from across town," I chuckled. "I'll get it," I left the kitchen and went to open the door. I was expecting to see Quentin but it was a handsome dark skin man standing there. "Can I help you?"

"Yeah I'm looking for Toi. Is she here?" The man asked.

"Um, who are you?"

"I'm Bless, an old friend," he answered with a friendly smile.

"An old friend huh?" I shook my head. "Wait right here," I closed and locked the door then went back to the kitchen. "Toi, why is that Bless boy at the door looking for you?"

I don't know much about Bless because Toi never gave me all the details. She told me he's her ex and Quentin's sister was dealing with him at the same time she was. Despite not knowing much about him, I do know if the new man pulls up and sees the old one here it's going to be some drama.

"He's at what looking for who?" Toi looked at me confused.

"The boy is at the door looking for you. I don't know what he wants but you better get rid of him before Quentin pulls up."

"This muthafucka," she mumbled while grabbing the meat tenderizer.

"What the hell are you going to do with that?"

"Smack the shit out of him with it if he doesn't get from in front of my damn door."

TOI

When I got to the front door I opened it coming face to face with Bless who had the nerve to be smiling like shit was cool.

"What the fuck are you doing here Bless?" The fact that this nigga was at my door right now had me pissed. How do I go from not seeing your ass for damn near two years to you popping at my house?

"Damn, why you look so angry? I told you I was going to see you again and like I told you the last time I saw you, you got some making up to do."

"You need to get your stupid ass on somewhere with this bullshit. I'm not making shit up to you, fuck from in front of my door."

"Ooh I like that feisty shit," Bless chuckled as if I was joking. "For real, grab your purse and shit so we can go."

"Nigga, I'm not going anywhere with you. Get the fuck away from my house!" I shouted. I didn't want to cause a scene but he was doing the most right now.

"I like the feisty shit but don't get stupid Toi. I gave you some time to get your mind right but like I said go get your shit so we can go." Bless said in a calm but stern tone.

"I'm not going with you. You think you're about to come back up here and disrupt my damn life? Nigga please, bye," I went to close my door, but he blocked it with his foot. "Move!"

"You're trying my damn patience Toi. Go get your shit and let's go."

"No!"

"Bitch-"

"Nigga finish that sentence and your brains will be all over this fucking porch!" Hearing Que's deep voice caused me to look behind Bless. Sure enough Quentin was standing there hand in hand with a little girl and holding a gun to the back of Bless' head at the same time.

Chuckling Bless turned around. "Oh look who it is, big Legend. This has nothing to do with you bruh, mind your business and move on."

"Nigga you stepping to my girl, it has everything to do with me."

"Your girl? Oh shit, you went and got the top nigga Toi? I can tell by the look on his face he's stuck on your ass," Bless laughed. "Damn, you must be throwing the pussy at him pretty damn good. I know what that's like, the pussy used to have me ready to kill too." He started to laugh again but it came to a halt when Que let go of his daughter's hand and began to bash this nigga in his face with the gun.

"Shit!" I grabbed the girl's hand and pulled her in the house while she screamed for her father. "Stay right here okay," I told her then went to Que and pulled him off of Bless who was on my porch bleeding from his damn face. The fact that he busted this nigga all in his shit didn't bother me at all. Bless deserved it but he was in front of my door with this shit and his daughter was standing right there.

"Toi get the fuck off me!" Que shouted in my face. I wanted to slap his ass and ask who the fuck he was yelling at but right now wasn't the time for that.

"No! Are you trying to get locked the fuck up? Your daughter is right there! He's not worth going to jail for, stop! Please?" Grabbing his face I made him look inside my house where Diamond was crying. My mother was kneeled down next to her trying to calm her down while the twins were standing there trying to be nosey.

He moved his face from my hands then looked at Bless who was slowly getting up. Que went past me and pushed Bless down my front steps.

"Stay the fuck away from her nigga. Next time it won't be shit saving your ass," he snapped then grabbed my arm and pulled me in my house slamming the door behind us. "Let me talk to you for a minute."

I couldn't object or agree because he was pulling me upstairs to my bedroom. "Get off me Que," I snatched my arm out of his grip once we were in my room with the door closed.

"What the fuck was that nigga doing here? YOU FUCKIN' HIM?"

"No!"

"Then why the fuck was he here and what was he talking about Toi!"

"Que we can have this conversation like two grown ass adults but you're going to stop fuckin' yelling at me like I'm your child! Remember what happened the last time you did this shit. Calm down."

He glared at me like he was ready to take my damn head off and sat down on my bed. "You right, I'm calm. I'll let you talk. What the hell was he talking about?"

"I used to date him."

"What?"

"I used to date Bless. I met him when I was 17 and we were together for almost four years. I ran into him when I was out with Mickey one night. He was talking about how I had to makeup something to him so he popped up over here. I didn't invite him, I'm not fucking him, and I don't talk to him at all."

"Wait you said you was with the nigga for almost four years. How serious were you because I don't ever remember him saying your name or even talking about having a girl."

"Why would you hear anything about me from him? How well do y'all know each other?"

The fact that Bless clearly knew who Que was didn't faze me because everybody knows him. Bless was in the streets so them crossing paths isn't shocking.

"Man, I grew up with that nigga." Que shook his head. "We came into the game together and when I took over everything I made him my number two. Everything was good, but he started getting sloppy."

"Sloppy?"

"Yeah, I guess he felt like because he was second in command that meant he could do whatever the fuck he wanted to do. That nigga would get into brawls and shoot-outs over little stupid shit. Then he kept fucking up with the product, not keeping count on certain shit the right way. I had to demote him, and I let him know he could get his spot back but he would have to work his way back up. Instead of being a man and doing that shit he tried to go behind my back and lock down his own deal with my connect."

"Grimy shit."

"Exactly; my uncle told me to get rid of him. Shit, even Tone told me to do it but I couldn't. Despite his fuck ups we grew up together so I told him he could either leave or I would have no choice."

"So that's why he left Jersey?"

"Yup, now he's back up here talking some shit about his cousin being missing. That's bullshit; he didn't give a fuck about that nigga. He's just up here looking for an issue."

"Well you done went and pistol whipped the man so now he has one," I sighed sitting next to him on my bed. "Wait, if you grew up with him that means your family knows him right?"

"Yeah," Que nodded.

"So he's known y'all his whole life?"

"Yeah Toi, what about it?"

"Well the boyfriend your sister was stalking me over was Bless."

"What?"

"Your sister and best friend were fucking around behind your back," I said it as straight forward as possible. "It had to be for a while too because the way she was acting over him, there is no way it was a onetime thing or something casual."

"I'm not even shocked," Que let out a bitter chuckle. "I'll deal with my sister and Bless. I don't want that nigga anywhere near you, you hear me?"

"Que I don't want man anywhere near me so you have nothing to worry about. You need to get downstairs and comfort your daughter. She doesn't know my mother; she's probably down there freaking out."

"Alright come on," he kissed me on the lips then we headed downstairs. We went into the kitchen and Diamond was at the table eating a cookie. "You good baby girl? Que asked after squatting down in front of her.

"Yeah, Miss Neva gave me some cookies."

"Good. Daddy is sorry for getting angry like that in front of you. It won't happen again, I promise. Okay?"

"Okay," she nodded.

Que kissed her forehead then went to my mother and kissed her cheeks. "Thanks ma."

"You're welcome. She's a sweet girl."

"I know, I wonder where she gets it from because it damn sure aint from her mama or mine." Que joked then grabbed my hand, pulling me towards him. "Diamond, this is my friend Toi. Toi this is Diamond."

"Hi pretty," I smiled at her and she smiled back showing me her two missing front teeth. As much as I can't stand this girls mama, I have to admit that she and Que made a gorgeous child. Diamond had a light complexion just like Isyss. Her long hair was pulled into two curly ponytails that went past her shoulders and she had big brown eyes just like her father.

"Hi. Daddy is she your girlfriend?" Diamond asked him. I looked at Que who was laughing.

"I want her to be."

"Oooh he likes you!" Diamond sang as if she was teasing us. "Do you like him too?"

"I don't know yet," I chuckled. "Do you think I should like him?"

"Yeah, he's nice. We go shopping, and watch movies at his big house."

"Big house huh?" I looked over at Que who had a smirk on his face. "You bought a house?"

"I been had a house, I'll show it to you soon." He kissed my cheek. "Aye ma, when are we eating?"

While Que and my mother talked I sat down next to Diamond and got to know her a little bit better. She told me she was turning seven in June, and that Que's whole family spoils her rotten. To my surprise she was very well behaved, well-spoken and she was obsessed with Disney Princesses, Moana being her favorite at the moment.

Honestly because of the obvious idiot her mother is I thought this little girl was going to be a piece of work but I'm glad I was wrong. Watching Que interact with her warmed my heart too. Nigga might be crazy but he's a damn good father. It had my mind thinking about how he would be as a father if we had kids.

MICKEY

"Are you done with your homework?" I asked Myles when I walked into my living room.

So far Myles was adjusting well to living with me again. I already had the original copies to all of his paperwork but I needed my mother to send me his school and latest medical records. I thought she was going to be a bitch and give me a hard time with it but she didn't. My threatening to quit paying her mortgage probably had something to do with it, but I don't care she gave them shits up.

I was a little worried about him starting at a new school when summer vacation was right around the corner but he loved it. He came home his first day bragging about the friends he made and he hasn't had any problems yet. I hope the energy is the same way next year because I would have to fuck somebody's child up for messing with mine.

"Yeah," he gave me his math work sheet and I sat down to check it.

"Okay, they're all right. Good job," I told him after reviewing it. I checked the rest and it was all finished and done correctly. "So you're smart just like me. That's what I'm talking about," I held my hand up and he gave me a high five.

"Can I go play my game now?"

"Yeah go head." Myles kissed my cheek then ran off to his room. I got up and went to my computer so I could check on a few things when my doorbell rang. "Who is it?" I asked when I got to the door. Instead of answering me they knocked on the door again. I sucked my teeth and opened it. "Who the fuck is…it.

"What's up baby?" Bryson said with a big smile on his face.

"Bryson?" When I saw him standing there my heart fell to my feet. Bryson still looked the same except for the fact that he clearly gained a great deal of muscle while he was locked up.

"You look shocked to see me ma, what's good?"

Once the initial shock of him standing at my door wore off, I cocked one of my eyebrows at his nerve.

"What the fuck are you doing at my door? How did you even get my damn address?"

"Come on now, you already know I get any information I need. You're not going to invite me in?"

"Hell no. Get the fuck off my porch right now."

"So this is how you want to act with me? The father of your only child?"

"The child you don't give two fucks about so mentioning him is pointless."

"So you're upset with me? I should be the one upset, I went to jail because of you bitch."

"Bullshit you went to jail because of your fucking self. Now like I said get the fuck off my porch before I get mad and you don't want that."

"Get mad Mickey, am I supposed to care? You can't beat me, we both know that."

"You're right but I can damn sure shoot or stab your big ass. Stay the fuck away from my house!" I slammed the door shut and locked it.

"That's alright! I'll see you again ma just wait!" Bryson shouted before letting out a loud unnecessary laugh I peeked out the front window and saw him walking over to a black Range Rover. Unsurprisingly Bless' bitch ass was in the front seat. Those two are thick as thieves, always has been.

Grabbing my phone I called Toi who picked up on the second ring. "What's up Mickey?"

"Tell me why Bryson was just at my fucking door."

"What? When the fuck did he get out?"

"I don't know but he's out and that bitch has my address." I sat on the couch and let out a deep sigh.

"That's not good, you need to move."

"Move? Why the hell would I move out of my house?"

"Mickey, you're about to act like you don't know how Brick is? He will keep popping up on you and it's just a matter of time before you end up in a damn fist fight. You have Myles again, and Brick having access to you is not good."

"I don't want to move."

"Well if you don't want to move get a restraining order on his ass. I think you should call Tone too."

"I was with you until you said that name."

"Mickey,"

"Mickey my ass, I'm not calling Tone. Fuck him."

"You're stubborn as hell. So what are you going to do if he tries some shit? You can't beat that nigga, I don't care how many bitches you've dragged."

"So what? I'll shoot his big ass. Toi, that nigga grew."

"What do you mean he grew?"

"The nigga grew, he's big as shit." Bryson has always been tall but now he's tall and huge. The nigga looks like a damn monster.

"Mickey you just need to go to the police station and get a restraining order tomorrow. I'm pretty sure if he's out early he's still on probation. If he comes anywhere near you he's getting locked back up and you cannot shoot him. That's jail time for you too. You're not a white person in Florida you're a black girl in Jersey. You will get a couple of years for that shit. Just do what I told you to do."

"Fine I'll go do that tomorrow. Oh even funnier, Bless was in the fucking car waiting for his ass."

"That's not shocking. They must read from the same book of bullshit because that nigga popped up at my house too."

"Are you serious?"

"Yeah and that's not it. He grew up with Que and because he was doing too much shady shit, he had to leave Jersey. That wasn't a decision he made himself."

"So he pretty much got ran out the state? That figures, his bitch ass."

"Que beat his ass on my porch. I could tell he wanted to kill that nigga."

"He should've; that was a chance to rid the world of a bitch ass nigga."

"Tell me about it. Fuck Bless though, what are you going to do about Brick?"

"I want him to leave me alone. Myles is enjoying himself up here so far. I'm trying to evolve and do better for us and this nigga wants to pop up? For what?"

"Mickey, are you shocked that he's out earlier than you expected or what because you knew as soon as he was released he was going to come see you."

"I mean I know but," I sucked my teeth. "Seeing him freaked me out."

Looking at Bryson had me feeling like my old self. Besides my father, Bryson is the only person in the world that I'm actually scared of. I feel like I put on a good enough act to convince him that he no longer had power over me but then again he could probably tell it was bullshit.

"I know it did and it should've. Brick is dangerous Mickey. He's a danger to you and Myles; you need to see about getting that restraining order."

"He hasn't done anything Toi, he just popped up."

"The nigga went to jail for putting his fuckin' hands on you. You testified against him, that's reason enough for them to grant you one."

"I'll look into it okay."

"Good. If not that you can still call Tone."

"Fuck Tone."

"Girl," Toi started laughing.

"What?"

"Why are you really mad?"

"I have a right to feel a way. He was on some extra shit on purpose. He's never acted like that even before we got together, but we break up and this nigga wants to be extra fuckin' friendly. Then he was kissing that bitch Cassie on top of everything else, HELL NO. Fuck that nigga! He can kiss my ass," I ranted.

Tone pissed me the fuck off at Legend's party. One of the things that attracted me to Tone was the fact that he's laid back but not boring. He'll party it up but he's never sloppy and he doesn't like women hanging all over him.

He's been like that since I met him, back when we didn't have anything going on. Now all of a sudden he's cool with having a bunch of hoe ass bitches hanging all over him. I feel like he was doing it on purpose, clearly he was drunk but I don't give a fuck. He's a grown ass man playing petty ass games, fuck him.

"I want to tell you to calm down but I would be hot too. You don't have to tell Tone, but I am telling Que to make sure somebody keeps an eye on both those niggas."

"Why?"

"I don't trust them. Bless isn't going to just let Que pistol whipping his ass go. Brick is going to lose his shit if he finds out you were in a whole damn relationship with another nigga. There is no telling where Kareem's sneaky ass is. I'm not taking any chances with them. I'm going to let Que know he needs to have his guard up if Bless is still in Jersey."

"I understand but I would rather Tone not know my business. So, if you could think of a way to leave me out of it I would appreciate it."

"I'll try not to mention you but if I have to I will; that's the best I can do."

"Mhm whatever, I'll take what I can get I guess. I need a fucking blunt right now." My thoughts were going in a million different directions.

Bryson being out is about to had me worried out of my mind. He swore to me the day he got locked up that he was going to make my life a living hell. Besides Toi and Bryson's friends knew I was the reason he was arrested.

After our last fight and I moved out and basically with Toi, Bryson would pop up on me. Every time he came around he was coming up with a new threat about how he was going to beat my ass once he got me alone. Of course if he ever got the chance he would surely put hands on me but that gave me more of a reason to stay away. I never gave him any type of reaction I just went on about my business.

One day I was on Toi's porch while Myles was at school and Bryson pulled up on me. He gave me the usual you better come home spiel but just like every other time, I didn't give him any attention. I guess he was sick of me ignoring him so he got in my face, looked me dead in my eyes and told me he would kill me and our son if I didn't come back to him.

I wanted to take it as one of his random threats but the look on his face told me he was dead serious. Noticing the fear in my eyes Bryson smiled like a Cheshire cat and told me I had one day to make my mind up.

When he left I broke down crying because I knew he would definitely kill Myles and I with no problem. He never loved our son, he just tolerated him. I didn't want to die but I didn't want to go back to the hell hole with him either.

I felt like my back was up against the wall and had no choice but to get him out of my life, I went to the police. Every time Bryson left a bruise on me I took a picture of it. I still had text messages and voicemails of him threatening me. When he put his hands on Myles I took pictures of the bruise he left.

He was arrested the very next day and I sent my son down to North Carolina with my mother thinking that was a safer place for him. Bryson got five years but it's only been three and he's out. He's probably on probation and knowing him, he's not going to abide by that shit. You can't put restrictions on a nigga like him because he doesn't care about rules or doing what's right.

Sure, I could go get a restraining order and I am just for precaution but it's not going to make a difference. That piece of paper isn't going to stop him from coming at me if that's what he really wants to do. As much as I don't want to leave out of my house I don't feel comfortable with him having my address. I have to and I have to get the fuck out of Jersey City while I'm at it.

BRYSON "BRICK" CAMPBELL

"Yo she was shook," I cackled when Bless pulled off from in front of Mickey's house. The look on her face brought joy to my ass. She was scared shitless and I could easily see it through her tough ass façade.

"Was she?" Bless laughed along with me.

"She tried that tough shit but I could see it in her eyes."

"So what are you going to do?"

"Oh I'm killing that bitch but I'll let her sweat for a little bit. I want her fear to build up so I plan on fucking with her before I end her life."

"What about Myles?"

"I don't give a fuck about the little nigga but I could turn him into one hell of a damn killer. I got plans for him."

"You think he remembers you? What makes you think he's going to let you turn him into anything?"

"He doesn't have a choice. He's young but Myles knows what it is."

The fact that I have a son rarely crosses my mind. I never really had a connection with Myles. Since the day he was born he was always up under his mama. The little nigga acted as if he didn't like me so I never bothered taking that father shit seriously. I would've liked for it to be different but

Mickey fucked that up. She turned him against me; that's one of the reasons she has to get dealt with.

The main reason is the bitch sent me to jail. I got five years behind bars for putting my hands on her. I was down for three and she didn't reach out the whole time. Didn't pick up a phone call, didn't write, bitch couldn't even put shit on my books.

Yeah I put hands on her, so what? If she did what the fuck I told her to do I wouldn't have to. My pops always said a woman's place is beneath her man. She's there to take care of the house, you and any kids that were conceived.

My mother used to piss my dad off all the time and it would result in her getting her ass beat. I was like Myles when I was around his age; extra protective of my mother. So much that I got in between her and my dad during one of their fights. I stood up for her and he whooped my ass like I was nobody to him.

When he was done, I thought she was going to take care of me, nurse me back to health or some shit. This bitch actually took it upon herself to whoop my ass too. My mother was actually mad that I jumped in the fight in her defense. In her mind I was supposed to keep my mouth shut and not say anything because she was getting punished for a reason.

After that I never attempted to step in their shit. I had both of them telling me that's how relationships were supposed to go, so I applied it to my own life.

Mickey and I met when she was a freshmen and I was a junior in high school. Besides the fact that she was beautiful, I liked the way she carried herself. She was confident and had no problem saying whatever she wanted to.

Another thing that got me with Mickey was the similarities in our home lives. Both of us had violent out of control niggas for fathers and weak bitches for moms. Now that I look back at it I realize we were both fucked up in the head. We had this warped ass mentality about what love is and how it's supposed to be shown.

I'm not a fucking idiot, I know putting my hands on somebody doesn't mean love. That shit is a big form I really don't give a fuck about you. When it comes down to Mickey, I loved her at one point but when I get angry I don't give a fuck about nothing.

Mickey is one of those females that can't shut the fuck up. She can't stop running her mouth and it's not like she's crying or some shit. Her mouth is reckless, she'll get disrespectful as fuck if it keeps going. It took me a good minute to train her ass and get her where I needed but she got there eventually.

To my recollection we were good until she did something that pissed me off one day. I hit her ass then Myles came out of nowhere and got into it. I smacked his little ass across the room and she got in her damn feelings. That bitch hit me with a lamp then dipped out at Toi's house. I would go over there to see her sometimes and she called the cops on me.

By that time there was no love there between either of us. She hated me and I could see it in her eyes every time she looked at me. That shit didn't faze me, I hated her ass too. The only reason we were still technically together was because she had Myles.

Having my son definitely spared her life the few times I thought about ending that shit. Now, I really couldn't give a fuck about that. I went to jail behind that bitch then I gotta hear that she was out here on some hoe shit too? Fucking niggas who got whole families at home and shit, yet she wanted to throw a fit every time I fucked somebody else.

Hypocritical ass bitch.

"I'm not trying to fuck your plans up or anything but it might not be that easy to fuck with Mickey. Especially if Toi gets involved," said Bless.

"What you mean?"

"I told you she's fucking with that nigga Legend now. I can almost guarantee she's going to get in his ear about looking out for Mickey."

"Man, I'm going to tell you just like I those little niggas on the block, Fuck Legend. I'm not scared of that nigga; I plan on getting him out the way just as easy as everybody else."

"Look we're on the same page but I'm just letting you know. What you mean you told the nigga on the block? What block?"

"I got a little something shaking on my grandmother's block. I got to stay there for a Minute so I'm making the best of it."

"Nigga you've been home for two weeks."

"So? I wasn't about to sit on my hands I need to get my damn money up so I can be straight?"

"I get that but you can't be reckless, like selling shit on a block that belongs to that nigga. Then you were talking shit about him too? To his people? You have to be smarter than that, Brick."

"Why does it seem like you speaking on behalf of that nigga? Didn't you just say he was fucking your bitch?"

"I'm not talking for that nigga, I'm telling you to go about shit the right way. You don't know Legend alright; you went through me for everything. It's bad enough you selling shit on his territory; you added shit talking on top of it?" Bless shook his head at me.

He was really going a little overboard in my personal opinion but I get where's coming from. Before I went to jail I had a nice little hustle going on. We weren't rich but it kept me, Mickey, and our child draped in the finest. I was working under Bless who was under Legend.

I've never met Legend or anybody that ran with him besides Bless. They were making good money together until Bless went and tried to get in with Legend's connect like that nigga wasn't going to find out. When he told me about it, I clowned his ass for being stupid. He was supposed to have Legend gone and out the way before trying some shit like that.

"So what do you suggest I do then nigga? Being broke isn't an option."

"Look I can get you some money but selling on his blocks is a hell no. You don't want to be on his radar, it's bad enough Toi might run her damn mouth to him about you."

"You need to get your bitch in line. Her nosey ass is always in my business. She's probably the one who told Mickey to lock my ass up."

"I got Toi, alright? Don't even worry about that."

"I'm not worried about her. If she gets in the middle of my shit she can catch the same treatment."

Toi isn't a part of my plan. Not because of the lack of hate, trust and believe I can't stand that bitch. I'm just not worried about her at the moment. Maybe down the line at some point or if she gets her nosey ass involved with my plans for Mickey, she'll be getting buried right after fucking friend.

TONE

"I'm coming to get her when I'm done handling my business. Damn, fuck off my phone. I'm making the money you keep asking me for." Legend ranted on the phone then slipped it back in his pocket after hanging up. Glancing over at him in the passenger seat I started laughing.

"Baby mama blues?" I asked with a chuckle.

"Man the blues aint even the word. I told her I was coming to get Diamond at three. It's not even one yet and she keeps hitting me up with the bullshit."

"Does she know about Diamond meeting Toi?"

"Unless Diamond told her she doesn't. I don't give a fuck either way. Toi is going to be around, she better get over it."

"So y'all back together?"

"We haven't had the official conversation but as far as I'm concerned we are. You need to fix shit with Mickey. She was ready to kill your ass at the party."

"I don't get why she's mad. We're not together."

"Nigga you're not about to act like your ass wasn't on some extra shit. Since when do you have bitches hanging on you like that? Then you had your stupid ass all over Cassie and you left with the bitch. You fucked didn't you?"

"Man," I shook my head. "I didn't leave with her ass, we went to my car."

"So y'all fucked in the car?"

"No we didn't. She sucked my dick in the car. That's something way different my nigga."

"Either way the shit was stupid. That bitch is grimy so why would you even go there with her ass?"

"I was drunk," I shrugged my shoulders.

"And you were being a little bitch about Mickey not speaking to you so did that extra shit to get at her. Go ahead and admit that shit."

"Fuck outta here."

"I see you didn't say I was wrong. You were trying to piss Mickey off and you did. Look at you," Legend started laughing. "You're always shelling out relationship advice and shit but you the one fucking up."

"Nigga I'm not fucking up. We're not together."

"So? You obviously feel a way about shorty if you did some stupid shit like you did. Even beyond Mickey, you let Cassie's stupid ass stupid ass near you. That's hustling backwards my boy."

"Nigga really? You finally get Toi to stop being mad at you and you turn into the hood version of Dr. Phil," I joked, making both of us laugh.

"Nah I'm not all that I'm just saying. I don't know what the hell is wrong with you and Yung's brains, even that nigga Barry; I can't go that long without seeing or talking to Toi. You niggas can keep playing with those females if you want to; I only have to bust my ass once to get it."

"What I do isn't Mickey's business so if she feels a way that's on her. We're not together."

"Alright, remember you said that."

"Man, whatever. What's the deal? You don't usually pull up on these little niggas. Yung usually handles them."

Legend called me earlier this morning talking about we had to pull up on some young boys we had working for us. He didn't go into details or explain why, all he said was we needed to head over there.

"I know that, he's how I heard about the shit. Supposedly it's some nigga moving his shit down there. I don't remember approving no shit like that and I damn sure don't remember anybody telling me they did."

"Shit, me neither. Who's doing it?"

"Some muthafucka named Brick. I don't know who the fuck that is. You ever heard of him?"

"Not to my recollection. You know anything about him?"

"Hell no, that's why we're going down here. Apparently, it's been some shit talking going on."

"About you?"

"Yeah; I don't give too much of a fuck about the he said she said bullshit but Yung told me it sounded like threats. I'm not for that shit."

"What kind of threats?"

"That's what I'm about to figure out."

We pulled up on the block and all eyes were on my damn car. Shit like that annoyed me because niggas stare like they've never seen a damn car before.

"Why they always with the staring shit?" I asked out loud. Legend heard me and started laughing.

"Nigga you pull up in a $200,000 truck and you're surprised niggas staring at you?"

"That aint the point muthafucka," I laughed too. Rolling down my window I waved my hand for Yung to come get his ass in the car since he was sitting on a porch with three other niggas.

He climbed in the back seat and immediately got down to business. Yung went into what happened with this nigga Brick or at least what he knew of it because he wasn't there.

"Getty was out here so he could tell you better than I could." said Yung. He opened the back door and called shouted across the street. Getty got up from the steps and came over to the car. When he got in the backseat I pulled off.

"What happened G?" Legend asked.

"Alright so for the past week some of our regulars weren't showing up like they usually do. I ran into one of them and they told me some nigga was selling some shit for the low. Auntie said his shit isn't as good, but it does its job and its cheaper. I had her point him out to me, big buff muthafuckas I never saw before. Bruh selling out of his damn granny house," Getty explained.

"Y'all approached him?"

"I did, I went to him to let him know he couldn't do that shit around here. I figured maybe he didn't know better or some shit. I told him why he needed to stop and he said fuck you. He was going to do him and if it was an issue you needed to come see him about it. I know better than to make a scene so I decided to let him walk until you told us what you needed us to do. I went to walk away from dude and he said that you needed to watch yourself, you got some enemies walking around ready."

Glancing over at Legend I could see the anger all his over his face. I understood the anger; words like watch your back and all that other shit can't be taken lightly.

"That's all he said?" Legend questioned.

"Yeah, but that's not even the big deal. We've been watching him since he said that shit and guess who keeps picking him up."

"Who?" I asked.

"That nigga Bless."

Upon hearing that name Legend and I looked at each other before we busted out laughing. Of course Bless would be cool with the nigga running his mouth about Legend. That's what snake niggas do, chill and mingle with those that are just like them. I knew this nigga wouldn't leave Jersey without being involved in some bullshit.

"Bless huh? Alright thanks for letting me know everything. Keep an eye on that nigga for me. Watch everything he does, anybody that comes to that house and all. As far as what he's moving; the nigga can't make money if he aint got shit to sell, right?"

"I got you Legend," Getty replied, realizing the instructions he was given.

We dropped Getty where he was and right before Yung was about to get out my car too, his phone started ringing.

"Hello? Oh shit for real! Alright I'm on my way now. FUCK! Yo, Tone take me to medical center."

"Why?" I turned to the backseat looking at him. "Fuck is wrong with you?"

"Taj is in labor, she's about to have the baby nigga."

"Oh shit, alright I got you. Close my damn door."

He shut the door and I sped off down the street. "Nigga you're about to have a son, get ready," I told Yung.

"What he needs to do is get ready for KeKe to be extra damn nutty."

"Man I'm not worried about KeKe. I haven't spoken to her since that shit went down with Taj. My mother picks Naima up and I get her from there. I don't have time for the bullshit with her."

"I'm surprised she let you go that damn easy. When you're dealing with a bitch that doesn't have shit to lose you have to watch yourself." Legend stated.

I shook my head chuckling. If either of them thinks KeKe isn't going to do some shit at some point they're delusional as fuck. A bitch like that never walks away unbothered. I'm going to shut up and let him see for himself.

* * *

"DAMN how long does it take to have a baby?" Legend said while we sat in the waiting area of the hospital. We've been here for three hours and Yung's stupid ass has yet to come and tell us if the baby was born.

"Sometimes it can be days." Toi answered him. She got up here about twenty minutes after we did. Unlike her damn boyfriend she was patiently waiting to hear about Taj and the baby. Legend has been complaining damn near the whole time.

"Days? See now that's just too much."

"Nigga, you act like you're the one pushing. All you have to do is wait, shut up." Toi told him, making me laugh.

"I'm just saying, it's been a long ass time. I still have to go get Diamond. You're coming with me to my house tonight right?"

"Why do I have to come with you? It's daddy-daughter day. Not daddy-daughter and Toi day."

"Yeah you're coming with me." Legend shrugged.

"Toi!" Hearing her name, we all turned to see Mickey coming over to us with her son right next to her. "Did she have him already?"

"Not to my knowledge we're still waiting," Toi answered her.

"Okay good, I thought I missed it. Myles sit down" Mickey said to her son and he did what he was told sitting next to Toi.

"What were you doing?"

"Looking at houses; girl that damn realtor had me all over Jersey. It was a nice four bedroom house I liked but that shit is in Monmouth County."

"Damn that's like an hour away."

"I know but it was the best one I saw. It has a nice big backyard, two floors, it's in a safe neighborhood and the school is right up the street. It's perfect, I'll be far away from y'all but you bitches know how to drive."

"They're really having a whole conversation like niggas not sitting here." Legend said. "Hi Mickey, damn."

"My bad I was in another world, hi Que." Mickey greeted him ignored my ass like I wasn't sitting right next to him.

'Who is that?" Legend pointed to Myles.

"This is my son, Myles say hi."

"What's up little man, damn you look like your mother." Legend chuckled. He was right; Myles does look just like Mickey's ass.

"Aye y'all," Yung came walking over to us dressed in a hospital gown and gloves with a smile on his face. "She had him, seven pound eight ounces."

"What's his name?" I asked him.

"Mecca. Y'all can come see him in a minute but she wants y'all two first." Yung pointed at Mickey and Toi.

"Okay, come on Mick."

They got up and started to follow Yung but I stood up and grabbed Mickey's arm stopping her. "Let me talk to you for a minute."

"Tone, let me go we don't have anything to talk about."

"I think we do. Just for a minute, alright?"

Mickey looked at Toi then at Myles who was staring at me like he was ready to take my head off if need be. "oi, take him and I'll be there in a second."

"Okay. Myles come on. She's fine, I promise. Que you come too." Toi took his hands and they walked off. Legend got up and went walking behind them.

Removing her arm from my grip Mickey crossed both over her chest. "What Tone?"

"Why are you moving?"

"Why do you want to know?"

"Because I know it's not for no reason. You love your apartment, so what's up?"

She chuckled then shook her head. "How's Cassie?"

"What?"

"How is Cassie? You had your tongue damn near down her throat. I know you know who I'm talking about."

"How do you know her?"

"That's not important for you to know."

"Look, that wasn't what it looked like. Cassie doesn't mean shit to me and hasn't in a long time."

"Good for you. Can I go now?"

"You didn't answer my question Mickey. I'm just trying to figure out why you're moving. You like your apartment, why do you want to leave it?"

"Myles is used to having a lot of room so I want a bigger space." She said with no type of emotion in her face. She was lying, I could tell but she wasn't going to admit it.

"Alright ma. You're lying but I'll leave you alone."

"Tone what I do isn't your business or your concern so you can believe whatever it is you want."

"So I'm supposed to act like I don't give a fuck about you? I told you we're going to have to see each other."

"You didn't give a fuck about me when you were all over bitches like I wasn't right there. You have the fucking nerve to sit back and act like not talking to you is so damn wrong but you were straight disrespectful the last time I saw you."

"I didn't intend for that shit to happen, alright? I was drunk and trippin'."

"I'm sick of grown ass men using being drunk as an excuse for the fucked up shit they do. My father used to use that excuse the day after he would beat on me and my mother. Bryson would say the same shit one he got sober. Being drunk doesn't erase shit if anything t magnifies the type of person you are. You knew exactly what you were doing!" When Mickey started getting loud, attracting attention from complete strangers I pulled over to the cut where there was more privacy.

"You're buggin' the fuck out yelling and shit in the middle of a damn hospital. I told you before we're going to have to see each other. Look at us right now. Our friends have a child together Mickey, acting like a bitch doesn't make anything easier."

"I let you slide with that bitch shit the last time because I was being rude to you after you were nice enough to come get me. You're not going to get too many more chances so watch that bitch word."

"I didn't call you a bitch."

"Saying I'm acting like a bitch is just a passive aggressive way of calling me one, nigga you aint slick."

"I'm not trying to call you a bitch, alright?"

"Shouldn't you be all up in Cassie's business why are you talking to me right now? I was doing really well ignoring you my nigga."

"Why you keep bringing that bitch up? It aint shit between us."

"So you didn't do anything with her that day?"

I wanted to tell the truth, lying isn't really my thing but the anger radiating off of Mickey made me feel like I had to lie. She clearly feels a way about Cassie and telling her the girl sucked my dick would probably make her lose her shit, so I lied.

"No, it was that kiss and that's it."

With her eyes squinted, Mickey looked me in the face to see if I was lying or not. "Mhm sure," she mumbled before walking off. That girl is going to be stubborn for the rest of her damn life.

LEGEND

"He was so cute, but why does he have to look like his big head ass daddy?" Toi said with her face all screwed up. She's been gushing over Mecca since we left the hospital. Since I rode with Tone to the hospital I got in the car with Toi when we left.

"It's his baby Toi," I laughed at her. "He's not supposed to look like his father?"

"Hell no. Look at Myles; he looks just like Mickey thank God. The world does not need another Brick around."

"Another what?"

"Brick, he's Mickey's baby father. Shit, now that I mention him you need to watch out for his big ass. He's real close to Bless."

"Oh really?"

"Yeah, he used to work for Bless; him and that punk ass nigga Kareem. I wouldn't be surprised if they were hiding him."

"They still haven't seen that nigga?" Mickey's cousin has been gone for damn near a year now. It's taking this long to get rid of his ass?

"He probably left Jersey, but he's not really anybody that needs to be worried about. He's only dangerous to people with a pussy between their legs. Brick is a little bit scary but it's mostly because of his size. That nigga is like 6'5 and he was kind of built before he went to jail. I can only imagine how big he is now."

I listened to everything Toi told me, not even bothering to speak on the shit I found out about this nigga Brick earlier today. This was the type of info I needed; shorty doesn't even realize she was giving me one hell of a heads up.

"Why do I need to look out for them?"

"Knowing Bless he's still pissed about you beating on him the way you did. He's not going to let that shit go and Brick is a supreme dick rider so I know he's going to back Bless up. I want you to be careful. You grew up with him so I know you're privy to what kind of nigga he is but I need you to watch him and yourself."

"I got you, trust me," I grabbed her hand and kissed the back of it. "Listen, when we get here you already know Isyss is going to clown when she sees you. Ignore her for me, alright?"

"I'm not going to lose my cool in front of Diamond. I'll let her mother be stupid on her own."

We pulled up to Isyss' apartment building and I parked. "I told her to be outside, now I gotta go up and there shit."

"Call her to come down. I'm about to go to the store real quick. You want something?"

"Nah I'm good, go ahead," I got out the car then went around her side and helped her out too. "You look cute ma," I complimented Toi when she stepped out. She was dressed comfortably in a pair of red and white Adidas track pants, a white cropped tank top and all white shell toes on her feet. Her hair was in a ponytail, and round sunglasses were covering her eyes. The only jewelry she wore was a pair of thin silver hoops and a Movado watch on her wrist.

"Please, I threw this shit on when Taj called me about her water breaking."

"And you still look good so it don't even matter and I'm not even trippin' on you not wearing a damn bra."

"Even if you did trip, I'm grown."

"That isn't the point. I'm surprised your prissy ass is wearing sneakers, I can't count on one hand how many times I've seen you wear them."

"Whatever Que let me go to this damn store. I need chocolate in my life."

"I'm all the chocolate you need baby," I kissed her cheek making her laugh.

"You aint even chocolate, you're more like caramel. I'll be back," she walked across the street to the store and just as she made it inside Isyss was coming out of her building with Diamond.

"What happened to three o'clock?" Isyss asked, giving me that stank ass attitude I've become accustomed to.

"You read the text I sent you so stop," I replied back then looked down at Diamond.

When I first found out about her I was scared as shit. I knew I wanted kids but I always thought I would have time to prepare and actually watch my woman have my child but that didn't happen. I missed the first six years of her life because of Isyss. Bitch gave me some spiel about thinking I was going to make her have an abortion when she got pregnant. I personally feel like that's bullshit but it doesn't even matter at this point.

"Daddy, is we still having our movie-thon?" Diamond asked me.

"It's are we and yes we are baby girl."

"Yay!" I laughed watching Diamond jump up and down in excitement.

"Que we need to talk," Isyss said, breaking me out of my laughter.

"About what?"

"I need to get the fuck out of this apartment. Diamond needs to be in a bigger space, where she has a backyard and all that other shit,"

"Aye watch your mouth," I corrected her. She was way too comfortable cursing in front of a six year old.

"She knows not to repeat me. Now back to what I was saying, I need to move."

"So move, what are you telling me for?"

"You can't get us a place?"

"Why do I have to get you a place? You want Diamond to have all that stuff, cool she can come live with me."

"Oh you really got me fucked up. You want to take her away from me now?" Isyss damn near screamed. If Diamond wasn't standing right there I would've choked her dumb ass.

"Who's taking what?" I heard Toi's voice behind me and Isyss did too because her eyes went wide and the anger flashed in them instantly.

"Really? You're about to have my daughter around this bitch? What the fuck is this supposed to be some happy blended family shit now? QUE YOU REALLY GOT ME FUCKED UP!"

"Diamond get in the car," I opened the backseat door and she climbed inside. "Put your headphones on okay," I closed the door then turned back to Isyss.

"I know you're ignorant as hell but all of that yelling and cursing didn't need to happen with her standing right next to your stupid ass," Toi spoke up before I could.

"Do you have a child? No I don't think so, so don't tell me what to do with mine. Mind your fuckin' business!" Isyss shot back.

"Bitch-" Toi started to curse her ass out but I covered her mouth with my hand.

"Chill get in the car and wait for me okay," I moved my hand, kissed her cheek and she did what I asked. "Why are you always making a damn scene?"

"Fuck you Quentin. You got that bitch around my baby when you know I don't like that hoe."

"You don't even have a reason to not like her. If anything you're always on the petty shit. Listen you can dislike whoever you want but I'll have my daughter around whoever the fuck I want to. She's going to be around Toi so you might as well let that shit sink in."

"I have full custody asshole; you don't have to see her at all."

"You want to play that game with me? Bitch I'm rich, I have legit money coming in, who the fuck do you think they'll give custody to if we went to court? Me? Or you? You don't even have a job and you live in a small apartment with your mother. Let's be fucking real."

Knowing what I said was true, she rolled her eyes then sucked her teeth. "Fuck you Que!"

"Unfortunately, I did that's why I'm still stuck with you," I went to the car got in and pulled off down the street.

"What the hell was all of that about?" Toi asked. I glanced in the rearview mirror to see if Diamond was listening or not but she wasn't. She was looking at her iPad with her headphones on eating a bag of cheese doodles.

"Why you give her that messy shit in my car Toi?"

"She's not going to make a mess."

"Yeah alright, let me see one cheesy fingerprint, I'm getting on yo ass."

"Sure you are. Back to Cruella, what was all that about."

"Bullshit as usual. Talking about she needs to move because Diamond needs more space, and a backyard and all that shit. I didn't disagree with her; I said my daughter could come live with me since I have that. She started bitching about me trying to take Diamond from her. That's when you walked up."

"Are you going to get her a new place?"

"Why should I? All she does is give me hell and irk my fucking nerves. If she wasn't a pain in my ass I wouldn't mind helping her out but she doesn't deserve shit."

"I don't like the girl but I think you should take it into consideration."

"What the fuck? Why?" My eyes glanced over in Toi's direction.

"Regardless of anything she has Diamond and she's kind of right about the space. Didn't you say they're in a two bedroom?"

"Yeah and?"

"Come on," Toi started laughing like shit was funny. I'm dead ass serious. I don't want to do shit for Isyss; why should I make her life easy when she's done nothing but fuck shit up since she's been back up here.

"Nah explain that shit to me because I thought you would agree with me. You don't understand where I'm coming from?"

"Que I get what you're saying, she's an ignorant son of a bitch cool I get it. I wanna snuff the bitch so you know I get it. What I'm telling you is, unless you're ready to have Diamond full time by yourself you should think about moving the girl. You don't have to buy her a mansion, but a nice little house with a yard in a better neighborhood for Diamond isn't a big deal Que."

"I give her enough money for her to move Toi. She better save that shit up and move her damn self."

"Would you quit being so stubborn and actually look at the bigger picture. I don't think it's completely fair that she's with you in some huge

MOLLYSHA JOHNSON

house during the weekends then sharing a bed with her mother throughout the week. Now, if you want her to live with you then fine but be real you work all the time. If it's not something with Tone it's something at the mansion, or you're at the damn barbershop. You think you'll be able to handle a six year old girl by yourself, all day every day?"

Everything Toi said was correct. I'm on the go the majority of the time so having Diamond 24/7 isn't something I'm ready for. Moving Isyss wouldn't be a big deal at all but I do enough. She doesn't have to worry about Diamond having clothes because I took care of that. I handle her medical needs, and anything else she needs on top of giving her $2000 a week when I drop Diamond off.

It's not like shorty is still working she quit her job not too long after I started giving her money. I see exactly what her motive so why should I play into it? Toi knows all of this but she's still telling me I should change my mind about the shit it's very telling.

"I'll think about it, that's all I can say right now."

"That's fine." Toi started going through her bag then pulled out a big ass pick wrapped in plastic. "This is about to be so damn good."

"Why the hell are you eating a big ass pickle?"

"You act like you don't eat pickles."

"I do but I don't just sit back and chomp on those shits, especially those big ass ones. God damn, are you going to eat the whole thing?"

"Yes, why are you making a big damn deal about a pickle?"

"I'm not making shit a big deal I'm just saying, that shit big as hell. Go ahead and east your pickle I'll leave you alone."

"Thank you damn. Now, where are we going?" She asked before taking a big bite out of her pickle. The crunch on that shit was loud as fuck too.

"You greedy as shit bruh," I laughed at her and she rolled her eyes in response. "We're going to my house, you know that."

"No I mean where do you live?"

"You ever heard of Oyster Bay?"

"No, where is that?"

"New York."

"Do you not have get togethers or some shit because you barely talk about it. You act like it's some secretive shit."

"Nah I have people over but I wasn't there all the time so it's not often. That's why I had the condo; my house is like an hour and a half away from the city so driving out there all the time was in the way. Now with Diamond coming over every weekend I have a reason to be there so I'm home more often. Besides, everybody doesn't need to know where I live so I keep visits to a minimum."

"Well you're finally bringing me, I must be special."

"You are but you knew that already. It's a reason I'm bringing you here. I want you to look around and tell me what you think about moving in."

"What?"

"I want you to move in with me."

"Que the last time I moved in something that belongs to you, I got put out."

"Why are you bringing up old shit?"

"Is it not relevant to this situation? I'm not trying to move into a house that I have no claim or right to."

"We can handle all that shit. I'm not letting you go again, I made that mistake before it's happening a second time."

"I don't know Que. I just moved back into my grandmother's house."

"You mean your house?" I corrected her. When Grams passed everything went to Toi including the deed to the house and custody of the twins.

"Well yeah," Toi chuckled. "Besides, I can't leave the twins with just my mother, they'll be wildin' out like crazy."

"Who said you were leaving them here? They can move in with us. I have nine bedrooms and a guest house your mother can move into so she can have her own space."

With a shocked expression on her face Toi looked in my direction. "You want my whole family to move in with you?"

"Yeah I don't mind. I know you're not going to leave them behind. Jayla and Kayla are damn near your kids so having them come would've happened anyway. You have custody of them, you couldn't leave if you wanted to."

"I don't know Que."

"What don't you know?"

"Uprooting our lives out of nowhere is a big deal."

"I know that, but didn't you want them out of Jersey City? I thought that was your ultimate goal."

"It is but still."

"Still what?"

"Que I'm in a place where I'm about to have my own business, finally working for myself. Granted I did the work to get the spa going but it wouldn't have been possible without you helping me out with the money. Now you're talking about moving us into your house. I just…I want to do something on my own for once."

"So this is about your pride."

"No it's not about pride."

"Sounds like it to me. Toi you've taken care of your family for years by yourself. Somebody taking some of that weight off your shoulders isn't a bad thing."

"I know that but it's a lot to think about. We're still working things out between us, you live a whole damn hour and some change away it's not that simple."

"We are still working things out but like I said, I'm not letting your ass get away from me again so bringing that up is pointless."

"Let me think on it, okay?"

"I can do that, take all the time you need. "

"Thank you."

TOI

"Toi get yo ass up, we're here," I heard Que's voice before feeling his hand come down on my thigh making my eyes shoot open in the process. I looked to my left and he was standing right outside the car with the door wide open. Diamond was standing there rubbing her eyes like she just woke up too.

"What the hell you hit me for?"

"I said our name and shook your ass but you didn't move. Come on ma, get up." He held his hand out for me to grab so I did and he pulled me out the car. I stretched m limbs while taking a look around at where we were.

When my eyes finally settled on the house we were in my mouth dropped a little bit. The brick colonial mansion we were standing in front of had my jaw to the floor. Besides the one time I went to Saint & Beautii's house I've never seen a place this big.

"Que this is not your house quit playing.'

"You think I just drove up on somebody's shit to play with you? Toi if you don't bring yo ass on." He walked towards the tall mahogany double doors.

I grabbed my purse from the car and shut the door before following him. When he opened the door to let us in I was a little nervous about going in. I don't think I prepared myself for the luxury I was about to walk into.

"Wow," I mumbled looking around. The entry ways soaring ceilings and a stunning double bridal staircase with stone handrails took my breath away. The latte colored walls fit the gold Carrera marble floors perfectly. "This is really nice Que, damn."

"I'm glad you like it. Diamond go put your stuff up baby girl."

"Okay daddy," Diamond took off upstairs while Que grabbed my hand pulling me in the other direction.

"Let me give you a tour."

It took us about twenty minutes to see the whole house. There were 9 bedrooms, including the two story master suite, and 12 huge bathrooms. The state of the art eat-in kitchen was huge and filled with every new appliance you could think of. He had a formal dining room, two living rooms, a wet bar and a great room with double high ceilings. The basement was turned into 3 separate rooms. One room was a home movie theatre, another had two bowling lanes and arcade games while the last one had four big screen TV's, a card table, a fully stocked bar, and a pool table.

After showing me the house we went to the backyard that had a basketball court, a huge pool and patio area. When he showed me around the guest house, I knew why he offered it to my mother. It had one floor, a huge master bedroom and bathroom, along with a living room, and fully equipped kitchen.

Honestly his whole place was like something out of a damn movie. I know Que is far from broke and the condo he let me stay in was top tier but this house is a lot. I don't know what I expected his home to look like but it wasn't all of this.

"Why do you need nine bedrooms?" I asked when we walked back into the main house.

"I want a lot of kids."

"A lot of kids? What is a lot?"

"At least six but I don't want less than four. It was just me and Mia growing up and she's five years older than me so it's not like we had a whole lot in common or really went to school together like that. Besides my mother raised us with just my uncle and aunts to help her so we never had that two parents in the household type of family. That's what I want for myself. I want to come home to a wife and a bunch of mini me's running around."

"I get what you mean, you know I was raised by my grandparents and they did a great job but it's not the same thing as a regular family."

"So you want kids too?"

"I do, I don't know about having six but I do want some. Shit, I pretty much raised twins so of course I want my own someday."

"What about marriage?"

"If it's built on the right things then yes I wouldn't mind marriage. I just don't want to be married for the sake of being able to say I'm someone's wife. I want a real commitment; I want to build a real life with somebody."

"I'm trying to give you that with me and you need time to think about it."

"Que moving in here isn't a commitment."

"You're right but it's the first step to it. It's not like you can't live with me, we damn near lived together when you were at the condo. I was there 95% of the time."

"It's not the same thing and you know it."

"Well I'm asking you to move in here with me and Diamond when she's here."

"My cousins will tear this house up."

"No they won't. You want more for your family and I want you with me so here we are. You think they won't like it or something."

"The twins will jump at the chance of living in a damn mansion and my mother will love this. I'm just…I don't even know this is crazy. Why do you want me to move in here so bad?"

"Why wouldn't I want to wake up to you every day? You don't realize I love you by now?"

My eyes shot up in shock. Did he just say love?

"You love me?"

"Hell yeah, you think I go this hard for no reason? Toi," he grabbed my hands, stood in front of me and looked me in my eyes. "I love you. That's not bullshit, I'm not saying it just to get what I want either. I really love you; so much that I'm not willing to let you go ever again in life."

"This is a lot at one time Que. I don't want to move in here with you then you find something else to be mad about and have you put me and my family out."

"I'm not going to do that shit again; I know everything I need to know about you. That was the point of us staying up till five in the morning last week talking about everything. You told me how you got into that robbing shit. You ran down the name of every nigga you did it too. I got the names of the people you would sell shit to. At this point I'm over all of that. You're not doing it anymore, your spa opens next week, you have your shit together. You were already a grown ass woman when I met you and I've watched you evolve into a better person. None of that old shit matter Toi."

"Are you sure? Promise me right now Que."

"Before I do that I have to give you something." He pulled a pair of keys from his pocket then put them in my hands.

"What is this?"

"Keys to the house, I'm serious about you moving in here. Toi I love you alright, I fucked up before and I did some fucked up shit. I'm sorry about that; it's not going to happen again I'm really in this shit."

"You're sure about this?" Que went into his other pocket and pulled out a small ring box. "What the hell?" he opened the box showing off a 6 carat heart shaped center diamond, surrounded by a double halo of inset diamonds. "I know you're not about to propose to me, I will faint on this fucking floor right now Que, no."

He started laughing. "Nah I'm not proposing, this is a promise ring." Que took it out and put it on my right ring finger. "I promise I will never do anything to hurt you and to upgrade your shit when the time does come for me to pop that question."

"Oh my God," I was staring at the ring in awe. This isn't the first piece of jewelry he's bought me by far but God damn.

I finally took my eyes off the ring and brought them back to his face. "Are you really sure about this?"

"I'm sure Toi, trust me."

I let out a deep sigh then let the smile I've been fighting off break out onto my face. "Okay Que, we'll move in here. But after my opening, I need to focus on that."

"That's good enough for me."

"Good, you better not fuck up my nigga. This is your last shot."

He laughed then kissed me on the lips. "I got you."

"Alright, let's go find Diamond and get this movie marathon started." We started making our way upstairs but I grabbed hand stopping him. "Oh yeah, one more thing; I love you too."

* * *

"OKAY GIRL, it's time for your entrance. The car is downstairs waiting on you. Are you ready?" Mickey asked when she came barging into my bedroom.

"Yeah, I'm ready to go," I answered after taking a deep breath.

Today is the day I've been working my ass off. All of the renovations were done, I hired my staff, and I'm certified with all my permits. Belle Melanin is officially about to be open for business.

I wanted it to be something small and simple but no, Legend Santana wasn't having that. He insisted on going all out for it but I didn't want some huge party. I'm running a spa not damn night club. I agreed to let him arrange for a few media outlets to come cover it. Catering but not full plates, a few appetizers, some champagne, light music and that's it.

My goal was to make some damn money not have these people thinking my opening day was about to be a free-be special.

"When I dropped Myles off with Taj she told me to tell you congratulations and that you better stack that money. She's so mad she can't come."

Since Taj literally just had Mecca seven days ago she wasn't able to make it to the opening. She was home with her baby and watching Myles for Mickey. I know she wanted to be here but she needs to sit her ass down and let her coochie heal before she starts coming out to celebrate anything.

"She just had a baby last week she better let her body recover. I'll call her when I get in the car. How do I look?" I did a quick spin for Mickey.

Since it was my grand opening I wanted to be classy but sexy and fun at the same time. I was wearing a black and white vertically striped sleeveless bodysuit. Over it, I wore a pair of white Stella McCartney high waist trousers. Red So Kate Christian Louboutin pumps were on my feet while my silver Rolex sat on wrist and the promise ring Que bought me decorated my finger.

My hair was now in a layered asymmetrical cut and my makeup was on point. I was rocking a shimmery light smoky eye, with a bold red lip. Personally I felt like I looked good as shit but I needed a second opinion.

"You look good. You're giving me rich boss bitch vibes, I love it."

"She's right, you look perfect," Que said when he came walking in the room.

Drool almost slipped out my mouth at the sight of him. He was wearing a white Dsquared2 button up shirt with the sleeves rolled up showing off the art work inked on his arms and fit his muscular body just right with some black slacks that fit just as well. He wore black Ferragamo loafers on his feet, a gold chain with a diamond flooded L, hung around his neck, and his gold and diamond Patek Philippe watch sat on his wrist.

Smiling I walked over to him and kissed his lips. "I see you shining, trying to show off on my day."

"I had to match your fly." He kissed me again then hugged me tight.

His *Greed Aventus* cologne lingered around the room and it damn near made my legs weak. I highly believe in the saying there's nothing better than a man who looks as good as he smells and Que is the perfect example.

"Match my fly? I'm good but I'm not even on it like you are."

"I know, so I came to fix that. Turn around and close your eyes."

"Why?"

"Just do it, come on ma. You don't want to be late."

I turned my back to him and closed my eyes like he asked me to. When I felt something cold hit my neck my eyes shot open and I reached up to feel what he put on me.

"Que what is this?" I went over to my mirror and looked at the diamond and ruby collar necklace he put around my neck.

"God damn," Mickey exclaimed from behind me. "Wow, that's nice as shit. You're doing it like that Que? Bruh my birthday is next month, I expect something real nice."

"I got you," Que laughed at her. "I'm riding with her so you can go ahead of us."

"Alright, see you at the spa. Don't go freaking before y'all get there either, you're wearing white remember that Toi." Mickey said before she went prancing out my room.

"She's a mess," I chuckled. "Thank you for this baby, this is really nice and expensive. Que you gotta stop spending so much money on me all the time."

"Why?"

I laughed at the confused expression on his face. "I don't need it that's why."

"So you don't want the matching bracelet?" He pulled a black box from his pocket.

"Que come on."

"What? I couldn't get one and not get the other. Look, I don't need my shit either but I have it. As far as I'm concerned if I have all this shit you and my daughter are going to have it too."

"You got Diamond a necklace like this?"

"It's not exactly like that; she's only six years old." Que laughed while pulling the ruby and diamond tennis bracelet from the box. "It's pretty close to it though. Shit, her name is Diamond it's only right I cover her in them. Come here, give me your arm."

I held my arm out to him and watched as he clamped the bracelet on my wrist. "Damn,"

"That shit is nice right?"

"Hell yeah I love it. Thank you," I gave him a kiss then stepped back before he could try to take it further.

"You ready?"

'Yeah, let's do this."

When we got to the spa it was packed full of people. Half of them I knew from around town but the other half was strangers. I had no problem either as long as they were here to spend money. After going around the room greeting and talking to people for a few minutes I went to the front where the DJ Que hired was and asked for a mic.

"Excuse me; can I get everyone's attention please?" I said through the microphone getting everybody to look at me. "First of all I would like to thank everybody for coming to the grand opening of my spa Belle Melanine." They all clapped. "This was a long time coming and I worked my behind off to get here so I appreciate the love you're all showing me today. I'm grateful for all of you but I have a few people I need to give special thanks too. First I would love to thank my grandmother who, as most of you know passed earlier this year. She's the beautiful woman on that big portrait right there," I pointed to the black and white picture of my grandmother that hung above the receptionist desk. They all looked at it then looked back at me. "She raised me to always go after what I wanted and do what I needed to do to become a better person. If she didn't teach me those things I wouldn't even be standing here so I'm grateful for her." They clapped again.

"My mother and my cousins, I love you guys. We've been having a rocky few months but we're making it. My best friends," I looked at Mickey. "One of them just had a baby and couldn't be here but I know she sends her love. Michelle," she rolled her eyes at me using her government name making me laugh. "Thank you for pushing me, encouraging and getting on me when I needed it. Lastly, to somebody who saw the potential in me from day one and helped me with damn near everything," my eyes landed on Que who was standing there with a proud smile on his face. "Mr. Legend Santana, for everything you do for me. I appreciate it and I love you more than you could ever know. Thank you for seeing something in me that I didn't even see in myself."

I was about to keep speaking until I saw Isyss walking her ass in my spa. When her eyes landed on me she smirked. Que must've followed my gaze because I saw him turn and start walking in her direction. Knowing how this bitch is with making a scene I decided to wrap this speech up.

"Well thank you guys for coming once again. Eat, drink, have a few treatments and enjoy yourself. Thank you for coming," I gave the DJ the mic back and walked through the crowd shaking hands with people while trying to keep my happy face on.

I finally got through the crowd and Mickey came walking over to me.

"Que pulled her in the hallway. I don't know why she's here but security can remove her ass real quick," Mickey said.

I shook my head. "No it's fine, she can stay I don't give a damn why she's here. As a matter of fact let me go say hello, I have to make every customer feel special."

"Toi," she grabbed my arm.

"I'm not going to fight at my own opening. I'm just going to go speak. I'll be right back," I moved my arm out of her grip then walked towards the hallway where I could hear them talking. I was about to have a little bit of fun right quick.

GENEVA

When I saw Toi walking towards the hallway I knew it wasn't anything good about to happen. I told Jayla and Kayla I would be right back before going in the same direction Toi was walking in.

"Toi," I called her name so she turned around. "Where are you going?"

"Que's stupid ass baby mama popped up here and I want to know what the hell is going on," she answered.

"Okay I'm coming with you, come on." We walked down the hall until we got to where Quentin was talking to some tall Spanish girl.

"Excuse me," Toi said after clearing her throat and getting their attention. "What's going on over here?"

"What we're talking about is none of your concern," the girl had the nerve to snap at Toi. "We have a child together so this is between us, mind your business."

"Bitch you're standing in my business or did you forget that quick? I don't care if you have a child together you're not special, the fuck?" Toi snapped back.

"Baby," Que came over to Toi and kissed her on the lips. "Calm down, don't let anybody get you out of character on your day, alright?" She didn't say anything, so he grabbed her chin making her look at him, "Alright?"

"Alright Que I hear you," Toi replied.

"Cool just chill," he said to her then turned to the other girl. "Isyss; I'm not going to keep telling you to watch your muthafuckin' mouth. I said it once let me say it one more time, she's going to be around Diamond so anything to do with her is Toi's business. I don't give a damn if you got an issue with it or not. Get the fuck over that shit."

"Fuck you Que, nobody is about to bow down to that bitch just because you fucking her. I don't give a damn if she's your woman if I don't want her around my daughter you need to respect that. I'm tired of you disrespecting me for this bitch."

"First of all, you need to chill with that bitch word and calm your ass down. Nobody is disrespecting you. You're just mad he's not willing to dismiss me for your ass like you're supposed to have some sort of privilege over me. Girl, stop with the drama. You're too damn old for it and it's not cute. Now, usually I would kick you the hell out but I'm trying to learn to have patience for bitches like you so I'm not going to do that. Go get a massage or something if you're the damn stressed; it's on the fifth floor," Toi told her in a calm and eerie voice. Something about her tone just felt off, it was a little scary.

"Don't try to act all high and mighty like you're some business woman. You're a con ass bitch. You wouldn't have this business if my baby father didn't pay for it. Fake ass independent woman."

I looked my daughter in awe because had this been me at her age we would've been scrapping already. I can't stand a disrespectful bitch, especially when you're disrespectful for no reason. This girl has no reason to have a problem with Toi, all her energy should be towards her daughter's father. But, jealousy makes people stupid sometimes; clearly this girl is the prime example of that.

Toi let out a bitter chuckle. "Okay, I was trying to be nice to you but you're ignorant so of course you don't see that or appreciate it. Know something though; this party of mine will be over at 8 PM sharp. If you're really feeling that damn froggy and you got such a problem bring yo ass on Pacific and Bramhall, I'll be home by 9 o'clock baby. We can gladly step in the street and I'll handle you accordingly; until then." Toi clapped her hands twice. "Security!" She shouted and two big cock diesel looking niggas came out of nowhere walking over. "Get this thing out of here, thank you." They grabbed Isyss up all the while she was screaming and showing the fuck out all the way out to the front door. We followed behind and we could see people trying to figure out what the hell was going on.

"I'm sorry everybody, we just had a little problem. It's handled keep having a good time!" Toi told the crowd then looked at Que and I. "Okay now that she's gone let's enjoy the rest of the party." She smiled then walked off.

"Do you think that girl is really going to come around there?"

"I don't know but I hope not. I have to go handle something tonight so I'm leaving early. If Isyss brings her ass around there call me."

"Alright," I nodded.

I looked around for Toi and saw her talking to Mickey. She was probably running down the whole situation to them and that means they're probably going to stay here with her waiting for something to pop off. Lord I hope that girl doesn't bring her ass back here.

The rest of the opening went without any problems. People were having a good time and taking full advantage of the treatments that were available. As the night went on, people started to leave. The twins and I stayed so I could help Toi make sure everything was cleaned and put away the right way.

It took us about 45 minutes to get everything perfect and it was only a little bit after 10. Toi locked up everything and we headed home. When we got in the house she went straight upstairs to her room while I sat in the living room and the twins sat on the front porch. A few minutes later Mickey came walking in the house and went upstairs shouting Toi's name.

"Auntie!" Jayla came running in the living room. "It's some girls outside looking for Toi."

"What?"

"It's a bunch of girls looking for Toi outside it's like six of them out there too."

"Wait what? When?"

"Just now; they pulled up the same time Mickey did."

"That's why she just came in here like that. Do you know who they are?"

"I don't know but some Spanish chick is running her mouth about Toi and Kayla is about to swing on her ass." Just as she said that we heard yelling and shouting coming from outside.

"Oh hell no," I rushed outside to see Kayla wrestling around on the sidewalk with some girl. I went downstairs and pulled them both apart. "What the fuck is going on?"

"Mind your business lady; this doesn't have shit to do with you!" Looking at her I shook my head when I saw it was Quentin's baby mama. This woman has to be damn near 30 if she isn't that already, out here fighting a damn teenager.

"If it involves my niece or my daughter it does involve me now like I said what the fuck is going on? You're fighting a sixteen year old girl when you're grown as hell."

"Fuck her and fuck your daughter, where the fuck is she anyway?"

"I'm right here, what's good." Toi came down the front steps with Mickey right next to her. Neither one of them were in the clothes from earlier they both had on t-shirts, leggings and sneakers on with their hair in ponytails. "You went and got your fucking squad like it's supposed to make a difference."

"You're talking too much right now you said come back bitch I'm here now what." The girl snapped back.

"Step the fuck up," Toi walked out into the middle of the street and the girl followed suit. They both squared up then Toi hit her twice in the face and kept swinging. The girl reached up and grabbed Toi's bun pulling her head down where she got two clean hits off but Toi lifted her arms and started landing punches on the side of the girls face.

"Damn bruh," I heard Jayla say and I took her phone from her hand.

"Do you have Quentin's number in here?" I asked her.

"Yeah."

I went through her contacts then hit his name and put the phone up to my ear while watching them still fight.

By now they were both on the floor; Toi was on top fucking the girls face all the way up. It was like that for a few seconds then one of the girls she had with her ran up and grabbed Toi by the hair and tried to pull her off. That shit didn't last long because Mickey ran over and hit the bitch on the side of the face and she hit the ground and just laid there. Did she just knock her out?

"What's up Jay?" I heard Que ask when he answered the phone.

"Quentin? This is Geneva I don't know where the fuck you are but you need to come to the house right now. Toi is out here beating the hell out of your baby mama and you might want to come save her ass," I said before hanging up and going over to where Toi was still fucking this bitch up. I pulled Toi off the girl and pushed her onto the sidewalk.

"LET ME GO!" Toi screamed at me but I didn't. "THAT'S WHY I FUCKED YOU UP BITCH! I TOLD YOU DON'T FUCK WITH ME!"

"Alright Toi, that's enough!" I shouted at her.

When I heard sirens in the distance I pushed her up the steps and in the house then shouted for Jayla, Kayla and Mickey to come inside too. I'm not worried about the girl trying to press charges or something. She came to our property acting out so she has no room to play victim.

"Toi, calm down, alright? You fucked her up. What else are you trying to do? Kill the bitch?"

"Fuck her! I told that bitch not to fuck with me now she's lying out there bloody as fuck. That's what the fuck she gets."

"You are too damn grown to be out here fighting over what? What was that for?"

"Ma you were right there when she popped all that shit earlier. It's my fault she got all that mouth but can't back that shit up?"

"No but you're an adult with shit to lose now. You have a business; you literally just came from a great opening of that business and you want to lower yourself to fight with a bitch who doesn't have anything. That makes a whole lot of sense Toi."

"You don't get it; she's been a pain in me and Que's asses since she's been around. I'm tired of that bitch. All she does is run her fuckin' mouth so she got punched in it."

"Who cares if she talks shit? You're beautiful and on your way to becoming very successful and they hate it. It's too many bitches out here talking shit and you ignore it just like you're supposed to do."

"I don't even know half the bitches that don't like me."

"Alright then so what makes her different from any other hater? Y'all don't like each other because you're both jealous."

"Jealous of what? That bitch doesn't have shit on me and Que can't stand her ass."

"He still has to deal with her, that's what you're jealous of. She can get on his nerves, be annoying on every level but she's never going anywhere because she has his child. Being with him means dealing with her and you hate that. She's jealous of you because you have his heart and no matter what she does she can't make him leave you alone or break you up."

"It's her mouth ma!"

"Let her talk! What can she do to you? You just proved the bitch can't beat you but I bet she still runs her mouth about you after this. You're about to be 23 next month, Mickey you're turning 24 next week you're both too old to sit back and let this petty shit get to you. Ignore these bitches if they want to hate you let them do that. You fucked her up, Mickey just knocked one of her friends the fuck out. Kayla got her ass too. It's over, let this shit go. If the bitch touches you fuck her ass up but if that doesn't happen you stay calm and let her talk shit."

Toi nodded her head in understanding. "Alright ma, I got it. I got you I won't fight her again or even act like that with anybody else."

"Good, now go clean your face. She scratched you up pretty good." The only thing that was wrong with Toi was the scratches on her face. The girl couldn't work her hands that well but her nails knew what they were doing.

"I gotta go get my son, I'll see y'all tomorrow or something." Mickey said before leaving.

Toi went upstairs while I went to the living room. As soon as I sat down I heard the front door open followed by Quentin's voice. "Toi!"

"She's upstairs Que!" I shouted loud enough for him to hear me. "Come in the living room for a minute."

When he came in I sat up on the couch. "Is Toi good?"

"Yeah she's fine all she has is some scratches."

"So she won?" Que smirked slightly.

"Boy it aint funny."

"It's not ma, you're right but Isyss deserved to get her ass beat. I'm sorry she brought that shit here, I'll handle her."

"Make sure you do. I don't need people coming around here trying to fight my daughter all the time."

"They won't, but y'all won't even be here that much longer so I won't matter."

"What? Why wouldn't we be here?"

"Toi didn't tell you?"

"Tell me what?"

"I asked Toi to move in with me and she said yes. Y'all are moving."

"Wait," I put my hand up laughing. "We're moving? To what? We're not all going to fit in a condo and don't you have a daughter that stays with you sometimes?"

"I'm not talking about the condo ma; she really didn't tell you anything about the house?"

"We're moving?" Jayla came in and asked. Kayla was right behind her looking for an answer.

"Were you listening at the door or some shit?" I questioned her and she nodded.

"Yeah I was being nosey my bad, but answer the question Que. We're moving?"

"Toi was supposed to tell y'all."

"TOI!" I shouted her name. "Come down here!"

"Alright I'm coming!" She shouted back. When Toi finally came in the living room Que went and grabbed her chin so he could inspect her face.

"You okay?" he asked her.

"Yes I'm fine Que. What are you doing here? I thought you were doing something with Tone."

"I was but ma called me about you and Isyss. Why didn't you tell them about moving?"

"Shit," Toi cursed under her breath. "I forgot; I've been running around like a chicken with the head cut off all week getting ready for the opening. My bad."

"Girl where are we supposed to be moving to and why didn't you tell us before you said yes?"

"I meant to talk to y'all about it but I really forgot. That's no bullshit, I wasn't thinking about it. But um yeah we're moving in with Que."

"She thinks you're talking about the condo baby," Que told her.

"Oh no, not the condo we wouldn't even fit in there. Que has a house in Oyster Bay, New York. It's a beautiful house ma."

"So you want us all to move in with you? Why would I live with my daughter and her boyfriend? That sounds off."

"You'll be living with us but not really. You'll have the whole guest house to yourself."

"Wait what?"

"I'll take y'all to see it tomorrow but it's more than enough room. Ma you don't have to be in the guest house, you can be in the main house with us if you want to. I just thought you would want your own space," Que said to me.

"How big is this house?"

"Big enough that he has to have a guest house in the first place. Ma, y'all are going to love it I promise." Toi assured us.

I looked at the twins and they didn't seem to be all that happy about the news. Honestly I wasn't that happy either but maybe my mind will change once we see the house.

"What about this house? You're not selling this house Toi."

"I know that ma; I would never even think to sell this house. You know I know better than that."

"Maybe we can rent it out when we're ready. Or just keep it for ourselves just in case. No offense Que I'm just saying, you never know what can happen," I suggested.

"You're good ma I know what you mean," he chuckled. "Y'all are going to love the house. You two will have your own rooms."

As soon as he said own rooms the twins' eyes lit up. "Own room?" They said at the same time then glanced at each other before turning back to us. "We're in."

"Okay Tia and Tamera," Toi joked making us laugh. "You'll have your own rooms, bathrooms, and the closets are big as shit."

'Toi you had us as soon as you mentioned separate rooms. We've been sharing for the last 16 years we need a damn break. Trust me, we are all for the move," said Kayla.

"So y'all are cool with the move. Ma, what about you?" Toi looked at me waiting for an answer.

"I'm okay with it. I'm not jumping to the moon but I'll be open-minded about it. I'm really in no place to complain anyway."

"Ma you're a grown woman who can do what she wants. I would just rather you be with us, I don't want you out here by yourself."

"I understand that so I'm okay with the move. I like the idea of being in my own space but close to you at the same time."

"Good. So we're out of here. We can start packing up this week."

"I'm about to call all my friends and tell them I'm moving to a mansion." Jayla shouted excitedly before running upstairs with Kayla right behind her.

"So we're doing this?" I looked at Toi who had a smile on her face.

"Yeah ma we are. It's time for a new start."

ISYSS RIVERA

Sitting in Maria's great room I was giving the performance of a lifetime while explaining my version of the fight between me and Toi. I was sobbing like a baby, tears, shortness of breath and everything. I should've gone into acting because I was selling this shit right now.

I hadn't actually talked to Que since the opening but that's because I wasn't answering his calls. There was nothing for us to talk about; I already know he wanted to curse my ass out. That nigga sent me a bunch of text messages going off on me for going to Toi's house.

The anger is confusing me because Quentin's dumb ass stood right there and heard that bitch tell me to pull up. If she didn't say that, I wouldn't have done it but of course he's going to take her side. Did I expect to get my ass beat? No, I didn't think the bitch could fight.

Mia told me she beat Toi's ass every time they fought and that she didn't have hands. She was definitely wrong about one or both of those statements because that bitch drug me. My nose, bottom lip and right eyebrow was swollen. My body was covered in scratches and bruises from being on the damn ground. I looked fucked up.

It's cool, I know how to get up and move on. It's not the first time I lost a fight and it won't be the last. I can't physically beat Toi, fine but I can fuck up their whole little love story. Que can act tough but he's a mama's boy at heart, there is no way he's going to get serious with a bitch his mother doesn't like. From what I've heard Maria say, she does not like Toi because she's too cocky. That's not it, she's not on board with Toi because Mia doesn't like her either. Maria is that kind of petty.

"I can't believe that girl put her hands on you," Maria said. "I told Quentin that girl had a problem with him having a daughter and he acts oblivious. Now look, she's fighting you because you're having a conversation about your child with him. That bitch better get right, because now she's really pissing me off."

"I told y'all she was a grimy bitch but your son is too stupid to see it," Mia added in her two cents. "You should press charges on her ass."

"No, I don't feel like doing that. Court is doing too much, I just want to move on but she keeps acting like I did something to her," I lied so easily. I know damn well I can't press charges on Toi when I'm the one who went to her house.

"And Quentin hasn't called and checked on you at all? I can't believe he's being this trifling. I'm going to let him have it as soon as his ass walks through the door."

"Huh?"

"I called him and told him to come by. He should be on his way now."

"I have to go," I got up and grabbed my things. Que knows exactly what happened; I don't need him busting me out in front of them.

"You don't have to leave; he's not going to do anything to you. Don't be scared of his ass."

"I'm no-" the sound of the front door closing cut me off mid-sentence.

"Ma!" I could hear Que's voice from the hallway.

"We're in the great room! Come here right now!" Maria shouted back.

Seconds later Quentin came walking in the living room looking so damn good. As much as I can't stand his ass, I have to admit Que is fine as shit. The black Nike sweat suit fit his tall muscular frame perfectly.

"What's up?" he spoke in an even tone until his eyes landed on me. "What the fuck are you doing here?" Que asked, obviously pissed off. His handsome face instantly went into a frown and his body language screamed 'I wanna knock your fuckin' head off'. "So you can't answer the fucking phone when I call you but you up for what?"

"Quentin don't talk to her like that. Look at that girl's face!" His mother shouted. She got up from the couch and walked over to him. "You're coming in here yelling and her face is all bruised up. She's the one who should have a damn attitude."

"Man, she bought that shit on herself. Nobody told her to bring her ass down to Toi's spa-"

"You mean your spa right? You bought it, didn't you?" Mia asked in a sarcastic tone.

"Mind your fuckin' business. Now, like I was saying, she bought her ass down. She bought her ass to Toi's house and got fucked up. That's on her. I tried calling her ass but she hasn't been picking up the damn phone."

Maria looked over at me like bitch what but then quickly turned her attention back to Que.

"Whatever Quentin, that doesn't matter right now. What matters is you getting rid of this girl."

"Getting rid of who? Toi?"

"Yes, she's caused nothing but problems since you started dating her."

"What the hell? Ma, with all due respect, I think you lost your fuckin' mind. Toi hasn't started anything, she came around one time how the hell is anything her fault?"

"You and Mia's relationship isn't the same. You barely speak to her when you come over here, and you're not going to stand here and lie Toi isn't the reason."

"She's not, at least not for me. Your daughter is the one that's salty about a nigga that was playing both of them. Since Mia likes running her mouth so much, did she tell you the reason she and Toi have a problem is because she was the side chick to Toi's ex?"

Maria had the same look of surprise on her face that I did. Mia said that Toi was the one playing the side chick.

"Que shut up, you can't talk about shit you don't know," Mia snapped.

"I know enough. I know the nigga you was playing side piece too was Bless," Que shot back and all our mouths dropped, Mia included. "Don't look shocked, you thought she wasn't going to let that fuckin' name slip?"

"Mia, is this the truth? You were sneaking around with Bless? Girl what is wrong with you?" Maria questioned.

"Nothing is wrong with me. How did this conversation become about me? We were talking about his girlfriend and her hand problems."

"Toi doesn't have a hand problem. You're the ones with the issue. Ma, you called me here for this? We could've done this shit over the phone; oh my bad she don't know how to answer that shit."

"Answer it so you could yell at me? It's not like you were calling to check on me," I finally decided to speak.

"You're right, fuck you. I'm not concerned about your ass because you stay doing stupid shit. I don't even know why you came to the opening. Don't give me that house bullshit because I told you when we were going to talk about it. You just wanted to be messy."

"You need to be concerned about her; she's the mother of your child Quentin. Why should that girl be involved in any type of discussion when it comes to you and Isyss."

"What?"

"She told us you won't move her because Toi won't let you. Damn," Mia shook her head in disgust. "You're that pussy whooped over her?"

"Yo, you really in here lying for real for real." Que said to me. "That's fuckin' crazy."

Toi is just your girlfriend, you have no ties or loyalty to her but you're pushing your whole damn family away because of her."

"How? I speak to my aunts and cousins all the time. I talk to Saint at least once a day. I'm not around every week because my girl wouldn't feel comfortable around you Mia so I avoid it. Ma, y'all have the issue, it's just y'all and you don't even know why you just backing up Mia."

"Besides Mia, she's proving herself to be a problem. Why is she okay with you not coming around your family whether she's uncomfortable or not?"

"She doesn't even know about the shit at Saint and Beautii's house so her opinion isn't even a factor. I choose to keep her away from y'all, I know what you'll do and she's not going to swallow your bullshit. I'm trying to avoid the drama but y'all keep it going listening to stupid shit. Toi did give her opinion about the house situation and you know what she said?'"

"I can imagine," Maria rolled her eyes.

"Nope, she told me to do it. Toi, the woman y'all hate so much told me to get this broad a bigger house in a better neighborhood when I was totally against doing shit for her ass."

"She should be telling you that, I'm not impressed. She's still not your family, nigga we are! I'm your sister, if I have a problem with her you should too! It's a simple as that."

"If that's the case, why the fuck are y'all on my neck for this bitch?" Que pointed at me. "Blood don't matter when it comes to her but I'm supposed to drop a good woman because y'all on some petty shit? Nah, I'm good on that. I'm trying to build a family with her and if y'all want to be a part of it get your shit together, if not then oh well. I'm out, Isyss I'm going to get my daughter from your mother since you're too busy lying over here to be with her." He shook his head at all of us then walked out.

Maria didn't say anything she just left out the room and went upstairs. Looking over at Mia I could see that she was upset.

"Are you okay?" I asked.

"No I'm not okay. All he does is take that bitch's side. What is so special about that bitch that niggas want to just fall at her feet. First Bless cut me off for that ho, now my own brother is doing the same thing. I'm sick of that bitch!"

"I know what you mean." Que is unfair when it comes to Toi; he acts like she can do no wrong and that shit is annoying.

"I want her ass out the way, it's clear he's not leaving her. I wish she would leave him."

"Oh please, she's not going anywhere Que is damn near perfect. He takes care of that bitch, he aint beating her ass, and he's not going to cheat on the bitch. Trust me, that nigga doesn't even look in the direction of another woman."

When I was working at the barbershop different women would come in, whether it be with their kids or a family member. It was some bad bitches practically throwing themselves at Que whenever he was there, and he always curved them. He wouldn't even entertain it, so I know trying to set him up in that way wouldn't work.

"I know, with his whipped ass. I hate that bitch, she needs her ass beat."

"Well don't look this way I'm not fighting her again. My girls could've gotten in it if her stupid ass friend wasn't there."

"We just have to catch her ass when Mickey isn't around."

"Didn't you just hear me say I'm not fighting her again?"

"Who said anything about us fighting her? You know people just like I do, and money is nothing. We'll get that bitch straight. You down?"

I looked at Mia and smiled. "This is why you're my bitch. Hell yeah I'm down and I know just who to call."

"Mia, I'm about to head to Beautii's house, she's over there going crazy," Maria announced when she came walking in the room.

"Why what happened?"

"Saint has two kids."

SAINT SANTANA

Walking into Beautii's salon I chuckled when everybody stared at me like they've never seen me before. I come in here at least twice a week to see my wife; I don't know why they always look so shocked. It's either that or they're scared, I'll put my money on scared.

"Where Beautii at?" I asked one of her stylist.

"She's in her office with an attitude," I shook my head and walked to her office and went straight in.

When she heard the door close she looked up from the papers on her desk then sucked her teeth.

"Why the fuck are you here Saint?" Beautii snapped at me. I didn't even do shit yet and she's coming at me.

"Whoa, watch your mouth. I came to see you, I can't check on my wife now?"

"Hell no, now get the fuck out and leave me alone."

"The fuck is wrong with you? You've had an attitude for the last few weeks for no fucking reason."

"You know damn well why I have an attitude. I looked you straight in your face a couple of times and asked you if you got that bitch pregnant and you said no. You're full of shit."

"You're still on this bullshit? I told you those are not my fucking kids. Let that shit the fuck go."

"Do I look fucking dumb to you Saint? I always wondered who their parents were because I couldn't figure out why they looked familiar. Now I know why, the complexion, the dimples, and they have grey eyes! It's no coincidence that Grace's daughters grey eyes just like yours."

I sat in one of the chairs she had in front of her desk then ran my hand down my face. "Beautii, those are not my kids ma."

She's been on this shit since she ran into Geneva and the twins in the supermarket. Everything was fine all day then she wants to come in the house going off about Grace and shit from over 15 years ago. I thought she was losing her damn mind until she said Geneva was Toi's mother. I had no idea about that, I knew Geneva had a kid but when she started getting heavy in that drug shit I never paid her much mind.

Plus I didn't know much about Grace and Geneva's parents to make the connection. Grace never invited me to her mother's house, I never bothered going and we never made any introductions. The only family of hers I met was her little sister Geneva.

All it took was for Beautii to take one look at those girls for her to come to the conclusion that they were mine. Once again she's losing her damn mind, they're not my kids.

"I can't believe that bullshit. Everything is telling me you're fucking lying Saint."

"Oh really like what?"

"Did you not hear me say they look just like you? Those are Grace's daughters, and they're 16 years old. Wasn't all that drama with her about 16 or 17 years ago? Oh alright, those are your daughters."

"I still don't think that shit, she never said shit to me about them being mine. You just fucking assumed it."

"I assumed because I know for a fact that you were fucking her, and then she ended up pregnant. Why would I not assume you?"

"You think I was the only nigga she fucked? Let's be serious."

"I don't give a one single fuck about anybody else. I care about you and the fact that you were fucking her. You got her ass pregnant."

"They're not my daughters damn Beautii! Fuck you want me to do?"

"Prove it. Prove to me those are not your kids."

"How the fuck am I supposed to do that?"

"It's called a DNA test nigga, take one then get back at me."

"Beautii really?"

She picked her phone up and scrolled for a minute then gave it to me. "Look at those girls and tell me you're 100% confident they're not yours."

I looked at the picture at the two identical girls. They're light sandy complexion, and deep dimples were identical to mine. I was going to dispute it because it's not really that hard to find a light skin girl with dimples, that doesn't necessarily mean they belong to me but when I looked at their big grey eyes, I was lost for words.

"Exactly, you can't say shit right? Those are your kids Saint."

"Beautii lis-"

"No, I'm not listening to anything; there isn't shit for you to say. You can save that shit for later. For right now what we're going to do is go talk to Geneva because if anybody knows it's definitely her."

"Are you serious right now?"

"I'm dead fucking serious, let's go." She got up from her chair then grabbed her purse and walked out.

I can't believe she's on this shit. Now we about to go over here and get caught up in some fucking drama because she wants to be petty. Grace has been gone for years and she's still mad about some shit from over ten years ago.

Grace was one of the few chicks I cheated on Beautii with when we were younger. I'm not going to lie and say Grace and I weren't rocking hard, we were. If I didn't love Beautii so much, Grace could've been the one to get a ring put on her finger if she wasn't on that getting high shit. She was too into drugs so I never took her seriously. I can't see myself wifing up a feen. I wasn't even about to do that bullshit.

When Grace turned up pregnant she told me it wasn't my kid so I took her word for it. Beautii wasn't trying to hear that shit but she let it go because Grace never came at us about her kids. I didn't even know she had twins until we were at Toi's spa opening. Beautii recognized Grace's sister Geneva then when she found out the twins were Grace's daughters and their age; she came at me with this Maury you are the father bullshit.

Now she wants to go to this house and approach Geneva's ass about her sister. I wasn't looking forward to this shit just because I knew it wasn't going to go well. Geneva and Beautii never got along just because of the relationship I had with Grace. Geneva was always on that if you have beef with my sister you have beef with me shit. Hopefully this shit doesn't go the wrong way.

When we got to Toi's house Beautii and I went up the front steps and knocked on the door. Seconds later it opened with Geneva standing behind it. Her arms crossed over her chest and her confusion was spread across her face.

"Hello Geneva," Beautii said. "Can you step out here so we can talk?"

"Talk about what?"

"Just some things I'm curious about. Are you going to come out or do we have to come in?"

"You're not coming in my house so stay right there." Geneva stepped out the door then closed it behind her. "What? I haven't seen y'all in years what do we need to talk about?"

"Your sister, I have some questions."

"It's been how long since my sister passed away, what the fuck is there to discuss."

"Calm down, don't curse at me."

"No I'm going to curse if I want to fucking curse. My sister has been dead for what? Almost 14 years, and you couldn't stand her so again, what the fuck do you want?"

"Maybe if you had that same aggression with your sister she wouldn't have overdosed." Beautii shot back.

"Bitch-"Geneva was about to go off but I cut her off before she could.

"Whoa, wait we're not about to do this bullshit right now. Beautii, come on, don't do that," I said, trying to get some control over the situation. "Geneva we're here because Beautii seems to think that your nieces are my mine."

"She thinks they're your what?" I chuckled.

"My kids; can you please tell her they're not so we can go home?"

Geneva let out a chuckle then sighed deeply. "Listen Saint, you know I respect you and I never had a problem with you so I'm not saying this to be funny or get this thing over here mad. They are your daughters."

"The fuck? What?" I asked in complete shock. I mean, looking at those pictures pretty much told me that they were mine but Geneva confirming it damn near knocked me off my feet.

"I fucking told you! I told you, I knew you got that hoe ass bitch pregnant!" Beautii screamed at me while tears ran down her face.

"Watch how the fuck you talk about my sister!" Geneva snapped at her. "I don't give a damn how the fuck you feel you're not going to be disrespectful right now. It's not going to happen so kill that bullshit."

"Shut the fuck up Geneva, you think I give a damn about disrespecting your bum ass? You don't even respect yourself, sucking dicks for a high," Beautii argued back.

"Better than swallowing nut for sport you miserable bitch. Tell all the drug jokes you want to I really don't give a fuck because that's not who I am anymore. Yes, they're his daughters. Grace didn't want to say anything because she knew your empty womb having ass couldn't have kids," Geneva spat. Beautii's face literally fell and I could see the heartbreak on her face.

Not being able to have children is one of the things Beautii struggles with the most. When she was 17 she was diagnosed with Endometriosis and the doctors told her the possibility of having kids were slim to none. Throughout the years we've tried to have kids but we've always come up with nothing. Of course I wanted kids but I knew about Beautii's fertility problems from the get-go so I chose to never make her feel bad or less than because she couldn't give me any.

I know hearing that I have kids by somebody else especially Grace of all people is really about to fuck with her mentally and emotionally.

"Yes bitch feel that shit, you want to throw out low blows and talk shit about my dead sister I can hit you where the fuck it hurts too."

Beautii shook her head and walked down to the car.

"Geneva man what the fuck? That wasn't necessary; you didn't have to take it there."

"She shouldn't have been talking shit about Grace when she's not here."

"Speaking of Grace, why the fuck did she lie to me about that shit and why didn't you tell me?"

"She made me promise not to say anything because she wasn't going to tell you either. Toi doesn't know so don't bother asking her about it."

I want to get a DNA test."

"Why?"

"What do you mean why? I want to know for sure."

"Saint they're 16, what are you going to do for them?"

"I don't know but I at least want to know for sure. One of y'all should've told me what the fuck was going on."

"What do you want me to do? Apologize? Not going to happen. I'll talk to them and see if they want to do it but if they don't you need to let it go."

"Hell no,"

"That's just the way it is Saint, they're young women. They're old enough to make that decision for themselves; I can't do it for them. If they want to know who their father is they'll take the test, if they don't then oh well. That's the only thing I can do."

"Alright well just let me know, Toi knows how to get in touch with me," I went down the stairs and walked back to the car.

When I got inside I looked over at Beautii who had her face in her hands sobbing. I knew she was hurt and I was the cause of it. We've been through a lot throughout the years but I don't think I've ever seen her cry so hard since I've known her.

"Beautii, baby I didn't know," I tried to grab her hand, but she snatched away.

"Don't touch me Saint! Don't ever touch me again!"

"Look I'm sorry alright! I didn't know they were mine, she said they weren't!"

"Whatever, just drive the car and take me home."

"Ba-"

"SHUT THE FUCK UP AND DRIVE SAINT!" Beautii screamed after slamming her fist down on the dashboard.

Usually I would check her ass for talking to me like that but I let it slide. She has a reason to be so angry, I'm not about to act like she's wrong for being upset with me. I might as well prepare myself for some shit because I know as soon as we go home the first thing she's going to do is call my damn sisters to run her mouth. I'm never going to hear the end of this shit.

TIANA "TAJ" JACKSON

Walking into Mecca's nursery I let out a small yawn before picking him up. "Okay, mommy's here baby, shhh," I rocked my son in my arms trying to calm him down. After I got his bottle in his mouth, he finally cut the crying out. "Greedy butt." Usually I would put him back to sleep so I could take a much needed nap but I had to get him dressed so I could take him to Anthony's house. He swore up and down he had something to show me that couldn't wait.

Three weeks ago gave birth to my son, Mecca Jamari Barnes after seven hours of labor. Being someone's mother is surreal on so many levels. I never knew I could love another person so much.

Mickey would talk about how much she loves her son and everything, but actually feeling it for my self was something different. I love my son more than anything or anybody in this world. I'll sacrifice my own life or take someone else's for that one and that's real.

After cleaning Mecca and rubbing down with lotion I put his clothes on him then laid him down on my bed so I could get dressed myself. It was still the middle of summer and hot as shit outside so I put on some black cotton short shorts, a white wife beater and my black and white Air Max 97's. It's not like I had much of a choice in my outfit anyway, I still can't fit my clothes.

During my pregnancy I gained 63 pounds and so far I've only lost four of them. Before getting pregnant with Mecca I was small as shit wearing a size 6 and now I'm at a 10. I'm not self-conscious about it because I gained in all the right places but it is something I have to get used to. I'm used to being small and now I'm on the thick side and I don't know what to do.

Once I was done getting myself together and getting Mecca's stuff in his baby bag I took his picture then posted it on Instagram.

After flexing for the gram a little bit we left and headed to Anthony's apartment. When I pulled up this fool was standing out front with a blunt in his mouth.

I couldn't help but shake my head; this is why I call his ass stupid. You know I'm bringing the baby but you want to get high. The fuck type of sense does that even make?

After I parked the car I got my son out of the car seat and grabbed his baby bag just as Anthony was approaching my car. "Give him to me." He tried to grab Mecca from me but I stepped back.

"Hell no you smell too much like weed and if your condo smells like that shit, I'm leaving. Take this," I gave Anthony his bag then we both went upstairs. Surprisingly his place was nice and clean, I guess he's not that damn dumb after all.

"Is he still keeping you up a lot?" Anthony asked like he was genuinely concerned.

"Yeah, but I'm getting used to it. What did you want to show me?"

"Oh yeah, I finished his room. Come on let me show you," I followed him to the room he decided to turn into Mecca's nursery.

When I walked in my mouth dropped a little bit, it was ridiculously nice. There was a nice crib almost identical to the one at my house, a rocking chair, changing table, and the closet was fully stocked with baby clothes, diapers, wipes and everything else he would need.

"Wow, this is really nice. This is why you called me over here?"

"Yeah I wanted you to see it. I figured sometimes I could take him so you could get some sleep. Like right now for example; go lay down in my room." He said before taking Mecca out of my arms.

"I'm fine."

"Who are you trying to fool? You're tired as shit. Just go lay down I got him, he's good."

I sighed a little bit then went to his bedroom and laid across his bed. Before I could even count to twenty I was knocked out.

* * *

OPENING my eyes I looked around the bedroom trying to remember where I was exactly. When I saw Naima's picture on the nightstand I remembered I was in Anthony's room. I stretched a little bit then walked out of his room and towards the living room. When I got in there I saw him sitting on the couch flipping through the channels while Que had Mecca on his lap playing with him.

"Anthony," I called his name out and they looked up at me.

"What's up Taj?" Que spoke up first.

"Hey Que," I spoke back. "Anthony, how long was I asleep?"

"For about five hours. He went to sleep, I fed him, changed him. He's good."

"Really? Thank you."

"What you thanking me for? It's my son too I'm not a dead beat ass nigga, I would think you would've figured that out by now."

"I never said you were a dead beat."

"Come here, let me speak to you." He got up from the couch then pulled back into his bedroom. "Are you good?"

"What do you mean?"

"I mean are you good. I get it we have a new baby but you're whole aura is off."

"I'm just…I'm just trying to get used to not sleeping as much and getting up with him. I'm glad he's not a crier like that but it's not easy being up with him all the time."

"So, call me and I'll come over there to help you Taj. You do know you can call me right?"

"I do now. I figured you would be working or something."

"I don't give a damn what you think I'm doing. If you're off that means it'll be harder for you to take care of him. I'm not going to let that shit happen. If you're tired and he's keeping you up call me. I'll come over and take him off your hands while you rest up. You didn't make him by yourself so I'm not letting you take care of him alone."

"Thank you."

"Taj, you need to stop thanking me. I don't need a thank you for doing what I'm supposed to." He shrugged his shoulders.

"No I get that but I'm going to say it anyway. I appreciate it."

"Well you're welcome. I do have another question."

"Okay, go ahead and ask."

"What's up with this?"

"What?"

"This," he pointed between us. "Us, what's up with us. You weren't trying to be together during your pregnancy and because I didn't want to stress you out I didn't press the issue."

"We're co-parenting with Mecca and that's it. What else is there supposed to be?"

"I mean you can stop acting funny with me."

"How am I acting funny? You were informed about everything my whole pregnancy. I called you to the hospital when I had him; I made sure you were there. I'm here right now bringing him to you. If I was acting funny I would be playing hide and seek with him but I'm not doing that."

"That's where you got me fucked up. I apologized for fucking our relationship up too many times for you to still act like this with me."

"How am I acting Anthony?"

"You're acting like you don't trust me."

"I trust you to a certain extent."

"The fuck does that even mean?"

"It means I trust you to be a good father to our son. I trust that if I ever need anything you would be there for me. As far as letting you back into my life and having you around me on a romantic level, no I don't trust you. I gave you my heart and you crushed it so no I'm not doing it again with you."

"Why not?"

"Nigga did you not hear me say I don't trust you? I can't trust you to go over your baby mama's house and pick your daughter up without touching her. I can't trust you to go out and not fuck somebody. If we don't have trust Anthony we don't have shit and that's it. We might as well stop talking about this right now. Do you want to keep him overnight or should I take him home?"

Anthony shook his head. I could tell he was frustrated because I wasn't giving him what he wanted but oh well

"Nah I got him, you can have a night to yourself."

"Alright, I'll call you tomorrow morning," I grabbed my stuff then went to the living room and kissed Mecca's forehead while Que held him. I said my goodbyes then left and headed home.

I'm convinced that Anthony lives in a damn fantasy world. He's a damn good father and I'll give him that, but he sucks as a boyfriend. I would be lying if I said I didn't think about getting back with him when Mecca was born because I did. After thinking about it I decided against it because despite wanting to give Mecca that complete family unit, I still don't trust Anthony.

Being with somebody I have doubt it would be a waste of both of our times. I don't have time to be wondering if he's fucking somebody, or lying about where he's going and who he's with. Until I can get that trust for him I'm not going to give him any false hope or put myself in a toxic situation.

ANTHONY "YUNG" BARNES

"She still aint fucking with you like that huh?" Legend snickered when I came back in the living room.

"Nigga make me take my baby from your shit talking ass."

"Fuck outta here you're not taking my God son anywhere." He laughed.

"Yeah alright, keep that God father energy when I need a damn baby sitter. You and Toi better be the best God parents on earth with how much shit y'all talk."

"Man, answer the question. She shut that ass down?"

"Shut up."

"I'll take that shit is a yes. Nigga leave her alone, I thought you were cool with co-parenting."

"That was before he was born. I thought the whole co-parent thing was going to be fine but now I don't want it to just be that."

"What, you want a family now or some shit?"

"Yeah man, is that so wrong?"

"Nah, nothing is wrong with it but are you ready for that shit? I know you love her, and you see her with your son so being a family comes to mind. But you have to give it some real thought, are you ready to be with her and only her. I think Taj has shown you more than once that she's not about to sit back and let you cheat on her ass."

"Who said I was going to cheat again?"

"That's why I asked you are you sure you're ready for that shit. Don't pull her back into something with you just to do the same bullshit."

"I hear you man, and I know what I'm going to do about Taj."

"And what's that?"

"Prove I'm not going to be on the same ole bullshit. That's all I can do right now."

"You do realize that in order to get Taj back you're going to have to get KeKe to act right, right? Imagine doing that when she's still pissed about that scar on her face," he said.

"She's still not letting that shit go."

The day Taj and KeKe got into it at the mall Taj didn't just beat her ass. She actually scratched the shit out of KeKe's face with the spike heel of a shoe. I thought once her face healed she would be good to go but that shit left a scar going from her left ear to her cheek and down to her neck. It's not a bad looking scar, it's not like its welted or left a keloid but you could tell something happened.

Every time I go to her house for my daughter she's on some depressed shit. KeKe doesn't even go out like that anymore talking about she's ugly because of the scar. She brings it up every chance she gets always ending with she's going to beat Taj's ass on sight.

I don't know about the beating her ass part, clearly, she can't beat Taj, but I do know how KeKe operates. She'll pick a damn fight and get into some shit just to prove a point; she doesn't give a damn about getting beat up. Taj doesn't need to be out here fighting and I know her temper, she'll fuck around and get arrested again.

If Taj and I were to get back together, KeKe would really lose her fuckin mind. I already know she's going to do the absolute most, so I have to figure out how to make that shit work.

* * *

"Aww look at him!" My mother squealed when she picked Mecca up from his car seat. "Oh my God, he looks just like you did when you were a baby. You must've been irking Taj's nerves something serious when she was pregnant."

"Maybe," I chuckled. "Naima isn't here yet?" I asked. Instead of going to her apartment to pick Naima up she and I agreed that meeting up at my mother's house would be better.

"No, KeKe hasn't brought her yet."

"Oh okay."

"So Taj let you get the baby by yourself?"

"I insisted she give him to me. She was tired as shit, I spoke to her this morning though. I'm taking him home tomorrow."

"Well I guess co-parenting is working out."

"For now, it hasn't been a problem. We're doing alright."

"That's good. I'm still mad at you for fucking that up," my mother reminded me.

My mother loves Taj, she loves everything about her. When they first met, she went on and on about how beautiful, smart, and independent she was. She had the same energy when she found out I cheated. I got cursed out for a good twenty minutes.

"You're not the only one; she's still hot at me too."

"So what are you going to do?"

"I want her back but I can't force her. The only thing I can do is show and prove to her that I'm not going to do that shit again."

"I think she'll come around. Just be the man I raised you to be, not the dog your hormones cause you to act like."

"I'm not a dog ma."

"What do you call cheating then? Despite that, I think she'll maybe come around, especially when she really sees how good of a father you are. You know Anthony, I'm proud of you."

"Proud of me?"

"Yes, I don't like what you're doing for a living. I would've rather you went to college and did the legit thing but I'm glad you're not stupid about what it is you're doing and I'm glad you're a damn good father."

"Thanks mama." Hearing my mother say she's proud of me really put a smile on my face. My mother had me when she was 18 years old and it's been me and her the last almost 22 years.

My father walked out on her the minute she told him she was pregnant. People tried to talk her into getting rid of me but she refused to. For years I watched my mother struggle to make a life for us with no complains. When I got old enough to make some shit shake on my own I went for it.

I ended up meeting Legend and Tone when I was 17 and they brought me in teaching me everything I needed to know. I've been with them since and I'm in a position where I could take care of my mother and my kids with no handouts. I'm not on Legend's or Tone's level yet but I'm doing well for myself and my family is taken care of.

"You're welcome," she sent me a pleasant smile. We sat around talking until we heard the doorbell ring. I got up and went to answer it.

"Pretty girl," I grabbed Naima from KeKe's arms and spun her around. "I missed you baby," I kissed Naima's chubby chocolate cheek then put her down. "Go find Grandma," I said, and she went off running in the living room.

Turning back to the door I looked at KeKe who was standing there with her arms folded across her chest. I could tell by the way her lips were twisted up she had an attitude, why I don't know because I didn't do shit to her.

"What's wrong with you Ke?" I asked.

"I heard ole girl had the baby," KeKe griped.

"That's why you're mad?"

"No, actually I'm mad because I see you posting pictures of her and the baby on your Instagram but you don't do the same for us."

"I post Naima all the time so what are you talking about?"

"You don't post me. You post that bitch and y'all baby why I can't be on your page too?"

"Are you fuckin' serious right now?" I was looking at KeKe like she was a damn dummy. That's literally the most asinine thing I've ever heard her say and trust me, some foolish shit has come out her mouth before. "What type of childish shit is that Ke?"

"It's not childish, I'm being real. Don't start acting funny because that bitch gave you a son. You don't even come by my place anymore."

"Man, you fucked up my relationship why the fuck would I come over there? Ke you need to drop this shit with Taj, alright? Both of y'all are parents, you have other shit to focus on."

"Drop what? I'm not dropping shit! Look at my fuckin' face! Fuck that bitch, she's going to see me watch. Payback is a real big bitch."

"I don't want to take it there with you but don't fuckin' play with me Ke. You started that fuckin' fight with her; nobody told you to pop shit if you couldn't back it up. I'm giving you one fair warning, leave Taj the fuck alone."

"Of course you're taking up for that ho. It's cool." She nodded her head. "I got you Yung, I got you," I was given a damn death glare before she walked off my mother's porch. I don't know what the fuck that was about but I hope like hell that girl isn't crazy enough to try some shit. I really don't feel like killing Naima's mother.

MICKEY

"So, Saint is the twins' daddy?" I asked Toi while we spoke on the phone. I was sitting at my vanity doing my makeup while Toi explained all the drama between her mama, Beautii and Saint.

"That's what my mother says. They do look like that nigga now that I think about it. I never made that connection between the two. But then again I didn't know Saint knew my mother and aunt so it is what it is."

"What did they say about it?"

"Jayla was fine, she actually seemed excited. Kayla on the other hand really didn't say much. But that's just Kayla in general she's not going to be all out there like that."

"She's probably not trying to give her hopes up. Sure they look alike but DNA could be a funny thing sometimes and no offense but your auntie was out there a little bit."

"I know what you mean. They did agree to take the test though so I guess we just have to wait and see what happens with that. Anyway, on to something else; Taj said Yung's mother is watching Mecca for her so she's for sure coming to the party. We're going to pick her up then head down there."

"Are you dressed? And who is we?"

"Oh Que has his driver and sprinter so we're going in that."

"Y'all are coming to pick me up?"

"No, you have your own special ride coming to get you."

"Wait what the fuck? What special ride?"

"You're the birthday girl, why wouldn't you have a special ride? Come on now, I told you shit was going to be super lit for you."

Laughing I shook my head, leave it to Toi to get extra. Tonight I will be turning 24 once the clock strikes midnight. To celebrate Que is letting me have a party at The Mansion. My plan was to get super drunk and just let loose. Since Myles has been back I haven't really been out like that besides Que's last party and I didn't even get the chance to have fun like I wanted to. So tonight, a bitch is getting wasted.

I'm not even ready yet."

"The person coming to get you knows that. They actually know you very well."

"Uh uh Toi, what are you up to?"

"Nothing," she laughed. "For real I'm not up to anything."

"Mhm sure. What is Myles doing? Is he being good?"

Earlier today after Toi closed up her spa for the day, she came to my house to pick Myles up so Geneva could watch him for me tonight. I offered to pay her but she told me no. She says she enjoys watching him and Que's daughter will be over there with them too so Myles will have somebody to play with.

"Yeah he's good. He's downstairs making personal pizzas with my mother and Diamond. Then they're going to watch a bunch of Disney movies and shit. They're going to have a fun don't worry about him."

"Okay good; kiss him for me before you leave out."

"I got you. I'm going to let you finish getting ready so I can finish too."

"Have you even started?"

"Yes I started-"

"SHE LYING!" I heard Que shouting in the background.

"Shut yo ass up!" Toi shouted back at him. "Anyway, I'm getting ready. We'll see you at the party. Have fun and be nice to your ride."

"Toi I feel like you up to something but whatever. I'll leave it alone, and I'll see you at the party."

"Alright, I know you're going to be bomb as shit in that outfit. I have some damn good taste."

"Don't sweat yourself," I laughed. "Thank you though, you know me so well."

"I know alright let me get my ass together, see you in a little while." We finally ended the call so I continued to get dressed.

My honey blonde hair was now platinum and I had it styled in a low, curly, invisible ponytail done by Taj. I was rocking a shimmery rose gold smokey eye with a sparkling pink lip. Toi took it upon herself to buy my party outfit while Taj bought my shoes. I love those bitches to death because they knew exactly what to get me.

Toi picked out a satin baby pink Dolce & Gabbana tulle bustier top and a leather high waist mini skirt of the same color. Taj did her thing picking out a pair of pink Giuseppe Zanotti snake chain sandals to go with the outfit. Triplet Mop Drop Rose gold and pink sapphire earrings a matching necklace and bracelet was the jewelry I decided to wear.

When I was done getting ready I looked in the mirror with a smile on my face. I looked damn good, and nobody could tell me any different.

I was getting my things together when I heard my doorbell ring. "I'M COMING!" I shouted before making my way to the front door and opened it. Seeing Tone standing there shocked me. I haven't spoken to or seen him since we were at the hospital for Mecca's birth.

"Tone, what are you doing here?" I asked once my initial surprise wore off.

"I came to take you to your party?" He answered while coming inside and closing the door.

"I'm going to kick Toi's ass, I knew she was up to something," I rolled my eyes. I knew Toi was up to some bullshit earlier, talking about a surprise ride. "Why did you agree to do this? I'm confused."

"I agreed to do this because I'm not trying to beef with you. I actually miss being able to talk and laugh with your mean ass. I'm not saying let's jump back into a relationship but I want to at least be your friend."

"My friend huh?" A chuckle left my lips. "Alright Tone, I'll try this friend thing with you but don't fuck with me. That means don't try my patience, I let you slide before with the disrespectful shit, this time I'm swinging first and asking questions later."

"I got you," he laughed. "You look beautiful, the blonde works for you. I like it."

"Thank you," I finally gave him a genuine smile.

"Happy birthday," he pulled out a long black box from his pocket.

"What is this?" I took the box and opened it to see a rose gold Rolex. "Wow, this is really nice Tone. Thank you. It actually matches my outfit too."

"I was aware of that." He took the watch from the box and put it on my left wrist. "Now you're really complete."

"I appreciate this, thank you."

"You're welcome shorty. So you're moving?" He looked around at the boxes sitting around my living room.

"Yup I'm out of here on Wednesday. Since you playing nice, you should come help me move. Your friend will be here."

"I got you. But come on ma, we got a drive to take."

"I'm ready," I grabbed my purse, phone and keys then headed out. When we stepped onto the front porch I saw a bouquet of black roses sitting right in front of my door. "What is this?" I picked them up and grabbed the card attached to them.

Happy Birthday Baby Mama, I hope you enjoy your last one

- Brick

After I read the card I had to grab the railing to keep my knees from buckling. My last birthday?

"What's up? Who is that from?" Tone asked with a concerned look on his face. I couldn't even fix my lips to answer his question I was in complete shock. If Tone didn't notice the flowers on the way in and I didn't see them when I opened my door for him that means Bryson literally just did this.

I guess Tone grew sick of me not answering his question so he took the card from me and read it.

"What the fuck? Who the fuck sent this? Mickey!"

"We have to get out of here right now," I rushed down the steps and over to his car. When I heard the doors unlock I opened the passenger side door and hopped in quickly closing the door.

Tone got in right after me then pulled off. "You care to tell me who and why some nigga is basically threatening you?"

"Brick is Myles' father."

"Brick...Wait Brick, he big as shit? Just got out of jail?" Tone questioned.

"Yeah, why you know him?"

"Nah not really, but I've heard of him. Why is he threatening you?"

"He's a psychotic ass nigga; I told you he used to beat my ass."

"Alright but why is he threatening to kill you is my question."

"He's mad at me because he went to jail for beating on me and stalking me after I left."

"The state pressed charges on his ass?"

"Nope, I did."

"So you're the reason he went to jail?"

"No, he went to jail because of his own actions. I just gave the information they needed to keep his ass there for a good while."

He glanced over at me then turned his eyes back towards the road. "Alright look, that shit is crazy but I'm not judging you. If the nigga was beating your ass you did what you had to do to keep him away from you."

"I'm glad you understand."

"I do and that's why you're not going back to your house."

"What?"

"You're not going back to your house; you and Myles are coming to mine until you're due to move."

"Tone that's not even necessary."

"No it is necessary. Mickey this nigga is threatening you, and he's trying to be funny about it so that tells me he isn't playing with a full deck. You said you're moving on Wednesday right? It's three days, let me help you for three damn days Mick."

"Alright, three days and that's it."

"Cool with me. Don't worry about that nigga alright, I got you."

"I'm not worried about him," I lied. I was scared to death of Bryson and he knows that shit. That's what annoys me the most. He knows the power he has over me and he uses it to his advantage.

"That sounded real convincing but I know you ma. The look you had on your face when you read that card is one I've never seen before. I've never seen you look so damn scared and I'm not feelin' that shit. I got you just like I said." Reaching over Tone grabbed my hand and intertwined our fingers.

When I felt tears welling up in my eyes I wanted to punch myself. I hate crying, it takes too much energy and shows the one emotion I don't like exposing; vulnerability. I've never had anybody care enough to protect me before. My mother let my dad do whatever he wanted to do to both of us.

Nobody ever attempted to get between Brick and I when he would start his BS besides Toi and Myles and of course they're no match for him so they couldn't do much. Tone saying he wants to protect me gets to me because it reminds me of why I fell for him in the first place. Then I'm quickly reminded that he left me and that shit actually hurts when I think about it.

The rest of the ride I chose to stay quiet. If I started talking I was bound to spill my feelings all in this car and I didn't feel like doing that. It's my birthday, I want to have fun tonight and worry about the rest of that annoying shit tomorrow.

By the time we got to The Mansion it was packed as usual. I know this is my party or whatever but I know for a fact that more than half these people are not here to celebrate another year of my life. I don't even fuck with too many people but this is how crowds at The Mansion usually are.

After Tone found a safe place to park his car we got out and entered the party together.

"The birthday girl just walked in the building HAPPY BIRTHDAY MICK!" The DJ, who I noticed was a local one from Jersey City named Wiz shouted through the mic before throwing on In Da Club by 50 Cent.

I waved and greeted the few people I did know and recognize before going to the section that had BIRTHDAY GIRL in gold balloons hanging above it. Toi, Que, Yung, Taj and the rest of Que's crew was already there turning up. I even noticed Dutch had her girl Giselle in tow.

"HAPPY BIRTHDAY!" Toi squealed when I got in the section, then she damn near jumped on my ass. "Yass I have good taste, you look so good."

"Thank you," I laughed. I could tell by Toi's face she was already on her way to being gone. Either they've been here for a minute already or she was pre-gaming in the house.

"Happy Birthday bitch!" Taj said before hugging me.

"Thank you boo. Okay Mecca did the body right, bitch you look good," I let her know. Taj has always been on the petite side but the baby weight she gained went to all the right places. She was wearing a satin leopard print Dolce & Gabbana ruched bustier midi dress with black Saint Laurent sandals. Her jet black hair was long down to her waist and was bone straight. Large thin gold hoops were in her ears and gold Cartier bracelets decorated her wrist.

"I told her the same thing, my bitch thick now!" Toi shouted excitedly.

"Thank you ladies; this ass is one of the pluses of pregnancy." Taj laughed. I looked at Toi's outfit impressed.

She was rocking a white Georgia Alice corset mini dress with red Gianvito Rossi *Marie* over-the-knee peep toe heels. With the excuse that she missed her hair, she added extensions so her body waves fell down her back. Between the big 14 karat Lana Vanity inside-out diamond hoop earrings, gold nameplate chain that had LEGEND written in diamonds around her neck and the diamond charm bracelet sitting on her wrist, my girl was dripping in diamonds. She even had the nerve to have a diamond trimmed, gold Patek Philippe watch on her left wrist.

"Okay bitch, you in here dripping in ice. I'm here for it," I said to Toi.

"Man listen, every time he picks something out for himself he buys me and Diamond something too. Well it started with just us, now he's spoiling the twins and my mama. He bought this watch because I moved in the house, and then bought them all tennis bracelets."

"Hey he has it to spend so let him." Taj shrugged and I agreed with her. It's not like Toi is begging him to buy her anything, he chooses to do it. So she better rock every piece he gives her, I would.

"Ayee your bottles are coming!" Toi shouted in excitement. She was a little too damn happy for me. The bottle girls came over with a bunch of liquor bottles, Ace of Spades being the main ones.

Que handed me a bottle of Ace and I popped it open taking a large swig from the bottle while Taj and Toi hyped me up. We drank for a little while then went down to the dance floor when they threw on G-Eazy's "No Limit".

After dancing through quite a few songs we went back to the section for a seat. Taj and I fixed ourselves a drink and sat across from where the guys were. Toi went straight to Que and sat between his legs while he sat on top of the white tufted sectional that furnished our area.

Yung was sitting to his right while Tone was on his left. Que was drinking from a bottle D'usse while Tone and Yung were on Hennessy.

"Your baby daddy is over there downing that liquor. I hope he didn't drive," I told Taj. From the looks of it Yun was going to be gone by the end of the night. He was drinking from his bottle like it was water.

"He didn't, we all came in Que's sprinter."

"Oh okay, just making sure."

"So you and Tone rode together?"

"Mhm, we did. Thanks to Toi's sneaky ass."

"And?"

"And it's a not even worth talking about right now. I'll fill y'all in on everything tomorrow but for now, let this be about fun."

"Cool with me, but just prepare for me to be hella nosey tomorrow. As a matter of fact if we don't get too fucked up let's go to brunch. I'll tell Toi before we leave."

"I'm with it," we hit the tip of our glasses together.

For the ladies, OK girl
I want to be your mother, ya father, brother,
Your sister your everything, you know?
Uh, goin' straight to the top baby

"Aww shit, Toi about to act up," I told Taj when we heard the intro to the Young Gunz classic No Better Love come on. Let Toi tell it, that's one of her top five songs of all time.

We both looked over at Toi who was on her feet rapping and singing along to the song but of course she added dramatics to it. Waving and moving her arms like she was on a stage.

"This is my shit though so I can't judge," Taj said and we both laughed then got up on our feet.

When it came time for the bridge I closed my eyes singing along. I was in my zone when I felt a pair of arms go around my waist. My first move was to turn around to see who was touching me but hearing Tone's voice in my ear calmed me down immediately.

"Ever since the day I saw your face

My mind told me you were the one that was down for me

And baby when I get laced,

I'm gonna do what you want I'll be there, truly

So don't you let a thing,

Turn you away from the love that you need, my dear

I don't want to play around wit ya

Cause I know I found lovin' right here" Tone sang in my ear before leaving a kiss on the side of my neck.

"Tone is definitely short for Tone deaf," I teased.

"Wow, a nigga try to be nice and shit with you and gets insulted," he said after laughing.

"I'm playing with you."

"Nah you dead ass serious," he said before taking a swig from the Hennessy bottle in his hand.

"You're not about to repeat your actions from the last party we were at are you?"

"Nah I'm good, I don't fuck with these bitches like that."

"Yeah alright, we'll see."

"If I did would you care?"

"Go ahead and do it. If you end up with a bottle across your head, you'll have your answer," I went over to Taj and told her to come with me to the bar. She grabbed Toi's arm and pulled her over to the bar with us. I ordered some shots and we drank them down quickly.

"Shit, that's hot." Toi fanned herself. "Are you having fun Mick?"

"Hell yeah, Tone trying to boo love and shit," I shook my head with a laugh. "Like I'm about to forget he dumped my ass."

"Well I do think you need some dick, I know you haven't had some since y'all broke up. That's a long ass time." Taj said and I nodded.

"It really is but oh well. I'm not fucking with him like that. He's not about to dump me and get some pussy just because you drove me to my party. He can use his mouth though," I shrugged then took another shot.

"Yo, either I'm drunk as shit or Brick just walked in here." Taj said after nudging my arm. We all looked over to where Taj pointed and sure enough it was him walking through the crowd.

"FUCK! He's here to fuck with me," I shook my head.

"You don't know that Mickey," said Toi.

"Toi he's here for me. The nigga just left black roses on my doorstep talking about he hopes I enjoy my last birthday."

"What? Are you serious?"

"Yes, he's here to try some bullshit," I looked at the bartender and waved him over to me. "Let me get a big ass bottle of anything, I don't care what it is." They looked at me confused but gave me a bottle anyway. "I swear to God if he fucks with me I'm busting him in his shit."

"Come on, we need to get back to the section before he sees you." Toi grabbed my arm and pulled me away from the bar.

TOI

As soon as Mickey grabbed the bottle from the bartender I knew we had to go get Que and Tone before Brick got to us. Usually I wouldn't think he would try some shit in a club full of people but if he's bold enough to pretty much leave her death threats, he's crazy enough to try anything.

As were walking through the crowd we were almost to the section when Brick's big ass stepped right in front of Mickey smiling. She tried to walk past him but he blocked her path. Due to the music being so damn loud I couldn't here exactly what they were saying to each other but by the pissed off look on Mickey's face I knew it was nothing good.

The only thing I could do was watch her actions and body language. The more upset she got the more she moved her hands. I pulled Taj close to me and told her to go get Tone. When she rushed off, I stepped in front of Mickey, put my arms around her shoulders, and pulled her close so she could hear me.

"Calm down, I see it all in your face. Don't let this nigga fuck your night up," I said while moving her back away from this nigga. I pushed her all the way back to we were by the bathroom. Little did I know he was following us the whole time. I was hoping he got lost in the damn crowd.

"I'm not sweating him he just needs to leave me the fuck alone and I'm good." Mickey said.

"You got my son bitch I'm never leaving you alone," I heard his voice behind me. "Looks like you still got your guard dog around. What's good Toi? You ready to give that pussy up yet?"

Turning around I looked Brick up and down. Mickey was right about him being bigger, he gained at least 80 pounds of muscle while he was locked up and it doesn't help that he was already tall as shit.

"Brick go somewhere with this disrespectful bullshit. For real, you're taking it too fucking far."

"Fuck you bitch I know you the reason she called the fucking cops on me anyway."

"Like you beating her ass didn't have shit to do with it right? Don't start with me my nigga you'll really get fucked up in here," I said truthfully. This was Que's club, every last one of his niggas was in this bitch and they will kill this nigga just off one word. He better watch himself.

"Bryson just go on about your fucking business. I don't want shit to do with you! Leave me the fuck alone!" Mickey screamed at him.

"Or what? Make me leave you alone! You thought you was about to get me knocked then hoe around and kick my back in while I was locked up and I wasn't going to do shit about it? Bitch you got me fucked up!" He started to come in her face but I pushed him back as much as I could but of course I didn't do much.

When I pushed him this nigga pushed me down to the floor then grabbed Mickey by her neck making her drop the bottle she had in her hand. Thankfully the shit didn't break. I grabbed the bottle and cracked it right over his head; I had to jump to reach him but I got his ass good. Immediately he dropped Mickey down on the floor and put his hands on his head.

"FUCKING BITCH!" Brick tried to grab me but out of nowhere somebody hit him from the on the side making him fall to the ground. Looking over I let out a sigh of relief when I saw Tone was the one to hit him. I was about to say something to Tone but he was too busy beating Brick's ass.

I got Mickey up off the floor just as Que, Yung, and a couple of niggas that run with them all jumped on Brick's big ass.

"Are you okay?" I asked Mickey and she nodded. Turning my attention to this ass beating that was taking place I wanted them to kill this nigga but I had to remember we were in a crowded ass club right now and that would not be a good look. I had to get my nigga before he did something stupid.

"Que!" I grabbed his arm and pulled him away from the rest of those nigga which was hard to do. "STOP BEFORE YOU DO SOMETHING STUPID IN HERE!"

"TONE DON'T!" I heard Mickey scream. Looking over this nigga pulled out his knife and had it to Brick's neck. Mickey went over and grabbed Tone's face and made him look at her. "I would love for you to cut this niggas head off but it's too many people in here! Stop okay?"

Clenching his jaw tight Tone looked from Mickey to Brick. "GET THIS NIGGA THE FUCK OUT!" Tone's yelling was cut off by gun shots ringing out.

"GET DOWN!" Que grabbed me and put his whole damn body over mine while pulling me into the bathroom. "Stay in here."

"Where are you going?"

"I'll be right back, just stay in here!" He shouted then went back out. In the middle of shit going haywire I didn't even get to see where Mickey went and I don't know where the fuck Taj was either.

It was a good five minutes of me silently freaking out at the obvious shootout that was going on outside. When the shooting finally stopped I waited for a minute before I left out the bathroom. I went out to the main floor and everybody was gone while it looked like a stampede came through.

I was about to make my way outside but click of a gun and the feeling of something pressed against the back of my head stopped me dead in my tracks.

"Take one more step and I'll send a bullet through that pretty ass face of yours," a familiar voice said from behind me. "Turn around slowly which your hands up."

I did as I was told and turned to see Kareem of all people standing there with a gun pointed at me.

"Kareem what the fuck are you doing? How did your ass even make it in here without getting beat the fuck up?" It's been almost a year since Bia died at the hands of this muthafucka, but nobody forgot about her or what he did. It's still people that want his head on a damn platter.

"Don't worry about that you just need to worry about listening to me. You're about to come on a ride with me. They got Brick the fuck out of here so I'm taking you. Fair exchange don't you think?"

"I'm not going with you, are you trying to get yourself killed? I'm pretty sure you already know who the fuck my nigga is, so you need to just leave right now while you got the chance," I wasn't scared of Kareem's ass right now. I knew for a fact he's not going to shoot me. If he couldn't show his face because of Bia, doing anything to me will have his ass dead before the sun could come up.

"Fuck you and that nigga. It's your fucking fault I can't walk around the fucking city like I want to. Trying to brain wash Bia into leaving me and shit. Mickey is lucky she got the fuck out of here."

"What is with you and your friend blaming me for the consequences to your own actions. You killed Bia nigga, that's not on me."

"SHUT THE FUCK UP! Like I said you're coming with me," he started to walk towards me, so I tried to slide past him and run but he snatched me by my fucking hair and pulled me back to the bathrooms. He pushed me inside then put his gun to my face. "Try that shit again I will blow your fucking head off."

"Get off me!" I screamed.

"TOI!" I heard Que yell my name.

"QUE!" I screamed at the top of my lungs only for this nigga to put his hand over my mouth.

"Shut the fuck up." Kareem whispered in my ear. Thinking fast I lifted my foot and stomped on of his making sure to use my heel as much as I could. "Ahh shit! Stupid bitch!" He let his hand go from around my mouth so I turned around and tried to take the gun out of his hands but he had a good grip on it.

We tussled over the gun until it finally went off.

LEGEND

"Is everybody out?" I asked one of the guards when he came outside.

"Yeah, Toi is still in the bathroom I didn't see her come out. I figured you would want to go get her." He answered.

"Alright thanks man," I went back inside my club that was pretty much all fucked up do to everybody trying to get the fuck out of here at one time. I was pissed the fuck off, niggas having a good time just so a bunch of pussies could fuck it up.

"TOI!" I shouted her name as I neared the bathroom so she could hear me coming.

"QUE!" Hearing her scream my name like that told me something was wrong so I ran to the doors. Before I could push it open a gun shot went off.

"WHAT THE FUCK? TOI!" When I busted in the bathroom she was standing there with her hands over her mouth while a body laid there on the floor. "Toi," I walked over to her and pulled her back some so I could see who this nigga was. "Who the fuck is that?" I asked her.

"Kareem.'

"The nigga who killed Mickey's cousin?"

"Yeah." She nodded her head.

"Come here," I pulled her to my chest then walked her outside to the van. "Get in I'll be right back." Once she got inside the van I walked over to the truck Barry was in. "How many?"

"Surprisingly none, niggas scrammed as soon as possible."

"It's a mess by the bathroom; make sure they clean that shit up. I'm dead ass serious, if anything goes wrong with that shit I'm taking that shit personal. They don't want that. The cops are bound to come sniffing around this muthafucka and I don't need a problem, you got me?"

"I got you, it'll be done. What you about to do?"

"Tone got that nigga in the fucking trunk. I already know what he's about to do. He choked and threatened Mickey, he's not about to see tomorrow."

"You're not heading over there?"

"Nah, I need to stay with Toi so I got to miss out on the fun a little bit. They're going to give you the tapes of what happened tonight. Look over them then hit me up; I need to know who the fuck started shooting."

"Alright, I'll look at them when I get out of here."

"Cool, hit me when you're done with everything," I slapped hands with him then went and got in the van with Toi.

"Where is everybody?" She asked me when I sat next to her.

"Yung got Mickey and Taj out of here; they're good. Tone went to handle that nigga Brick," I closed the van door and the driver pulled off. "What happened? He came in the bathroom? I didn't see anybody going in."

"I came out the bathroom and he put the gun to my head talking out the side of his neck. He and Brick was on some blaming me bullshit."

"What you mean?"

"Brick said I was the reason Mickey put his ass in jail-"

"Mickey got him knocked?"

"Yeah, he was beating on her and stalking her once she finally left him. Then Kareem said I had Bia ready to leave him when that was Mickey if anything. I never really got in the middle of he and Bia's business, but I guess since he couldn't get to Mickey, he tried it with me."

"Alright so what happened after that?"

"I tried to go past him but he pulled me in the bathroom. When I screamed your name he put the gun to my face. I stepped on his foot and we tussled for the gun; I guess he pulled the trigger and thank God it was turned his way when he did."

I kissed her forehead before she rested her head on my shoulder. "I'm glad you're good and I'm sorry. You shouldn't have been in that position."

"You don't have to apologize."

"No I do because I shouldn't have left you in the bathroom. You'll never be put in that position again; I'm going to make sure of it."

"What are you going to do?"

"You don't need to know everything but as far as you go if you're not with me, or in this van you're not going anywhere."

"What? Que I have a business to run."

"And I'll make sure you get to and from work but you are not going to be anywhere by yourself. Until all this bullshit is dead this is just how it's going to be."

"Okay Que, I understand."

"Good," I closed my eyes trying to get my mind under control. Shit went left tonight and even though the people I care about all came out of that bullshit fine, it could've went way worse. Niggas had a gun to my girls head ready to kill her and that shit has me hot. Kareem is dead, Brick will be dead soon but neither of them are the ones that started the damn shooting.

The name Brick didn't go over my head so if my gut is correct I know who came to wreak havoc in my shit along with those niggas. I told Barry to get and look at the tapes but I don't even need to see that shit to figure out who it was. Everything was pointing at one person and there's no way I'm wrong. Bless was behind that shit.

MIA SANTANA

"Did you hear about the shoot-out at your brother's club?" Isyss asked as we moved things around her new living room.

Despite all the bullshit Que was spitting about not taking care of Isyss, he moved her and Diamond into a brand new town house in Syosset, New York which is only a quick drive from where he lives. I personally feel like she should've had a real house and not a townhouse but that's just me. She likes it so I'll leave it alone.

"No, I didn't hear about that. What shoot-out?"

"Girl, everybody is talking about it. One of my people called me and told me about it. Apparently Mickey was having a birthday party," we both rolled our eyes at the mentioning of that bitch. "Niggas started shooting in the club, and from what I heard Bless was one of them."

"What?"

"You heard me; he shot up your brother's club."

"Wow. I bet it was over that Toi bitch."

"You think they're beefin' over her?"

"Hell yeah; she used to fuck with Bless now she's fucking with my brother. If they're beefin' it's definitely over that hoe."

"Do you think it's over you? I mean, Que could be feeling a way about his sister fucking his friend."

"Oh please, Que doesn't care about me or what I do. If it's not about that hoe it doesn't matter."

I know for a fact whatever Bless and Que's problem is has nothing to do with me. What I want doesn't matter to niggas and look what they have in common; Toi. I swear to God I hate that bitch. Everything is always about her.

Bless wanted to drop me all of a sudden because of that bitch, and now my brother is putting her before our whole damn family. It isn't even just about me; Quentin has pushed away our mother too. Since the situation at her house they haven't really spoken.

"So you think Bless did that because of her? Damn, what is the obsession with that bitch?"

"I don't know but I'm sick of her and that funky ass attitude of hers. You're holding out on this shit; we can get that bitch touched."

"Alright say we do that, when Que goes off who is about to be at the mercy of his anger?"

"He won't know who did it. With all this shit with Bless going on we're going to be the last people he thinks of."

"I don't know Mia; I'm not trying to get on that man's bad side."

"Oh please you've been on his bad side. You think he got you this house because he wanted to? Hell no, you made him feel guilty and threatened him with child support. Besides this town house is nothing, he moved Toi and her whole damn family in with him."

"What?" By the surprised look on her face I knew she didn't know about Que's new house guest. "What you mean he moved them in?"

"They live with him and I'm not talking about in that stupid ass condo. They're living in his house, the house your daughter goes to every weekend."

"What the fuck? He moved that bitch in and didn't even tell me?"

"Yup, I heard my uncle telling my mother. They're all living there, her mother and those bastard twins."

"Aren't those Saint's daughters?"

"Supposedly, but their mother was a damn crack head, so who knows. Fuck that, focus on the real issue. What are you going to do about him moving her in? She's probably the reason he didn't tell you. You know she has his mind gone."

"Man fuck her, I'm going to ask him why he thought moving her in the house my daughter lays her head in was cool without talking to me. He knows me and that bitch don't get along so she could be on some evil shit and mistreat my daughter. I'm not cool with that shit and I want to know what the fuck he was thinking."

"That's not it though. He bought her a damn ring, a big ass diamond ring. Now why is he only giving you a couple thousand dollars a month when he's dropping hundreds of thousands on her? That sounds like he's putting her before his daughter and I bet she's behind it all. I'm telling you, that bitch is the problem."

"So what do you think we should do?"

"We're going to get this bitch out of the way."

"Are you trying to kill her?"

"No, I'm not stupid, but I at least want that bitch to get the point. As long as she's with Que, shit will continue to happen. I'll make her life a living hell, I explained this to you at my mother's house. You need to be on the same page before that nigga has Diamond calling that bitch mommy."

"I will kill that Que, he better not ever disrespect me like that."

"Well do you want to do this shit or not?"

"Fuck it; let's get this bitch out the way."

"Thank you for finally seeing the light. First things first, we need to send her a message."

TONE

I walked in my living room to see Myles sitting on the couch watching TV while Mickey sat across from him typing away on her laptop and talking on the phone at the same time. They've been here for the last three days and were due to leave tomorrow since that when she picks up the keys to her house.

When I told Mickey she could stay with me until it was time for her to move, I prepared myself to be annoyed. I'm not used to living with a kid, I thought Myles was about to act like he had no sense but he was the total opposite.

If he wasn't watching TV or playing his game he was talking to me about cars, which I've learned is one of his biggest obsessions. He'll sit on his tablet or iPad looking up cars all the time and he could legit have a full blown conversation about them all day if you entertained him that long. He's a cool little kid and he's not all over the place, Mickey has a good one on her hands.

"Damnit, okay I'll be down there as soon as I can. Thank you." Mickey said to whoever she was on the phone with. "I have to go get the keys to the house right now."

"Why? I thought you were picking them up tomorrow."

"That's what I thought too but the realtor just called me saying he has a family emergency or something so he won't even be in the state tomorrow. Myles put your sneakers on and come on. We can go get your haircut when we come back."

"Okay," Myles got up off the floor and went upstairs to the bedroom he and Mickey slept in. I told her they could take my room and I would be in the guest but she didn't want to do that.

"I can take him," I volunteered.

"Take who?"

"Myles, I can take him to get a haircut."

"Oh. You don't have to do that; I can go when I get back."

"Mick, it's 2 in the afternoon, you're about to drive an hour to get down there. By the time you come back and that's if it's not traffic out the ass it's going to be late and crowded as shit. I can take him; you don't trust me or something?"

"No, it's not that, he just doesn't know you like that. I don't want him feeling uncomfortable."

"You don't pay that much attention because little man has been talking my head off since he's been here. He's cool, we're good. I'll ask him when he comes down."

"Alright, if he wants to go he can. It's actually better for me anyway." She got up from the couch and put the lap top away then turned her attention towards me. "Thank you."

"Don't worry about it."

"No for real you've really been here for me and I appreciate it. I feel like I owe you something."

"You don't owe me anything; I didn't do it to get something from you."

"I know that but I still want to do something. How about I cook for you?"

"Cook? You know how to cook?"

"Yes I know how to cook. I don't like to but I can. I'll cook dinner for all three of us tonight; since we move tomorrow it could be like a final thank you."

"Alright, that's cool with me."

"I'm ready ma," said Myles when he came downstairs.

"Tone is going to take you to get a haircut. Are you okay with that or should I take you?"

"Tone!" He shouted quickly.

"Well damn," Mickey and I fell out laughing. "Why did you answer so quickly? You don't want me to take you?"

"You're a girl ma, I'm always around girls," Myles told her.

"Oh well excuse me, go ahead with Tone then and act like you have sense Myles."

"He's going to be fine; you go handle your business."

"Alright, alright I'm out. I'll call you when I make it there." Mickey grabbed her purse, cellphone and keys then headed out the door. Two minutes later my phone was ringing so I answered it.

"Yo,"

"Mick just left, we're on her."

"Alright, don't lose her and don't let her spot you either. I don't feel like hearing her mouth."

"We got you."

"Alright," I ended the call then slipped my phone back in my pocket.

Since everything went down at the party a few days ago Legend felt like we needed to have eyes on the girls until he can deal with Bless. Taj and Toi were cool with being driven around everywhere but I know how Mickey is. Having somebody following her around all day isn't about to fly with her so I figured she doesn't have to know she's being watched. She's protected and that's all that matters.

"You ready?" I asked Myles.

"Yeah,"

"Alright come on." We left the apartment and headed out to start our day.

After getting his haircut we swung by McDonald's then went by my parents' house to kill some time. When we walked in the house I could hear my mother singing Celia Cruz at the top of her lungs from the living room so that's where we went first.

"Ma!" I shouted to get her attention and scared the shit out of her in the process.

"Ahh! Antonio! Tan estupido! Why would you scare the shit out of me like that?"

"My bad," I managed to get out between my laughter. It was so funny Myles was cracking up too.

"It's funny? Laugh when I slap you." She came over and smacked the shit out of the back of my neck.

"I'm sorry ma," I told her once my laughter died down. "Alright for real, that's my bad. You shouldn't be in here with that shit so loud though, you didn't even hear me come in."

"So? The door was locked."

"That's not the point ma."

"Whatever Antonio shut up and tell me who this handsome little boy is."

"This is Myles."

"Well hello, I'm Luciana this big head boy's mother. You can just call me Miss Lucy."

"Hi Miss Lucy," Myles said to her.

"Whose child did you kidnap?"

"I didn't kidnap anybody this is Mickey's son. She had some business to handle so I volunteered to have him with me for the day."

"Oh really? Hmm we'll talk about that later. For now, I bet Myles would love to go play in the little playground you insisted on putting in the backyard."

"Playground? Can I go?" Myles looked up at me.

"Go ahead, ma you'll keep an eye on him?"

"Yeah I got him. Your father is downstairs in that damn room of his if you want to see him. Myles and I are going outside to have a little fun. Do you drink lemonade Myles?" My mother grabbed his hand and they walked towards the kitchen while I went down to talk to my father.

"Aye pops, why you always locked down here?" I asked when I hit the bottom step.

"Your mother was up there singing like she was auditioning for American Idol, I didn't feel like hearing that shit. What you doing over here?"

"Just came to check in on you real quick. I got Myles with me,"

"Myles? Mickey's son?"

"Yeah, she had to go pick up the keys to the house she's moving in so I took him with me. He's a good kid, you'll like him."

"I'll take your word for it. So you're taking her son out and shit, what's going on there? You two back together?" He asked when I sat next to him.

"Nah it's not like that."

"Why not?"

"It's just not."

"Alright well is it because of you or because of her?"

"Pops the shit is complicated."

"I have time, go ahead and explain it to me."

I ran down everything that happened with Brick at Mickey's birthday party and gave a little bit of the backstory between the two.

"So he's no longer a problem right?"

"Nope, and neither is the nigga who killed her cousin. Now we just gotta handle this nigga Bless and we shouldn't have any more problems," I shrugged.

"All of that happened and you're not back together?"

"Nah," I shook my head.

"Nigga," Pops said while giving me the side eye.

"What?" I laughed.

"What the hell are you waiting for exactly?"

"What you mean pops?"

"I mean it's obvious you care about the girl, shit I'm banking on love since you done went and got rid of two niggas for her and it aint even been a full year that you've known her. People don't do shit like that for somebody they don't give a damn about."

"I never said I didn't care about her, that much is obvious."

"So what are you going to do about it? You still mad about that old shit?"

"No, I honestly forgot that's why we ended in the first damn place."

"That should tell you how stupid the shit was. From what you told me about her, she's a good woman who's been through some fucked up shit. I think you need to figure out how to get back with her."

"Have you met her or some shit and never told me because you always pushing this tem Mickey shit like you know her."

"I don't know her personally I know what you told me. I still don't agree with you ending it the way and when you did, that shit was stupid. I know you, and I know you wouldn't be down here talking to me about the girl if you wasn't thinking about fixing it. Save us both another headache and make that shit work. I told you once and I'm going to tell you again, if she gets another nigga don't come crying to me over the shit."

"Whatever pops, come upstairs so you can actually meet Myles. Shit, you keep spending all your time down here if you want to; I bet your wife fucks this room up."

"She aint fucking shit up, Lucia likes to act tough but she aint doing nothing." We got up and went upstairs.

After spending a few hours with my parents Myles and I finally decided to head out. By the time we were preparing to leave my mother was damn near trying to force me to give her Mickey's number so they could arrange a time for Myles to come back.

You would think she would just ask me to bring him back but neither of them gave a shit about me coming over, their focus was on him. I wasn't shocked at all because Myles is the type of kid you would love to be around. He's smart, always happy with a smile on his face and he's respectful I'm an only child with no kids so my mother hasn't had the chance to do the whole grandma thing and having Myles around gave her a taste of it. Now she doesn't want to let him go. I didn't give her Mickey's number but I told her I would make sure she meets and talks to Mickey so they could make something shake.

Since Mickey was cooking dinner I decided to pick up some ice cream for dessert so we stopped at this ice cream place downtown Jersey City. While we were in line waiting for our stuff I felt a tap on my shoulder so I turned around. When I saw it was Cassie standing there I sucked my teeth causing the smile on her face to drop into a frown.

"Damn, you don't seem happy to see me," she said to me.

"I'm not, why would I be?"

"Well the last time I saw you, we were good. What's the problem now Tone?"

"I was drunk and on some other shit, I still don't fuck with you shorty," I shrugged my shoulders. I haven't seen Cassie since she sucked my dick in my car at the mansion. That night I was drunk, trippin' and even though I refuse to admit the shit out loud I was trying to piss Mickey off. That's the only reason I entertained talking to the bitch at all, now that I'm sober and in my right mind she can get the fuck out my face.

"Really Tone?"

"Yes really, what are you even doing here? Last time I checked your ass lived in the heights."

"I do but I work at medical center, I'm on my break so I wanted something from here. Tone look, can we talk please?"

"Nah I'm good on that."

"Our ice cream is ready," Myles said after tapping my arm. I went over and paid for our stuff while Cassie followed behind me.

"Who's kid is that?" Cassie pointed at Myles.

"None of your damn business," I grabbed the bag from the cashier then looked at Cassie's annoying but beautiful ass. "Forget about what happened alright? It meant nothing, I still don't fuck with you like that so just drop it," I grabbed Myles hand and we left.

"Who was that?" He asked once we were back in my car.

"An old friend."

"She a bird?"

"Is she a bird? What you know about birds Myles?"

"My mama said birds are always begging or desperate. She wasn't begging but she was desperate for your attention."

"Well your mama was right about that. She doesn't need to know about running into that bird though, you hear me?"

"Yeah I got it."

When we got back to my place we went to the kitchen so I could put the ice cream in the freezer. Mickey was bent over in front of the oven checking on what looked like a pan of corn bread.

"Alright, you got it smelling good up in here," I said, getting her attention. She put the pan on top of the stove then used her knee to shut the oven door.

"It's going to taste good too." Mickey replied then looked at us. "How did it go today? Were you good Myles?"

"Yeah he was good, so good my mother is ready to harass you to bring him back," I told her.

"Your mother?"

"Yeah we swung by my people's house for a little bit, they love his little ass."

"Oh really? Well aren't you just everybody's favorite." She kissed the top of Myles' head. "Go wash your hands so we can eat okay?"

'Okay," Myles ran out the kitchen leaving Mickey and I standing there.

"So you two had a good day? That's what's up, thank you again for real."

"You don't have to keep thanking me, I told you that."

"I know I know but I just want you to know I'm grateful for everything. I know I'm not the most sensitive person or whatever," she chuckled. "But I do appreciate everything you've done for me and Myles."

"Don't worry about it, I told you I got you and I always keep my word. Remember that. Now what did you cook?"

"Oh we're about to tear some shit up okay. We got some fried ribs, Myles loves them. Corn on the cob I know you don't like it off the cob fuckin' weirdo," we both laughed. "And some potato salad, it's good too."

"You sure? You know everybody can't make that shit right."

"I know that but mines is bomb trust me."

"Yeah alright, we'll see," I chuckled just as my phone was going off. I got it from my pocket to see Legend was calling me so I answered. "Yo,"

"Aye bruh, is Mickey with you?" He asked, by the urgency in his voice I could tell something was wrong.

"Yeah she's right here, what's up? You good?"

"Nah man, come to medical center something happened to Toi."

The fuck you mean something happened to Toi?" Mickey almost dropped the bowl in her hands when she heard me but caught it just in time.

"Somebody jumped on her ass and this wasn't no normal fighting shit. Niggas did this shit with a fuckin' purpose. I don't even know all the details just come by the hospital right now."

"Alright I got you, we'll be there in a minute," I hung up and looked at Mickey.

"What happened to Toi?"

"Legend said somebody jumped on her. He doesn't know everything and neither do I, so we just need to go to the hospital, alright?"

"Somebody jumped her? What the fuck happened?"

"I don't know Mickey but we gotta go if you want to find out. I need you to control yourself, alright? Don't go in this hospital on some other shit. You can stay here and I'll call you when Legend gets an update."

"Tone I'm not staying here. My best friend is in the hospital because somebody jumped on her and you think I'm staying here? Hell no, I'm going."

"Then act like you got some damn sense. Okay?"

Mickey ran her fingers through her long blond Mohawk released a deep breath then looked at me. "Fine Tone, I'll be cool now can we go?"

"Cover the food up, I'll get Myles." She turned back towards the stove and I grabbed her arm pulling her to my chest. "I'm sure she's fine, you know Toi is strong. Don't think the worse," I kissed her forehead then let her go.

I walked out the kitchen to get Myles with a million thoughts running through my mind. One of the main ones being I hope I didn't just accidentally lie about Toi's condition.

TOI

"Toi are you sure you're okay by yourself? I can stay if you need me to." My main receptionist Brianna asked when I stepped off the elevator. We closed 20 minutes ago and everybody was either packing up to leave or already left not too long ago.

"No I'm fine, I have to fill out these order sheets. I'm not trying to bring it home with me. I can't concentrate with that man of mine there," I laughed.

"You're lucky you have one, but alright I'll see you tomorrow. Have a good night."

"I'll try to, good night," I waved to her then walked to my office.

I was more than ready to go home and lay down I've been here all day. Today we had our first bridal party and it had me going every which way. It was at least 15 women and they were using every one of our treatments.

Thankfully I have yet to have a slow day since I've opened. With the usual crowd we have every day and the bridal party that came in, I was tired as hell. This has been my busiest day thus far and I wasn't done because I had to fill out order sheets. If I realized how much I was going to be worked I would've worn some sneakers instead of heels.

As soon as I sat down at my desk my phone rang. When I heard the

Fabolous and Tamia ringtone I knew it was Que so I answered then put it on speaker and sat it on my desk. "Yes baby?"

"What are you doing ma?"

"I'm in my office filling out these order sheets. Once I'm done I'll be ready to go."

"Alright well I'm still taking care of something, so I'll get dropped off there," he told me.

"See if you took your car this morning you wouldn't have to come by here but alright."

"There is no point if we're both coming to the same place, I'm saving gas and saving the environment."

"Yeah alright if you say so," I laughed. "When are you coming?"

"In like forty five minutes, if you get done before that call me and you can just come pick me up in the van."

"Okay, I'll talk to you later."

"Later ma," I hung up the phone then went on back to my order sheets.

It took me a good thirty minutes to finish all the sheets then put them away so I could fax them out tomorrow morning when I get back here. After double checking everything making sure nothing was left on and cleaned like it needed to be, I grabbed my stuff so I could leave.

"Are you ready Toi?" the driver Pat asked when I walked outside. I don't know what Pat's personal life is like but I do know if he has somebody they're very understanding because Que has him on call all the time. If Que calls he comes no questions asked and he gets paid a pretty nice penny to drive us around. Shit he comes in handy for me when it comes time to pull down these heavy ass gates.

"Yeah I'm ready," I went in my purse to grab my charger so my phone could get some juice on the way home, but it wasn't in my bag. "Damn, my charger is still in my office."

"I'll go get it then I could pull the gates down for you. The van is unlocked you can wait inside."

"Okay, that's fine with me," I gave Pat the keys to the lock then he went inside. I pulled my phone out and called Que who picked up on the second ring.

"What's up baby girl? You ready to go?"

"Yeah, I'm done with everything so we're about to come get you. Where are you?"

"I'm at the barbershop. You know we're going to have to bring something home to eat right?"

"We can just order once we get there or you can call my mother and tell her to order something."

"That'll work. Are you in the van already?"

"No, I'm going now, Pat went inside to get my charger then he's going to lock up," I started walking across the street to my car until I heard my name.

"AYE TOI!"

Turning around I was met with a fist going across my face making me drop my phone. I wanted to see who the fuck hit me but a second punch immediately followed the first almost knocking me to the ground. Backing up some I dropped my purse out of my hands and swung on the person in front of me.

I was getting it in with them until I felt my hair being snatched in two different directions with punches being dropped on both sides and behind me. I tried to swing back but it was too many hits coming in from too many directions.

The punches kept coming until I was on the ground, that's when the kicks to my side back and stomach came raining down. There was no way I could stop the kicks so my first thought was to guard the reason most bitches hate me anyway, my face.

With every kick and punch delivered to my body I felt myself getting weaker. I was almost out when I felt my hair being snatched so that my head was pulled forward. Feeling somebody on the side and back of my neck caused a scream to come out of my mouth.

"Don't fuck with Mia bitch!" One of my attackers shouted then dropped me back on the ground.

I wanted to grab my phone but I couldn't move. I went to try and lift my head to see where my phone was, but I was either punched or kicked right in my face, that's when everything went black.

LEGEND

Clenching my fist I paced the hospital waiting room anxious to hear anything from the doctor. I knew I looked like a mad man right now but I really didn't give a fuck. They're lucky I'm not tearing this place up.

"Que you need to relax, I understand you're upset but you need to calm down," Mickey said. She was sitting next to Tone with Myles in her lap looking at his tablet.

"How the hell am I supposed to do that Mick? Somebody beat the hell out of my girl and left her on the fucking street and you want me to calm down?

"Tone talk to him, if he keeps that hostile shit up they're going to kick his ass out. Weren't you getting on me about being calm?"

"She's right man, just sit down and relax. You need to tell us what the fuck happened anyway." Tone came over and pushed me down in one of the chairs. "Who did this shit?"

"I don't fucking know, I was talking to her on the phone then I heard somebody say her name. After that it sounded like her phone dropped and I heard scuffling then the line clicked off after that. Pat called me like a minute later telling me she was on the side of the van knocked the fuck out. He called the ambulance and that's all I know. I told him to go back to the spa and look at the tapes but they had on ski mask and shit."

"Were they bitches?"

"He said from what he could make out it looked like three men."

"That's fucked up," he shook his head. "Who would do that shit to her?"

"The same nigga that just tried me two days ago," I answered him. This had Bless written all over it, Toi doesn't have problems with anybody else that would try some shit like this. Sure it's some chicks that don't like her over some petty bullshit but it's not deep enough that they would send a trio of niggas to touch her.

Of course he would try to go for Toi. He's salty I have her, and he's salty I beat his ass for disrespecting her. Now his homeboys are dead, along with the cousin he came up here looking for in the first place. He has every reason to try some bullshit with me but going through Toi is taking it too damn far.

"You really think he did it?" Tone looked at me as if he was asking if I was sure.

"Hell yeah, who else would do it? I'm over this stupid shit. I let that nigga breathe when he tried me before. This nigga didn't die the other night like his two punk ass friends; you would think he would get the fuck out of dodge. But nah, he stays up here and sends some niggas to touch my girl, I'm off this shit. I want it done tonight. You put the word out there; I want that muthafucka in my warehouse before the fucking sun comes up."

"Alright man I got you, but you have to chill. I know you don't want to get kicked the fuck out so relax. Did you tell Geneva?"

"Nah she's an hour away, it makes no sense for her to drive all the way down here and I don't want her on the road while she's mad. I'll call her once I know what's going on."

We sat in the waiting area for another thirty minutes before a doctor finally came out looking for us.

"Are you La'Toia's family?"

I got up and walked over. "She's my wife, how is she?" I know Toi and I weren't married yet but fuck that, he doesn't need to know that. I don't want anything holding me back from getting information about her.

"As you know she was attacked, and they beat her pretty badly but she's stable. Her ankle is sprained, and she has two bruised ribs. We'll tell you how to treat that before she leaves so you don't have to worry about it. The bruising on her face was a little severe but she should heal just fine. She had two lacerations on her neck; thankfully they weren't deep or damaging. All she needed was a few stitches. We want to keep her here for a few days just to monitor how she's doing but if taken care of properly she will heal just fine."

"Okay," I let out a sigh of relief. "Where is she now?"

"We're getting her set up in her room. Once she's settled in a nurse will bring you up. We gave her something for the pain so she should sleep through the rest of the night but she will be in pain when she wakes up."

"Alright, thanks man."

"The police have come by but since she's asleep they left. They will be back here in the morning."

"Okay that's fine," I went over to Mickey and Tone. "She has bruised ribs, a sprained ankle and they had to give her stitches on her neck but she's stable. She's more than likely going to be asleep for the rest of the night. They're going to move her to her own room."

"Well I just want to see her for a quick second then we can go. Are you staying the night?"

"Yeah I'm staying. I'm can't lay in that damn bed knowing she's here so there's no point in leaving," I answered Mickey.

Sitting down I rested my head in my hands trying to get my mind right. I was feeling a mixture of emotions. On one hand I was grateful to God that Toi was okay but on the other hand I was pissed the fuck off. There's no reason she should even be in this fuckin' position. I could literally break that niggas jaw with one hand I was so pissed off.

Actually using my bare hands to end his fucking life seems like the best idea at this point. Pulling a trigger wouldn't give me the satisfaction, it's too quick.

"Who's here for Henderson?" We heard someone ask. I got up ready to answer them until I saw who it was standing there. "Cassie?"

"Legend?" She looked at me confused then her eyes went to Tone and Mickey. "Oh and what is this?"

"Cassie, don't come over here on your bullshit," Tone said to her.

"I didn't even say anything but since you want to bring shit up let's go there. You acting funny with me but what? You playing step-daddy to this hoe's son? You know she snitched on her baby daddy right?"

"Yo, my son is right here, you better get this broad under control Tone, I'm not playing." Mickey spoke in a calm but stern tone. I could see by the look on her face she was ready to knock Cassie's head off her shoulders. It had me confused because it's clear they have their own past and I don't think it has anything to do with Tone's ass.

"Can you tell us what the fuck you came over here to say instead of doing this childish bullshit?" Tone asked Cassie harshly.

"No what's childish is being all over me one day then playing me like the shit didn't happen." Cassie shot back.

"Oh my God, is this about that damn party that happened how long ago? Bitch get over it, it's been months." Mickey said before shaking her head. "He don't want you, oh well move the fuck on."

"I wasn't talking to you Mickey so mind your damn business!"

"Alright, look relax with this yelling shit. Cassie, she's right that shit was how long ago? Let it go ma for real."

"All y'all did was kiss, it aint even that deep."

"We only kissed? Is that what he told you?" Cassie laughed. "You know what I'm not even about to do this back and forth anymore. The fact that this nigga clearly lied to you is funny enough. Legend, Henderson is in room 320."

"Alright," I said before she walked off continuing to laugh.

Mickey put Myles on his feet then got up. "Mickey wait let me expl-"

"Nah I'm good, you don't have to explain anything. Let me check on my friend and we can go," she grabbed Myles' hand and they went over to the elevators.

"You need to handle that, don't forget to do what I asked."

"I got you don't worry about it." We went up to Toi's room and went inside. Seeing the bruises on her face only intensified the anger I was already feeling. There was dark bruising on the upper right portion of her face. Her face looked puffy due to the swelling. She didn't look like herself and it was fucking with me heavy.

Grabbing a chair I sat it right next to her bed and grabbed her hand in mine. If I didn't already know I was in love with Toi, this night would've proved it to me. The fear that came over my body when I figured out what happened to her wasn't normal. In the life I live, I've seen and become immune to a lot of shit. Things that get to regular people don't bother me at all but the thought of Toi being hurt had me damn near over the edge.

Images of Bless' head getting blown off plagued my mind. There was no way I was about to function correctly with this nigga still breathing. Who comes for a woman and what type of punk ass niggas even agree to do the shit. At this point everybody involved has to die.

"Legend, man we're out," Tone said.

"Alright. I want this shit done tonight Tone," I replied never taking my eyes off Toi.

"I got you man. Come on Mick."

For hours I sat there staring at Toi, silently thanking God she was going to be fine. I don't pray as much as I should and I'm not really the get up and go to church type of nigga but I was begging and calling on God from the time her phone cut off mid-sentence.

When I called Geneva and told her what happened, of course she immediately started crying and praying to God that Toi would be okay. It took me five minutes to calm her down enough so I could tell her Toi was going to be fine. I promised her I would make sure I got her here in the morning hopefully before Toi wakes up.

The clock read 4:57 A.M when I felt my phone vibrate in my pocket. I pulled it out and saw it was Tone calling so I answered.

"Yeah?"

"It's done, we're waiting on you."

"Alright," I got up from the chair and kissed the top of Toi's head. "I'll be right back ma I love you." Walking out the room I went to the nurse's station and personally gave them my number letting them know to call me even if it's the smallest thing, I want to know about it. She promised she would call me so I left.

When I walked in the warehouse Tone, Yung and a few other niggas were standing around Bless who was lying on the floor knocked out. His hands were pulled behind him and handcuffed together.

"Y'all had to hit the nigga?" I asked, getting their attention.

"He wasn't trying to go without a fight so he had to get put out," Yung answered. "Toi good?"

"She will be. Wake this nigga up, I want him to feel everything. Pour water on his ass."

Tone poured a half bottle of water on Bless' face causing him to jump up looking around the room. He looked confused until his eyes landed on me. I could see the realization of his fate coming across his mind.

"What's up playboy? I hope you had a good day, my shit was fucked up."

"Man what the fuck is this shit about? You mad about that fuckin' party? Nigga your people are good, I know you did some shit to Kareem and Brick."

"I didn't do shit, I don't even know who the fuck you talking about. What I do know is my girl is laying in a hospital bed right now and I think It's because of you."

"Fuck is you talking about? I didn't do shit to Toi!"

"I would probably believe you if my shorty wasn't laid up with her ribs and shit fucked up. Three niggas! THREE GROWN ASS MEN JUMPED ON HER! Everything is telling me it's you! Who the fuck else is dumb enough to try me? As much as you violated throughout the years I've been letting your punk ass slide. Now I'm done with that shit, clearly you take my patience for weakness."

"I didn't do anything to Toi!"

"BULLSHIT! Who the fuck else has any reason to do some shit to her? You could at least be real and admit the shit."

"I'm not admitting to some shit I didn't do. Fuck is you still talking to me for anyway? Go ahead and do what niggas wanted you to do as soon as you stepped up for Saint."

"Fuck is you talking about?"

"You really wanna act like niggas didn't want me out the way as soon as you got to the top."

"Clearly you still breathing so what those niggas said didn't matter! Yeah, my uncle don't fuck with you, Tone don't fuck with you, hell a lot of these niggas didn't fuck with you. What the fuck did I do? Kept you on anyway, even when you kept messing up I kept you on. You went and did some grimy shit and I let you fuckin' live, you went down south did your own thing and I didn't bother your ass at all. Now you back up here doing mad bullshit for what?"

"Nigga fuck you, you killed my cousin!"

"And? Scrappy was a thief ass nigga. You know the game you know how shit goes. He fucked up, that was on him. That shit doesn't justify your sneaky ass behavior, like fuckin' with my baby sister. Cheating on Toi to do it, it's funny how shit works out."

"Man Mia came on to me, she a little ho it aint my fault if you can't see that."

'Fuck Mia, I'm not surprised by her ass but you should've known better nigga. You knew you weren't about to be in a relationship with her ass, you knew you had a girl. A good girl at that and you fucked that up along with fuckin' my sister's head up. I get why she's so fuckin nutty now."

"Man, just do what the fuck you gonna do alright, fuck all this talking shit."

I let out a bitter chuckle. Nigga got a smart ass mouth but can't admit to his shit, fuck they do that at?

"You know what you right," I went over to the wall of tools and weapons that was on the side and grabbed a large sledgehammer. "Alright my shorty had a fucked-up ankle," I told him before swinging the hammer back and crashing that shit against his ankle.

"AHHH! SHIT!" Bless screamed through clenched teeth.

"She had a few bruised ribs," I swung the hammer at his side as hard as I could. When I heard a crack a satisfying smirk came on my face. He screamed out in pain again. I made sure to show the other side of his body the same attention. "What else was it Tone?" I stepped back

"Stitches on her neck and her face is bruised."

"Right." Using the sledgehammer I beat this niggas entire body into a bloody pulp. By the time I was done with him his face was unrecognizable. Blood was all over the floor, my clothes, hands and face. If I had time to kill I would cut him the fuck up and send his mama a different body part every week. Lucky for him I had better shit to do right now.

Bending down I snatched the diamond B pendant chain from around his neck. "I'll keep this for a memory of why you can't give niggas shit," I stood up straight then looked at my crew. "Clean this shit up and burn this nigga's body."

I dropped the hammer on the ground and went back towards my office.

My warehouse wasn't your typical thing. I had this shit set up like a legit business. I got central air and heat in this bitch and everything

When you come inside it's the dirty area; we handle everything; like when what took place with Bless happens since there's an incinerator in the room. Walk through a pair of double doors on your left that's where our product is handled during work hours. If work isn't being done there is no product anywhere on this property, not for anybody outside of Tone and I to know about at least. Straight to the back we got our conference room, that's where we have all our meetings and do the counts.

Attached is my private office and bathroom that has a full bathroom inside of it. I feel like it's always important to have a private space for yourself everywhere you go. Especially here, all types of shit happens in here. I have to be able to get cleaned up and change clothes.

After taking a quick shower and changing clothes I left the warehouse not saying shit to anybody. I took my ass straight back to the hospital so I could check on Toi. The sun was up and shining with not a cloud in the sky and it was just about to hit 8 A.M. When I walked in her room the nurse I gave my number to was checking her vitals and Toi was silently watching her.

Hearing the door close they both looked in my direction. "Mr. Santana, I was going to call you as soon as I was done checking her vitals. According to her she woke up forty-five minutes ago but she only called for a nurse ten minutes ago so she could use the bathroom."

"How is she?"

"She's feeling it kind of tough but she's fine as she could be. We're going to get her something to eat so we can give her something else for the pain."

"Alright, thank you."

Once the nurse left the room I sat in the chair next to Toi's bed grabbing her hand. "I'm glad you're okay baby," I kissed the back of her hand. "This will never happen again," I said and she looked me in the eyes. "I handled it."

"H-how," Toi winced in pain.

"Your ribs are fucked up, so it's going to be tough for you to breathe and speak a little bit," I let her know and she nodded.

"You don't kno- "

"I do and trust me I handled it. Relax, alright?"

"Phone," she held her hand out so I gave her my phone. After unlocking it and going to a memo pad app she began to type something out.

"Who do you think did it?" Toi typed out.

"Bless, I handled it already," I answered. Her eyes went wide for a second and she quickly shook her head no. "What you mean?"

"Mia did this shit. One of those dudes said her name."

"Are you sure?" I asked and she nodded. "Fuck!" I gritted through clenched teeth. "So, he wasn't lying, damn," I shook my head. A part of me felt bad but the other side was saying oh well, he violated anyway and there was no way he wasn't going to try something. "So Mia did this shit to you? I'll handle it, don't worry about it."

"I'm not worried about her; I'm worried about you. You look stressed and I don't like it, I'm fine. I'm in pain like fuck but fine."

I read the message chuckling a little bit. "You shouldn't be in this position period but I'll try to chill out a little bit. Your mother is coming today."

"When she does, you need to go home and go to sleep. She can stay here with me until you get at least a few hours to rest. Don't argue with me about it either. Just do it, when she comes you go home."

"I don't have to go home ma; I can stay and sleep right now. Besides I'm not even tired."

"LIES! I can see it all over your face. You've been up all night. Go home and go to sleep when my mother comes, please.'

"Alright, I got you, but I won't be gone long I promise," I put my head down on the bed exhaling. "I'm glad you're okay ma, you have no fuckin' idea."

TAJ

"Okay Lace, you're good to go," I told my client after I removed the cape from around her neck. Her waist length Fulani braids took me four hours to do but it was worth it. I killed it as usual.

"Thank you Taj, oh my God this is so nice."

"You're welcome my dear," I walked her to the front so she could pay then walked her to the door. As I was going back to my station Beautii came walking out of her office.

"Taj, no sneakers remember." Beautii pointed at the black huarache's on my feet.

"Sneakers are fine as long as their black was the rule that came out your mouth. This isn't the first time you've seen me in sneakers" I said back. Beautii wanted her business to be chic as possible so we could only wear sneakers if they were all black. If you can't work in heels then flats will do but slippers and that other shit was a no.

"Well we changed that rule last month."

"When I was on maternity leave? Right okay."

"Things change Taj, I'm sure you know how that is."

"Alright Beautii, whatever," I went to my station taking a seat while I waited for my next client. I'm not about to go back and forth with Beautii's tough for no reason ass.

"Why does it seem like she's been on you since you've been back?" Nessa, the stylist that worked next to me asked.

"I don't know but it's getting on my nerves," I answered back.

I've been back to work for a week now and since then Beautii has been acting real funny with me. She nit-picks at me about small shit, like about my sneakers for instance. I've been working in this bitch for a good while now and she's never had a problem with black sneakers. Now when I'm gone, you change shit and I don't even get told about it? Mind you I've been wearing black sneakers all damn week.

"Well if that annoyed you, you're really about to be mad. Look at the front." Nessa motioned towards the front of the shop.

"What the fuck?" I cursed under my breath at the sight of KeKe's dusty ass standing in my job. It's bad enough her mad ass is sending insults and subliminal shit on social media. I blocked her and the hoe made new pages to stalk me on. If it's not her it's one of her goofy ass friends trolling on my page.

Before Mecca, I would've pulled up and beat the shit out of her but I can't do that reckless shit anymore. Lucky bitch.

"Never mind, I see her." KeKe told the receptionist before making her way over to me. "I heard you were starting back at work this week."

"What the hell are you doing here and why are you looking for me? We don't have shit to talk about." I countered.

"No we do, seeing as how our kids are siblings we need to talk about quite a few things. You need to understand that my daughter is number one in Yung's Life and that's not going to change because you trapped him. Make sure you and that baby of yours knows your place."

"Okay I'm convinced you lost the majority of your mind and because I'm at work I'm not going to slap the shit out of you. My son isn't second to anybody and neither is Naima. They're both his first priority, now are we done with this stupid ass conversation?"

KeKe chuckled taking the sunglasses off her face. "I bet you really think you're the shit. That's your biggest problem, you and those rat ass friends of yours. You think you can't be touched, oh wait shorty was touched. I heard they got her ass good too," she laughed a little. "I wonder how those scars are going to be for her, I mean you don't seem to give a fuck about what you did to me."

"I don't, you started that shit. You decided to fuck with me, I didn't do shit to you."

"Look at my face! You didn't do anything to me?" KeKe screamed making everybody look our way.

"No I didn't, that scar is on you. You think throwing that shit in about my friend was funny, bitch get out before I spit in your face then beat that ass all over again," I got up from my chair furthering my warning that I wasn't playing with her nut ass.

"Do it then! Hit me bitch!" KeKe screamed again. I went to knock her head off her shoulders but Nessa blocked it.

"Yo chill Taj she aint worth it! You got a baby to think about! Fuck that bitch," Nessa said in an effort to calm me down. Beautii came rushing over with all the dramatics in the world.

"What is going on? Taj are you about to fight a client?" Beautii questioned slowly crossing her arms over her chest.

"She's not a client she came in here to pick at me, and I told her to leave. At this point I'm defending myself," I answered her.

"Fuck you bitch, you aint defending shit. You mad I said something about your bird ass friend, fuck both of y'all."

"Alright that's enough!" Beautii shouted. "You need to go, right now and don't come back to my shop with this foolishness."

"Whatever, I'll be seeing you around bitch," KeKe cursed at me before storming out.

"Taj, are you serious?"

"Look, I didn't start that. I didn't ask or tell her to come here running her mouth, she did it on her own. I tried to hold my composure but she kept going. I'm sorry but it's not on me."

"You should've dismissed yourself and went to the back or come and get me you know better Taj. You were about to fight in my business over nothing."

"I just told you what happened Beautii."

"No I think I heard what happened. This is about what happened with Toi? And because she brought it up? Who cares about that?"

Tilting my head to the side I gave Beautii the most confused expression I could muster up. Is she serious? Now everything is making sense. Toi told me about Saint possibly being the twins' daddy. She also told me about Geneva and Beautii getting into it so there would be a chance Beautii stopped fucking with her.

I didn't think Beautii would act like this, she's known Toi for years and they've always been close. Why would she act funny with Toi because of something that has nothing to do with her? All of that would also explain why she's been acting weird with me. I never took her as the petty type but obviously I was wrong.

"That's funny, before you found out who her mother was you would've cared. Who cares about Toi? Really Beautii? You've been calling her your niece for the longest time. Shit, I met her through you. You always went on about how smart and beautiful she is but now it's who cares? Are you really that bitter about a dead woman?" I asked.

Even though I knew there was no chance in hell she was going to admit fault or answer my question, I had to ask. I've never seen a woman her age switch up so damn fast. It's like lady you're too damn old for the childish shit.

"Don't talk about what you don't know or understand Taj. My personal life doesn't have shit to do with you stirring up drama in my shop."

"I didn't stir up anything, that bitch came in here. How is that my fault? You know what Beautii just do whatever it is you're going to do. You clearly have a problem with me because I'm friends with Toi."

"I don't have a problem with Toi."

"Okay, whatever you say," I shrugged my shoulders.

"You know what Taj, how about you get your things and leave since you think I have a problem with you. Look for another job while you're at it."

"Excuse me?" I had to be hearing her ass wrong, did she just fire me?

"You heard me, get your things and get out. You're fired."

"Wow," I said before I started laughing. I had to laugh, it was either find the humor in this situation or I was going to hit this bitch. "It's cool, I don't feel like working for a bitter ass bitch anyway."

"Bitter?"

"Yes bitter, you're a bitter ass bitch. You're firing and feel a way about me because Toi is my friend. You feel a way about Toi because her auntie used to fuck Saint. This just in; Saint used to be the biggest whore out here and I do use the term *used to* loosely. Everybody fucked Saint! Get over it," I got my things together from the back and proceeded to get the fuck out of her salon.

When I got in my car, I pulled my phone out and called Toi. She's been out the hospital and at home recovering for about a week now. Hopefully she's awake and not sleep or high as shit on pain meds.

"Yo." When Que's voice came through the phone I sucked my teeth.

"Que is Toi awake?"

"Yeah she's in the tub, you good?"

"Not really but I will be. Can I speak to her?"

"Hold up let me bring her the phone," Que said. "Aye ma, Taj wants you on the phone."

"Taj baby, what's up?" Toi said when she got on the phone.

"A headache is what's up. How are you doing?"

"I'm alright, still in pain but it's not as bad as before. Taj bitch get you a Jacuzzi tub. Que made this shit extra hot put some Epsom salt and rubbing alcohol in this bitch. Oh my God talk about perfection."

"Hot water works wonders I know that life. But listen; tell me why Beautii just fired me."

"What? What you mean she fired you?"

I ran down the entire story to her and she was laughing and mad as hell at the same time by the time I was done.

"Yo something is wrong with the bitches in that family, they all petty and childish as shit. Are you good? What are you going to do?"

"I'm fine, I can easily get a job at another salon tomorrow if I want to but I don't know if I want to do that. I've been working for Beautii since I got my license and that was straight out of high school. Shit I'm tired of having a boss."

"Well the business you're in, it's not hard to freelance and get your own shit going."

"I know and I'm thinking about that. Hell, I should open my own damn shop and take all her customers. Ole bitter ass."

"Seems to be a family trait."

"Has he said anything to his sister?"

"Nope not yet and I don't want him to. He'll end up hurting her ass; it's bad enough his mama already on him about me anyway."

"His family is a trip."

"Girl tell me about it but shit, they're not related to me so fuck it. I'm worried about hi though, I don't want him to be ostracized by his family over me."

"If they love him like they're supposed to he won't be. Don't worry about it."

"It's whatever but back to you. I like the idea of you having your own shop. Not even just to get back at Beautii's ass but just business in general. You're a bomb ass hairstylist, and you're about your money. Go ahead and open a shop, it's not like you don't have the money."

"Who said I did?"

"Taj who the hell are you fooling? One you haven't spent the money from your parent's estate yet. Your house is paid off, and you pay all your bills on time so you don't have credit issues. Girl, open a damn shop and hush," Toi ranted quickly making me laugh.

"You think I should?"

"Hell yeah and I will be a faithful customer. I'm not putting any more money in Beautii's shit, fuck that bitch."

"I'm glad I have your support."

"You'll always have my support but you knew that already."

"Well thank you. I'm about to go get Mecca and take my ass home. I was thinking about coming to see you this weekend but shit it aint like I have work the rest of the week. I'll be there tomorrow; I still have yet to see this house."

"Neither has Mickey, I wanted to do a dinner here or whatever to celebrate us moving in together but now I'm all fucked up so I don't feel like it."

"We'll save that idea for Mickey's new house. Have you seen it?"

"She showed me some pictures but I haven't been there. That sounds like a good idea, talk to her about it and I'm cool with it."

"Alright well I'll see you tomorrow, I'll call you. I love you bitch."

"I love you too, later T." When we ended the call I sent Anthony a text letting him know I was on my way to get Mecca before I pulled off down the street. Five minutes later he texted me back telling me it was okay to come straight up to his apartment so that's what I did when I got to his building.

"How are you off work this early?" Anthony asked when he came walking from Mecca's room holding him after I came into his apartment.

"Your baby mama came to the shop running her mouth. Beautii had a problem with it, we exchanged words and her stupid ass fired me," I grabbed Mecca from his arms and kissed his chubby cheek. "Hi stinky, did you miss me?" I baby talked as I went to the couch to sit down.

"What the fuck? What you mean she fired you? Why would she do that? Y'all cool."

"We were until all that shit happened with her and Toi's mother. She's been nitpicking at me all week for the smallest shit. I low-key think she was just looking for a reason and that bitch you have a daughter with gave her one."

"What did KeKe do, Taj?"

"She came in there telling me I need to understand that Naima come first and that Mecca will always come second to her. Then she said some shit about what happened to Toi and how we swear we can't be touched; she was extra mad about the scratch on her face as if I was supposed to give a fuck. For real Anthony, I really don't want to go to jail so I'm telling you now get that bird under control. She got one more time to say something stupid and I'm going to leave that bitch with more than that stupid ass scar."

"I'm going to handle that."

"How? Please tell me how you're going to handle it because you've been saying that shit and nothing gets done."

"I said I'll handle it and I mean that, alright? Damn, why you coming at me?"

'I'm not coming at you."

"Shit it sounds like it to me but whatever."

"Alright look, I'm not trying to fight with you or come at you but you have to understand my side."

"You think I'm stupid? I get it, she's a bitch to you when she has no right to be. I'm going to handle the shit, trust me on that. She will not be an issue for you."

"Okay, I believe you I guess."

"You guess," he chuckled. "You can't give a nigga a break for nothing. It's cool though, I get it. What are you going to do about work? I mean that's if you even want to work."

"Yes I want to work. I'll probably free-lance for a little bit but I'm thinking about opening my own shop. It's not like I don't have the clientele to do so especially if I hire bomb ass people."

"Your own salon huh?"

"Yeah, what do you think?"

"I think it's a good idea. Honestly, it's a bomb ass idea. Shit, I might want in."

"Want in? Boy bye I'm not working for you."

"I'm not asking you to work for me. I'm saying we could work together."

"You don't know shit about hair?"

"But you do, I'll handle the logistics you worry about everything else."

"What? You want to be business partners or something?"

"Exactly; I need some shit to invest in anyway. Why not invest in you?"

"Sounds like you're trying to pull on of your friends' moves."

"Nah, Toi's spa is hers, he really has nothing to do with it. I'm trying to build with you. I'll be in the background; nobody has to know I'm involved."

"Let me think on that for a little bit. It's not really a good idea to mix business and pleasure."

"Man it hasn't been pleasure between us since you got pregnant."

"That's your fault not mine. Did you feed him yet?"

"Nah he had just woken up when you came in. He's changed though so if you want to feed him before you leave go ahead." Anthony said before going in his pocket and pulling his phone out when it started to ring. "Damn, it's a good thing you came early. I have to go handle something."

"Handle something?"

"Yeah, lock up when you leave, alright?" He grabbed his keys off the mantle.

"Is that business?"

"Yeah it's business shorty," Anthony chuckled. "I gotta go, remember to lock my shit up." He came over and kissed Mecca's cheek then left out his apartment just that quick.

"Well let's get you ready to go," I said to Mecca as if he knew what I was talking about while I walked back to his room.

YUNG

"Aye, the count was on point. You can head out if you need to," Legend told me when he came walking out of his office in the warehouse. "You good? You've been on some quiet shit today."

"I'm good I just have a lot on my mind."

"What's up? Are you and Taj going at it again?"

"Man, KeKe call herself going to Taj's job to start some shit and Beautii ended up firing her."

"Toi told me about that. Beautii has been on a war path since that shit with Saint. Is Taj good without her job?"

"Taj got money out the ass from her parents that she doesn't even touch so she's more than good but even if she didn't I would've taken care of it. You know that. I'm just trying to figure out how to make KeKe stop with the bullshit."

"Have you talked to her?"

"Yup and she doesn't listen. At this point I'm just ready to take my daughter from that bitch so I won't have to deal with her."

"Are you sure you're ready for that level of responsibility? Naima is 2 and you have a brand new baby. That isn't easy to pull off."

"I know that but KeKe is getting on my damn nerves. All she does is bitch about Taj, and stupid shit like posting her and Mecca on my Instagram. She's still mad about that scar on her face and she told Taj that Naima is basically number one in my life and Mecca will always come second. She's doing too damn much."

"Well nigga it's time to put your foot down if you don't want to deal with this on-going baby mama bullshit. Let her know what it is, no chaser. Make sure she knows you're serious about whatever it is you two talk about."

"I hear you man, hopefully that shit works. I really don't want to have to kill my daughter's mother but I Damnit will before I deal with a fuckin' headache for the rest of my life."

"Well if you're serious about the custody thing, I can get you some pay stubs to show that you have a legit income coming in."

"Shit I might just take you up on that," I got up and slapped hands with Legend. "Let me go talk to this girl and get this shit straight. I'll see you around."

"Alright good luck nigga."

I left the warehouse and went straight over to KeKe's place. When she let me in I could see by the expression on her face that she was unhappy to see me but I don't give a shit.

"What are you doing here Yung? Your bitch went and told on me?" KeKe blurted with her arms folded across her chest.

"What the hell is your problem Ke? For real, what's the problem? I take care of Naima, I'm here for Naima, you don't have to do shit but look after her and you're still on some other shit. Fuck is the issue with Taj?"

"Why is she so special? I've known you for years and gave you our first child but you act like I don't even matter and I don't want my daughter feeling like that."

"Fuck is you talking about? I don't treat you any different than I've always done. The only thing I no longer do for you is fuck your stupid ass and you fucked that up by running your fucking mouth. Naima is never going to come second to anybody and neither is my son, those are my kids I don't favor one over the other."

"Pssh," she waved me off. "That's bullshit; you're already doing it by treating that bitch better than me."

"You want me to treat you like Taj? Is that it? I'm sorry I can't do that."

"Why?"

"You're not her, you don't work, you're not financially independent and more importantly I'm not nor have I ever been in love with you. Come on Ke, we both know we were never in a relationship. We never talked about being in one, we were just two people who liked to fuck and we got Naima out of it."

"So she was a mistake is what you're saying."

"No I'm not saying that at all, I'm just saying we didn't plan her. Look, I know you're mad about what happened to your face, but this childish bullshit has to stop. I'm not about to keep doing it with you."

"Well you won't have to because I'm moving to California with my mother and Naima is coming with me."

"What? Say that again," I needed shorty to repeat herself because I know I was hearing all the way wrong.

"I'm moving to California, I know you heard me the first time."

"If you want to move there that's fine but you're not taking my fuckin' daughter with you. Fuck out of here with that."

"You can't tell me what the fuck I can and cannot do with my child Yung. I'm going, there's nothing in Jersey for me. It's not like you give a fuck about me for real."

"You're right I don't but I care about my daughter and she's not leaving so you can forget that shit."

"Yeah right, watch me take her right along with me. We leave tomorrow."

"You got me fucked up," I pushed past her going down to Naima's room and picked her up from her crib.

"Put my baby down Yung! I'm not leaving here without her!"

"Then I guess you aint leaving," I turned to face KeKe's beautiful yet selfish ass. "Like I just told you, you can go if you want to but she isn't leaving."

"That's not fair! You don't give a damn about me but you're trying to keep me here!"

"Leave Ke! Leave if you want to but she's not going, I'm not about to keep repeating myself. I'm taking her with me, you call me when you make your mind up."

"If you leave here with my child I'm calling the cops."

"Call them, my name is on her birth certificate. I have rights to her too, keep playing with me Ke and I'll take your ass to court for full custody."

"How?" She began to laugh. "You're a damn drug dealer, nobody is about to give you custody."

"Can you prove that shit?"

"What?" her smile dropped.

"Can you prove that I sell drugs? You don't even know what the fuck I do, all you know is who I'm around and those niggas are legit as fuck on paper. I can get paperwork proving my income, I don't have a criminal record but you got how many mug shots? Let's see petty theft, simple assault, trespassing, and some more shit right?" I ran down KeKe's little criminal record. She's never been charged with a felony or did real jail time but shit it's more than what's on my record. That's good enough for me. "Who do you think they'll give custody to?"

"Fuck you! I hate your stupid ass!"

"Good the feeling is fucking mutual. If you want to leave Ke by all means do you, I don't care but she's not going. Now you can either stay here and act like you have some sense or you can go to Cali with your mama and not give me any trouble. If you do that I'll make sure you get her for summers, every other holiday shit I'll even get you a little spot out there as long as you don't irk the shit out of me. Play with me if you want to, I'll push for no visitation an make sure she doesn't remember your dumb ass. You sleep on it and let me know what the fuck your decision is," I sent her another glare and walked past her making sure I grabbed one of Naima's hoodies that were hanging up on the way then left the apartment al together.

When I got home I put a sleeping Naima in the crib in her room then went down to my own bedroom. To my surprise Taj was laying in my bed with Mecca asleep. The lights were off and the 90's R&B station from the Pandora app on my TV was playing at an even volume. All the lights in my apartment were off and everything looked to be in place. I heard music playing but I figured she left my TV on so I didn't even know she was still here.

I carefully picked Mecca up and went to put him in his crib then went back to my room. "Taj," I shook her, and she jumped up looking around. She looked confused until her eyes landed on me then she relaxed some.

"Shit, I didn't know where I was for a second. What time is it?"

"Almost 10, I didn't know you were still here. I thought you were going home," I turned my light on to see she was wearing one of my t-shirts.

"I was but Mecca threw up on me when I was getting him dressed so I washed him up and put my clothes in the washing machine. Then he shitted and I mean one of those shits where it comes out the diaper and goes everywhere. I had to clean him again all the while he was screaming his head off. I just got him to go to sleep," she looked down at her watch. "Thirty minutes ago. I'm taking him to the doctor tomorrow because today he was totally out of character. Thank God he doesn't have a fever but I just want to make sure he's alright. He's usually a good baby, his big head self was on one as soon as you left."

"It be like that sometimes, glad it wasn't me," I chuckled.

"Of course you are," Taj laughed. "Well let me get up and go my ass home. Can you get my clothes from your dryer please?"

"Yeah I got it," I went into the hallway to the dryer and pulled her clothes out.

When I walked back in my room I was stopped in my tracks seeing Taj pull my t-shirt over her head. I was used to Taj being small, she picked up a few pounds during her pregnancy but she was wearing it well.

Her caramel colored legs were thick as oatmeal making the tattoos on her legs even sexier. Her hips spread giving her an hourglass shape and what used to be a small c-cup; her titties were sitting up perfectly in a bra that had to be at least a double D. Not to mention that ass definitely grew and it was getting to me.

"Anthony," Taj snapped her fingers in my face bringing my attention to her face. "Are you okay? I said your name like five times."

"Shit, yeah I'm good my bad. I zone out, here," I put her clothes in her arms and sat at the foot of my bed watching her. She was talking about something but I wasn't listening I just liked watching her move around.

Realizing she was about to slide her jeans on I stood up gently grabbing her arm to stop her. "What are you doing?"

"Shhh," I brought her face close to mine and kissed her halfway expecting her to pull away from me, but she didn't. It started off as just a simple small kiss grew into a full blown make out session within a matter of seconds. When we finally separated I watched him lick his lips with lust all in his eyes.

Stepping back from her, I pulled my black joggers and shit off then picked her up and sat on the edge of my bed with her in my lap. I grabbed my remote and turned up the volume on the TV.

When Jagged Edge's I Gotta Be came through the speakers I could feel her smile against my neck. "What you know about this?" Taj pulled back looking at me with a smirk on her face.

"I know they're good to fuck to." Grabbing her ass in my hands I squeezed it then slapped it hard as shit, making a deep moan leave her mouth.

"You know I'm not for the games right? Don't take it there with me if you're not ready to do right." she said now kissing my neck, slowly sucking on it.

"I know that, I'm not even about to game you ma,"

"How can I be sure? How do I know you're not going to fuck tonight then pull the same bullshit?"

"I learned my lesson; I'm not doing anything to lose you ever again. I promise you that, I just need you to let me show you," I answered her. "I gotta be the one you touch. Baby, I gotta be the one you love. I gotta be the one you feel," I sang softly in Taj's ear. She lifted her head then ran her tongue across my lips and kissed me. "You heard me?"

"I heard you baby," she moaned in my ear as she grabbed the ten inch monster inside my boxers. I grabbed a handful of her hair and pulled her head back as I attacked her neck again. Her soft moans were like music to my ears. I pulled her shirt over her head then removed the bra she had on underneath releasing those pretty titties. I attacked them with my tongue while she moaned loudly.

"Mmm that feels so good."

She pulled my wife beater over my head and she licked and sucked all over my neck and chest. Getting off my lap she got down on her knees. I felt Taj's soft hands pulling my dick from my boxers. She looked in my eyes as she wrapped her pretty full lips around my dick. She licked and sucked slowly around the head of my dick while keeping eye contact. When she pushed my dick to the back of her throat and past her tonsils, I groaned.

"Fuck," I said grabbing a hand full of her thick hair.

She slurped before saying, "You like that daddy?"

"Fuck... yea," I felt myself on the verge of a nut, so I pulled her up, laid her on her back and dove into that pussy with my tongue. I took her clit into my mouth and sucked slowly. I watched as she arched her back and licked her lips. Licking and sucking slowly I slid my index and middle finger inside her tight hole.

When she began to wiggle underneath me I knew she was about to cum. I removed my fingers and began attacking her swollen button with my lips and applied more pressure with my tongue. Before I knew it she was releasing right inside my mouth. Her nectar was sweet. The shit was all over my lips and beard.

Grabbing my face she pulled me up so that we were facing each other. "Come here," she said wiping my beard with her hand and then kissing my lips, "I taste pretty damn good." Picking her up, I laid back on the bed and lowered her down on my dick. "Sh-shit," Taj cried out.

With her thick hips in my hands I moved her up and down slowly so she could get used to my size. Once I knew she would be able to take it, I flipped us over so that she was on her stomach.

"Up baby," I mumbled after running my tongue up her spine causing her to arch her back just like I wanted her to. I entered her from behind making her yell out. She began easing forward running from me. "Uh un fuck you doing? Don't run from me ma."

"Fuck! I feel that shit in my chest."

"Stop being a pussy. Throw this ass back," I slapped her ass hard gripping it in my hands. She began rocking her body slowly, it felt good as fuck because her drenched walls were sucking me in like no other but she was playing games. I slapped her ass again making her whine. "Stop fuckin' playing man," I grabbed her by the waist and slammed all ten inches inside her. She screamed out in pleasure and pain as I pushed in and out of her with force. If she thought I was about to play with her ass, she had me fucked up.

I grabbed a handful of her hair and wrapped it in my hand as I hit that pussy with skill. I wanted to make sure she was feeling every inch, with every stroke I gave. "What the fuck?" Taj whined loudly, she sounded like she was near tears the way her voice cracked.

"Shit," I grunted when I saw her sweet juices covering my dick when it slid out of her. Gripping her waist tighter I rolled my hips into her spot.

"Oh… my… God! Anthony! Yes! Right there!"

"Here?" I started hitting her wall repeatedly. I watched Taj grip the sheets in her small hands as she continued to scream out in pleasure. Thank God for thick walls because my neighbors would've been calling the cops on my ass with how she was screaming.

"Fuck I wanna cum baby! I wanna cu-cum!"

"Cum for daddy, soak this dick baby," I slapped and gripped her ass in my hands.

"O-Ooh shit!" I went deeper and deeper until I felt her juices running down both of our legs and my nut was shooting full force into her.

"Shit!" I shouted before slapping her ass again. We both fell on the bed out of breath.

"My body feels numb," said Taj after her breathing slowed down.

"That's what good dick does to you."

"Shut up," she laughed turning to face me. "I meant what I said about you playing with me."

"I meant what I said too. Seeing you with Mecca changed a lot for me, I want a family and I want it with you. I love you and I'm willing to fight for this."

"Mecca made me look at you differently. I knew you were a good father because of how you were with Naima but it's something about seeing you with our son that feels different. It's like I see the man I know you have the potential to be if you would just stop fucking around and doing stupid shit."

"I know and I'm telling you I've learned my lesson."

"We'll see, but don't play with me Anthony. I'll really cut your ass this time."

"The sad part is I know you dead serious," I laughed. "I got you, alright? We do need to talk about something though."

"That would be?"

"Naima is here and I might have Naima full time now," I continued. "I don't know yet but depending on what KeKe does tomorrow will determine it."

"Why? What happened?"

I told her everything that happened at KeKe's apartment. "I'm tired of the bullshit so she has a couple of options. She can either stay here, take care of Naima and act like she has some sense, or she can move to Cali and leave Naima here with me and we'll co-parent to the best of our ability. If she tries me I'm going for full custody and I'll make sure she won't ever see her again."

"Well I'm going to support whatever decision you make. As long as we're good, the kids are good, and there isn't a bitter bitch making pop ups I'm good to go."

"So we're really doing this shit?" I smirked at her and she nodded with a smile on her face.

"Yes we are, just don't make me regret it."

LEGEND

"You good?" I asked Toi while we sat in her doctor's office. She was here getting another checkup making sure that she was healing correctly. Her whole purpose was to find out if she could go back to work but she isn't going back if I have anything to do with it; at least not right now anyway.

"Yeah I'm fine. I'm just happy I can breathe without feeling pain. You think she'll give me the go ahead to work?"

"She probably will but it won't matter."

"Why wouldn't it matter?"

"We'll talk about that later."

"No let's talk now. Que I've been in the house for four weeks. I didn't even get to celebrate my birthday like I wanted to. I'm not about to stay in the house if I don't have to."

"You act like you haven't been out the house at all."

"Going to register the twins in school for the year doesn't count and you only let me do that because my mother couldn't."

"We'll talk about it later Toi, okay?"

"Whatever fine, later," she shrugged her shoulders. We sat in silence for a minute when her doctor finally came in.

"Hello, I'm sorry to keep you waiting. How are you feeling La'Toia?"

Dr. Anderson, a tall slender black woman with long dreads pulled back into a ponytail asked her.

"I'm good; finally breathing without feeling like somebody is drumming on my ribs."

"Well I'm glad you're feeling better. Let's check you out and we can discuss some things."

"Discuss some things like what?" Toi asked.

"You'll know when we discuss those things," Dr. Anderson laughed. "Lift your shirt for me. I want to see how the bruising is coming along." She examined all of Toi's injuries impressed. "You're doing really well La'Toia. What have you been doing?"

"She sits in the hot tub all day," I said with a chuckle.

"A hot tub?"

"Yeah it's been the best thing ever." Toi looked up at Dr. Anderson who had a look of worry on her face. "What's wrong?"

"You have to stop with the hot tub thing and we need to do an ultra-sound right now."

Toi looked over at me confused, almost as if she was looking for me to tell her what was going on but I couldn't. I didn't know what the hell the problem is or what's going on.

"What's wrong? Is she okay?" I hopped up from my seat and grabbed Toi's hand.

"According to the blood test you took the last time you were here you're pregnant, that's one of the main reasons I wanted you to come in today."

"WHAT!" Toi and I shouted at the same time.

"You're pregnant, you can't be any more than six weeks and I assume that because when you were hospitalized nothing came up. We need an ultra-sound just to make sure everything is okay since you've been spending so much time in your tub."

"Wait so what happened to her didn't affect the pregnancy?"

"Depending on how far along she is, there's a chance she wasn't exactly pregnant just yet. If she was, more than likely she was only a week into her pregnancy."

"Which means?"

"It means it was too early for your body to show it through whatever examinations they did. Or she was too early for any damage to be done. We won't know for sure until we get a look." Dr. Anderson got her prepped and ready for the ultrasound then pointed to the screen. "There is your baby."

"Oh my God, I'm really pregnant," Toi spoke after her mouth hung open in shock for a few seconds. "So is everything okay?"

"From what I can see you're fine and you're looking to be about five weeks. I need you to give the hot tub a rest. Long hot showers are a no too, you can't overheat yourself." The doctor got everything straightened then threw her plastic gloves in the garbage. "So, I'm going to give a prescription for some prenatal vitamins. Unfortunately you can't take your usual pain medication. Aspirin and ibuprofen are off limits, that means no Advil or Motrin. I'm going to prescribe you Tylenol; you have to be very careful with how you take it, okay?"

"Yeah I get it," Toi nodded quickly.

"Well, congratulations. I'll let you get straightened up and get everything you'll need," Dr. Anderson said.

"Thank you," I told her before she walked out the room. "Well damn, I wasn't expecting that at all."

"Neither was I. So what are you thinking?"

"What do you mean? You're pregnant so we're having a baby. Can you come up with a reason why you wouldn't want to have it or even question having it?"

"No I'm just checking your thoughts about it.'

"Shit I'm good," I laughed. "You already know how I feel about kids."

"Yeah you supposedly want five."

"I want six but I'm willing to go down to five."

"Oh you're willing to go down?" she chuckled. "Que shut up. Let's focus on your daughter and this one we have coming. Speaking of, when is Diamond coming?"

"I'm getting her from my mother's house today." As soon as I said that it's like a light bulb went off in my head. Toi is five weeks pregnant; she was attacked four weeks ago. The fact that she was early on could've played a part in why she didn't lose it. Had they pulled that shit two or three weeks later our child would be dead.

A flash of rage went through my body and Toi must've felt it because she snatched her hand out of mine then looked at me confused. "What's wrong with you? You were about to break my damn hand."

"My bad, I'm just thinking about something. Come on, get dressed so we can go."

I helped her get dressed, we got her prescription and copies of the ultrasound pictures, then we left the doctor's office.

While I drove I glanced over at Toi a few times and she was staring at the sonogram every time. "Toi, you good?"

"Yeah I'm fine, I'm just in awe. I'm going to be somebody's mother, that's something I have to get used to."

"It's not like you don't know you'll be a good mother. You helped your grandmother raise the twins and even though they're a little out there y'all did a good job."

"Thank you baby, I'm still in shock a little bit but I'll be fine. Speaking of the twins, they finally agreed to do the DNA test."

"What changed their minds?" Toi asked the twins weeks ago if they wanted to know if Saint was their birth father after Geneva told them what happened. They immediately said no, they didn't care to know who their father was at this point. They didn't give a damn that it might be Saint either; they weren't trying to hear it.

"Kayla said they thought about it and felt like God forbid something happened to me permanently they wouldn't have any other family besides my mother. They love her but they have an opportunity to know their father so they're taking it."

"I'll let him know, more than likely Beautii will be at my mother's house," I told her and I could see Toi roll her eyes. "Come on man."

"Come on what Que? Fuck Beautii, she flipped the script on me over some shit that has nothing to do with me. I'm good on her ass and if it comes back that Saint is the twins' father, she better watch her muthafuckin' mouth."

"She's not going to talk about the twins alright, Saint isn't going to let that shit happen."

"I'm not worried about that, they'll check her ass if anything. I'm talking about her speaking on their mother. She was two when they died and yes she was far from perfect but I don't want her putting shit in their heads about her."

"Like I said Saint won't let that happen, alright? I know Beautii did some bullshit, especially firing Taj and what she said about you, but despite her feelings if he is their father, he's going to make sure they're good."

"Alright I hear you Que but I'm telling you Beautii has one time to try my cousins and one more time to come at my mama."

"Geneva came at her too Toi, remember all the shit she said about Beautii not being able to have kids."

"Was she lying?"

"What your mother was out there doing isn't a lie either but nobody wants that shit brought up. Both of them were going below the belt Toi."

"I don't give a flying fuck she went to my mother not the other way around. Beautii needs to watch her damn mouth like I said. I don't give a shit about what you talking about fuck her feelings."

"Look I know how you feel ma, I get it but at the same time that's my family. Be real Toi."

"I am being real and I'm dead serious. You don't want me involved in that shit. Your mother already doesn't like me. I'll really give her a reason to hate me by fucking her sister in law the fuck up."

"Don't talk about my mother, alright? You pushing it now."

"You just said something about mine."

"Toi, shut the fuck up-"

"You shut the fuck up," she shot back before I could even finish my damn statement.

"You need to chill alright, like I said that's my family."

"And? If my mother is correct, the twins are your family too so we should be on the same page. I'm not about to sit back and let Beautii treat or talk to them any kind of way.'

"Neither is Saint, alright? Damn, relax. They didn't even take the test yet and you acting like you have no sense."

"You know how I feel about my family and the way Beautii switched up on me tells me she's not to be trusted."

"I don't know how many times you expect me to repeat myself but that shit is a wrap. I hear what you saying, I understand you I get it but you gotta chill with all that hostile shit. Not even for them or me, it's about you and my baby. You're pregnant and still healing, stop getting all worked up over shit you don't have to worry about. Saint isn't going to let Beautii do shit to those girls, and if he can't step up you know I got them. Until we get the DNA results, I'm not talking about this shit. You want to talk about it talk to the twins' or Geneva because you like to argue with me about it and that's fuckin' annoying."

I love Toi to death but once she gets her mouth going she doesn't stop. She has a bad habit of getting a little too disrespectful. I don't give a damn that she doesn't like my mother, I get why but that doesn't mean she's about to sit there and talk shit in front of me either. She'll probably try to kill my ass if I started going off about her mother.

Like the big baby she is, Toi crossed her arms over her chest all the while rolling her eyes. "Alright Que, damn; why are you always giving me a lecture?"

"Why do you always need to hear one? Fix your face," I playfully plucked her bottom lip since she wanted to sit over there pouting.

"Stop," she swatted my hand away. I could see the corner of her lips starting to turn up and she was doing her damndest to stop it.

"Go ahead and smile, you know you want to."

"Whatever Quentin, can you just drive?" Toi said with a laugh.

I took her to get her prescription then drove her home. I had to go get Diamond from my mother's house. Since what happened to Toi I avoided being in the same room with Isyss and my sister as much as possible. My mother picks Diamond up from school every Friday then I get her from there.

In a perfect world Toi could come with me and chill at my people's house for a minute but no, everything is all fucked up. My aunts don't necessarily have a problem with Toi but Beautii has turned them on Geneva completely. Nothing I say changes their mind; they have Beautii's back to the end. They don't want to meet Geneva or speak to her because Beautii repeated what was said about her not being able to have kids. Now granted that was fucked up, she conveniently left out what she said about Grace and Geneva's addiction. They're not feeling the idea of her and she feels the same way so as of right now getting together isn't happening.

When I got to my mother's house I spotted Mia's car sitting in the driveway. The logical part of my brain wanted me to call my mother and have her bring Diamond outside so I wouldn't have to see her damn face.

But there was another part of me that wanted to break her fuckin' neck for what she did.

Mia and Isyss has been on my shit list since Toi told me what happened. Now adding on to the fact that we now know she was fucking pregnant has me even more pissed at her. Toi didn't hear them say anybody else's name but i refuse to believe Mia did all that shit on her own.

Knowing how Isyss is especially when it comes to the way she ass kisses my sister, I'm more than 100% sure she had something to do with that shit. If not she at least knew about that shit. There is no way I was going to be able to see either one of those bitches without choking their dumb asses.

Getting out the car I went to the front door and tried to open it but it was locked. For some reason that shit set me off so I started banging on that shit like the police.

Seconds later the door opened with Mia standing on the other side of it. Pushing through I snatched her up by the neck and lifted her off the floor.

"WHAT THE FUCK IS WRONG WITH YOU!" I shouted at her. Her eyes were bulging out of her head and I could tell she wasn't getting any air but fuck that, she doesn't deserve to breathe.

"QUENTIN! QUENTIN PUT HER DOWN!" My mother's scream snapped me back to reality so I dropped Mia to the floor. As soon as I did my mother's hand went across my face. "Have you lost your mind? You don't put your hands on any woman let alone your fuckin' sister! What the hell is your problem?"

"Your daughter is my fuckin' problem! Ask her what the fuck she did to Toi!"

My mother's head quickly whipped around towards Mia. "You did that to that girl? You had somebody jump on her?"

"We did and so what?" Mia snapped as she got up off the floor. "You choked me over that bitch? Fuck her and fuck you too! I'm glad she got her ass beat!"

"Really? Why would you do that to her Mia?"

"Fuck her ma! All he cares about is that bitch! Somebody already chose her over me before, now my own brother is putting her before me! You're supposed to be my blood!"

"This is what you're mad about? Some punk ass nigga you had no business being with? You were dumb enough to be that niggas side chick and you want to be mad he chose her over you? The second bitch never gets chosen Mia, the fuck is wrong with your brain?"

"Whatever Que that shit doesn't have a damn thing to do with you choking me over that bitch!"

"She's pregnant! You could've killed my fucking child, you lucky choking you is all I did! I told you before she isn't going anywhere and now that's she's carrying my baby she's always going to come before you, get the fuck over it."

"Oh please! Isyss had your baby and you don't give a fuck about her so why is Toi so special?"

"Isyss didn't even give too much of a fuck about Diamond before I stepped and she realized she could benefit from her. The fuck you thought I don't speak to her mother? She barely took care of Diamond; her mother did everything. I know more than you bitches think I know."

"Can both of you shut the hell up?" My mother said then looked at me. "Toi is pregnant?"

I nodded. "Yeah, and she almost lost it because of your dumb ass daughter."

"Why didn't you tell me?"

"We just found out today, what does it matter?"

"It matters because since you been with Toi you've put this family on the back burner. You're never around anymore and when you do come around it's nothing but drama. Why do I have to hear from Saint that you moved her in with you?"

"Are you serious right now? I tell you that your daughter almost made my girl lose our baby and you're questioning me about some shit that really has nothing to do with you? Yeah I moved her in so the fuck what? It's my house I don't have to tell nobody shit. I'm tired of you muthafuckas questioning me about what the fuck I'm doing."

"Watch your mouth Quentin; I'm still your mother! I'm telling you, you need to get your priorities straight. You've only known that girl for a fucking minute!"

"What's your point?"

"My point is this family comes first, we come first. It's our blood running through your veins not hers."

"I really see where Mia gets this selfish shit from. I care about my family, I love y'all to death but I don't give a fuck about who y'all do and don't like. You have a problem with Toi because Mia doesn't like her and you know the dumb ass reason why but you're still sitting here dick riding her ass. I'm over this bullshit, DIAMOND!" I shouted for her. Seconds later she came running downstairs.

"Hi daddy," she said before I pulled her in for a hug.

"Hey baby girl, let's go," I grabbed her hand then looked at my mother and sister. "Mia, don't call my phone, don't ask me for shit you cut the fuck off. Tell your mother to take care of you," I sent both of them a death glare then walked out the house with Diamond.

MICKEY

"Myles!" I shouted for him when I walked into his bedroom that he's barely in unless it's bedtime. In order to monitor how much time, he actually spends on his PlayStation, I hooked it up in the living room instead of his. He'll fuck around and be on it all night while I have my ass in the bed asleep. "Come here!"

"Yes?" he asked when he came up.

"Which one are you wearing tomorrow?" I laid out two different sweat suits. Both were NIKE branded but they were different colors. There was a gray and white one with matching Retro 10's, and the other was red black and white with Retro 1's to go with it.

"The red and black one," he answered me.

"Okay well go put it in your overnight bag then go ahead and get in the shower so you can get dressed. We gotta go," I walked out of his bedroom and down to mine.

We've been in our new house for a couple of weeks now and we love it. Myles started at his new school and seems to be adjusting well. Living in the suburbs is something new to me, I'm a city girl through and through but it's comfortable. I don't feel the need to watch my back like crazy an it's refreshing to go to be without hearing a bunch of yelling or police sirens every damn night.

The only thing I hate about my new home life is there are no corner stores around here. If I get the munchies or just want something quick to eat I can't walk across the street for a turkey and cheese anymore. Now I have to drive out to the nearest 7-Eleven and they don't even sell the stuff I'm used to. I guess I gotta get used to not having hood shit.

I went to my bedroom so I could shower and get dressed too. Today I was taking Myles to Tone for their little overnight excursion. Since his 8th birthday is tomorrow, Tone promised they could have an all boy sleepover at his house. It's going to be Myles, Tone, Que, Yung, Mecca even though he's a baby he was invited something about a boy is never too young to have man time, and a couple of Tone's little cousins along with his dad. They're staying at Tone's parents' tonight then tomorrow I'm throwing him a birthday party at Skyzone.

Besides helping me move Tone has really stepped up and become a big part of Myles' life over these last few weeks. They talk everyday on the phone, and it's to the point where Tone has asked if Myles could come to his house sometimes on the weekends. There was a slightly petty part of me that wanted to say hell no but that would hurt my son more than it would satisfy me so I didn't do that. Despite how much he does for Myles, Tone isn't my favorite person.

I was about to get comfortable with him and really let my wall down again until Cassie's bird ass put it out there that he lied to me. It wasn't even just what she said that got to me, it was the look on his face that confirmed it. I still don't know what happened because I haven't let him tell me yet. I honestly don't want to know because it's not going to do anything but piss me off. The thought of them touching period makes me want to go off so I could imagine how I would feel if I knew the whole truth.

Also it wasn't even just the fact that something happened that had me pissed. Tone went on and on about how he doesn't like liars and he couldn't trust me yet he stood right in my face and did the very thing he ended our relationship for. It seems like lying is a problem and off limits when it's done to him but if he's the one handing out bullshit it's not a problem. Maybe one day we'll talk about it but today aint it.

Once Myles and I were both ready to go we left and I dropped him off at Tone's apartment. They were going to do their whole man day thing while I ran around getting everything together for Myles' party.

"Michelle Whitfield?" I heard behind me while I stuffed the bags from Party City into my trunk. I turned around to see two men casually suited up standing there.

"Who wants to know?"

"I'm Detective Norris this is my partner Hanson. We would like to ask you a few questions." One of them spoke up.

"Questions about what?"

"You'll find out when we ask you those questions. We need you to come down to the station for a minute, it won't take long. You can just follow us or we can drive you."

"No, I'll drive on my own thanks."

"That's fine, we'll see you in a little while Ms. Whitfield." When they walked off I got in my car and made my down to the station. The whole time I drove, I was trying to figure out what they would want to question me about and came up with nothing.

When I got to the station, they brought me to an interrogation room and instructed me to sit down. Detective Norris sat across from me with a smile on his face.

"Ms. Whitfield, can I call you Michelle or Mickey?" he asked. I chuckled at his little tactic, saying my nickname is a way for them to let me know they've done their digging about me.

"Michelle works fine. What is this about?"

"Well a few weeks ago someone came in and filed some missing person reports. Were you aware that your ex Bryson Campbell was released from prison some months ago?" he asked. It took everything in me not to bust out laughing. *This is what I'm being questioned about? Wow.*

"Mhm I was."

"And?'

"And what? He's out, what does that have to do with me?"

"A lot seeing as how we know you're the reason he went to jail."

"No he was the reason he went to jail. I didn't make him do the things he did."

"No but you reported it and with the volatile relationship you two had

I know seeing him walking free couldn't be too easy."

"What is the point of this? He's out okay and? Why am I here?"

"Well Mr. Campbell is missing and it was bought to our attention that he was last seen at your birthday party. Nobody has seen him since then, have you?"

"Nope, he popped up on me, tried to start an altercation, and he was escorted out. I haven't seen him since then and I don't want to. If he's missing good for him, I can't help you locate him."

"Well you know what's funny is your party ended in a shoot-out."

"Uh huh, so?"

"So? That's not odd to you? Your abusive ex pops up on you at a party, it ends in gunfire and he's now missing."

"Maybe he's on the run, shit I don't know and I don't care where he is."

"Of course you wouldn't care. He was beating your ass for years why would you? You know what's funny is the person that filed the missing person's report filed one on somebody else too and your name came up in both situations."

"What are you talking about?"

"Do you know who Kareem Hudson is?"

"I wish I didn't, but I do. What about him?'

"Oh yeah that's right, he murdered your cousin. What's funnier is he was last seen at your birthday party too."

"Was he?" I asked putting on a dumb face. "I didn't see him there," I said truthfully.

"Well he was there and now just like Bryson he's missing. Tell me something, who threw your party?"

"My best friend did."

"La'Toia Henderson, right? A party at the mansion isn't cheap, how did you two swing that?"

"We know people, how is this relevant?"

"People like her boyfriend Legend Santana?" Detective Norris raised an eyebrow. "Oh I'm sorry Quentin Santana. Do you know who that is?"

"I know Quentin, again how is any of this relevant?"

"I'm just trying to figure out what's going on Michelle. Your abusive ex and the man who murdered your cousin in cold blood showed up to your birthday party and haven't been seen since. Your best friend is in a relationship with the person we believe is responsible for every drug moving through New Jersey, Surely getting rid of the men that caused you so much pain wouldn't be too hard of a task for him."

"Look, I don't know where Bryson is. I don't know where Kareem is either. As far as Quentin is concerned he's a business man, a very hard-working one. Instead of standing there and trying to mind fuck me into doing your job for you, maybe you should be on the streets tracking them down. One is a murderer and the other I'm sure has violated his parole by now so go handle those criminals as you see fit. Now, if I'm done here I would like to go on about my business."

The detective let out a dark chuckle then nodded. "You're free to go Michelle."

"Thank you," I got up and got out of there as fast as I could. When I got to my car and got far enough away from the station I called Tone who answered on the second ring.

"You calling already? He's fine Mick," Tone said when he picked up.

"Where are you?"

"We just got to my parents' house? Why?"

"Is Que there?"

"Yeah he just got here, you good?"

"Not really, I need y'all to meet me at your apartment. Right now, can your parents watch Myles for a minute?"

"What's going on Mick?"

"I'll tell you when I see you. I'm on my way to your apartment just meet me over there okay?"

"Alright, we'll be there in a little while."

"Okay," I ended the call then let out a frustrated scream. I'm not worried about me because I didn't do anything at all but the fact that they brought Que's name up shook me a little bit. I didn't get the feeling that they were trying to blame me but it was more than obvious they were leaning towards trying to put it on Que.

I waited outside of Tone's building for a good ten minutes before he and Que finally pulled up. When they got out of the car they came over to me.

"What's up Mickey?" Que asked when they walked up. "What's

going on?"

"Okay so I was at Party City putting shit in my trunk when two detectives came up to me."

"Came up to you for what?"

"Asking me about Bryson and Kareem, somebody supposedly filed a missing persons report on them. They know they were at my birthday party."

"So they're thinking you did it?" Tone polled.

"Not really, it seems like they're trying to put it on you Que."

"The fuck?"

"Yeah basically they trying to say if you did it your motive would be the fact that I'm your girls' best friend. I don't know how far they're about to go with this shit but that detective sounded like he was building something against you."

Que shook his head then ran his hand down his face. "Thanks for telling me. Do me a favor though, don't tell Toi about this shit. I want to see how far they take this shit, if something comes of it I'll let her know. Until then just let her be, I don't want her pregnant ass stressing."

"Pregnant? She's pregnant?" I looked at him confused. When the fuck did she get pregnant, and why didn't I know?

He sucked his teeth and sighed. "We weren't supposed to say shit until she got further along," he chuckled. "Yeah man she is pregnant, don't say shit, alright? Let her tell you herself."

"Aww oh my God, okay I won't say anything but yay I have a god baby coming."

"For real Mick, she's going to be pissed if you tell her I told you. She wants to let you and Taj know, don't tell Taj either."

"I got you. Y'all can go I just wanted to let you know what was going on," I told them.

"Good looking out Mickey," Que said before giving me a small hug and going back to the car.

"Are you going back to your house?" Tone asked.

"I was planning on it."

"You can stay here if you want to. It's closer to Skyzone anyway. Here," he went in his pocket and gave me the keys to his apartment.

"Okay that'll work. Thank you."

"Nah, thank you. I'll hit you later so Myles can speak to you." He kissed my cheek making my heart damn near jump from my chest then went back to his car while I went to mine.

"Lord give me strength," I mumbled under my breath. I'm going to fuck around forget I'm supposed to hate his ass and end up fucking him.

* * *

"Happy Birthday to Myles, happy birthday to you!" Everybody sang right before Myles blew the candles out on his pull apart cupcakes that were shaped in a large number eight with red, white, and blue icing. About an hour ago, we filled Myles, Diamond, Naima, and Tone's little cousins with pizza before sending them back out to play in the large indoor trampoline park that is Skyzone.

I personally feel like it's the perfect place to take kids, all they do is jump around and play all day. By the time you feed them, bathe them, and get their little asses in the bed they're knocked out for the rest of the night.

Myles has been bouncing around like a chicken with his head off all day. Tone said he was in play mode from the time they got up to eat the breakfast his mom made them. When he got to the Skyzone he damn near knocked me down when he hugged me. To say he was excited would be an understatement.

Everybody clapped as Myles stood there smiling. He turned to me since I was right behind him and put his arms around my waist. I thought he was just hugging me until I looked down and saw tears going down his face.

"What's wrong?" I quietly asked him but he didn't answer me. Taj was standing right next to me so I asked her to start passing out the cupcakes then walked off to the side. Once we were out of earshot, I unwrapped his arms from my waist and wiped his tears away. "Why are you crying? I thought you were happy."

"I am happy," he replied. I looked Myles in the eyes which wasn't hard to do since he wasn't that much shorter than me.

"Oh, these are happy tears, okay," I pulled him in for a hug. "I'm glad you're happy, I love you."

"I love you too."

"Alright come on let's go eat these cupcakes." We went back over to the table and joined everybody else.

"Everything good?" Tone looked at me and asked.

"Yeah everything is fine."

"Alright, aye Myles we doing dodge-ball after y'all finish those cupcakes," Tone went over to Myles while I went over to Toi. She still hasn't said anything about her pregnancy, and I was itching to talk about it. Knowing how Toi is she'll cop an attitude if she finds out she couldn't be the one to tell me. I wish she would hurry up and say something, I have some questions.

"Tone and Myles so cute," Toi pointed out when I sat next to her. "What's the deal?"

"What are you talking about Toi?"

"She's talking about you and Tone looking like a little family," Taj said when she walked up. "Are y'all back together?"

"No, we're just getting along. It's actually because of Myles we're even speaking. They have their own situation going, ending it would be hurting my son so I'm tolerating him."

"Girl please you are doing more than just tolerating that man," Toi continued. "I think you need to get out your feelings and try to fix shit with him. It's clear that it's still feelings there."

"Nah I'm good on that."

"See you say shit like this but then you want to be mad if he looks at another bitch," Taj blurted. "You still love his ass, he obviously still loves you. He's great with Myles, hell if I didn't know any better I would think he was his father."

"They can have their relationship if they want to, why does it have to involve me? We broke up February, girl it's damn near October, that's what? About seven months, we're over. I wish y'all would realize that. As a matter of fact let's drop the subject."

"Fine with me, I'll drop the subject. I do have a question though."

"That would be?" I looked at Toi.

"Are you good with money? Because between you moving and starting up your business, I know you have a lot going on. You still pay your mother's mortgage?"

"Yeah but I'm good. Toi I know how to save money. I wasn't chasing it all the time because I was low, and I flipped it."

"Flipped it how? Don't tell me you about to be a drug Lord."

"Hell no, it's called knowing certain people I can hand $500 to today and get $2000 the very next week. How they get that shit is not my concern as long as I get my money back I'm good. Don't worry about me, I'm always going to be good, I know what I'm doing."

"Well you know if you need anything, I got you, alright?"

"Yeah, I know, but don't worry about me. Are you good?"

"I'm fine, Que still wants me to relax some more so I'm not back at work yet, but we compromised on two more weeks of me taking off. My manager got it though; I'm on the phone with her half the damn day."

"What about you Taj? No more baby mama issues?"

"No, she's gone to California so Anthony has her full time now which means I pretty much have her full time too. It's fine though, as long as her mother isn't getting on my damn nerves, I'm good," Taj answered.

"That ditzy bitch thought he was going to let her go live across the country with his daughter?" I shook my head. KeKe had some nerve trying to make Yung choose between his kids. I guess she thought he was going to either choose her or just become a checkbook father. The broad didn't expect him to tell her he'll file for custody.

"Bitch didn't think all of that shit through but she's gone so fuck it. Toi, did the twins take the test yet?"

"Yup, we should be getting the results next week. I'm nervous like it's me."

"Well it's going to change all of your lives," I noted. "It's been you the twins and your grandparents for the longest time, now they're about to have a damn daddy. Saint is their father they look just like his ass."

"I know, I'm just cautious of how it's going to work out with Beautii's bitter ass. Speaking of, I heard she's losing clients and employees."

"She is," Toi laughed. "That shit with Saint must be getting to her because she's been on some real bitchy shit lately with everybody. The bitch lost my clientele which is a good percentage of what was coming in that muthafucka anyway. She fired Nessa and Kelly."

"Nah she didn't fire her only nail tech, Kelly was bringing that shmoney in that bitch."

"She did which is damn stupid. The more she fucks up the more calls I get about how much she's fucking up. I'm really about to get a damn shop going, Kelly already told me she'll come with me if I got a space and so did Nessa."

"Well get your money then girl."

The rest of Myles' party went without a hitch. He had the time of his life and just watching him smile all day put a smile on my face too.

When we arrived home, I made Myles take a shower and told him he could play the game if he wanted to, but he was in his bed knocked out right after he put his pajamas on. I took a shower and was about to take it down until my doorbell rang.

"Who is it!" I shouted when I hit the bottom step in the foyer.

"Tone!"

"Oh," I went over to the door and opened it. "Hey, what are you doing here?"

"Some of Myles' gifts are in my car; I figured I would drop them off."

"Okay, well you can bring them in."

"Alright," Tone ran back to his car and within two trips brought in all of Myles' presents. "That should be it. Where is he? Sleep?"

"Yeah he played himself something crazy today. Thank you for coming and for last night too."

"Mick, why are you always thanking me for something?"

"You do that when you appreciate something that's been done for you. You don't have to be here for Myles but you are and I'm thankful for it. A real father isn't something he's ever had, it's not like Bryson gave a fuck about him or even tried to have a relationship with him."

"He's a good kid so I don't mind it, besides bonding with your son has to happen if I plan to be a part of your life."

I gave him a skeptical look. "A part of my life?"

"Are we about to stand here and act like it's not still something here?"

"That doesn't matter because you're full of shit."

"What?"

"You broke up with me because you didn't trust me-"

"You lied to me."

"So did you. All you and Cassie did was kiss?" By the 'what the fuck' frown that came on his face I could tell I caught him off guard with that one.

TONE

When Mickey bought that Cassie shit up I sucked my teeth then took a seat on her living room couch. I forgot all about that shit and when Mickey never brought it up, I thought she did too. I should've known better, women don't forget shit like that.

"Come on man, fuck Cassie. That bitch is a non-factor," I told Mickey as she stood in front of me with her arms folded.

"Non-factor my ass, who is she to you? It's obvious y'all know each other because that bitch was real deep in her feelings. What's the deal Tone?"

"Remember the ex that lied about having a miscarriage? I told you about it a long ass time ago."

"She was the ex?" she asked so I nodded in response. "Wow, Jersey is too fucking small."

"You're right about that. How do you know her?"

"Kareem was her cousin and she used to instigate shit between him and Bia. Telling shit she should've kept to herself or she would just flat out lie so he could attack my cousin. She thought the shit he used to do to her was funny."

"That's fucked up," I shook my head. Hearing that about Cassie didn't even shock me, nothing about that bitch surprises me anymore. Anybody that can lie about having a miscarriage clearly has issues.

"Yeah it is and I hate that bitch so you need to tell me what the hell happened between y'all that night and don't lie."

"She gave me head in my car but that's it."

"Tone."

"What? I'm dead ass serious; all she did was give me head. I lied to you about it because you were already pissed at me and I didn't want to make it worse. That's all that happened; I wouldn't fuck that bitch again with the next niggas dick."

"Alright, I believe you. What's done in the dark always come to the light so I'll find out if you're full of shit."

"Well I'm not lying," I grabbed her by the waist pulling between my legs.

"Tone, let me go."

"No."

"Why not?"

"I miss you,"

"Oh nigga please, you dumped me remember?"

"Did that shit hurt your feelings or something? You always bringing that shit up."

"Yes it hurt my feelings nigga so you need to let me go. I don't have time to play with you."

"Who said I was playing? I'm dead serious; I love and miss you Mickey."

"What's your point?"

"Don't even act like that with me," I looked up at her. Mickey is fuckin' beautiful and she knows it, but I don't think she realizes how much. Everything about her face and body is perfection, so much so that I often wonder what our kids would look like.

"Act like what?"

"Like you don't want me."

"Nigga, I don't."

"I think you're lying."

"I don't give a fuck about what you thin-" Instead of hearing the lie that was about to come out of her mouth I stood to my feet and shut her up with a kiss. To my surprise she kissed me back, and it wasn't some simple shit she kissed me like she really meant that shit until she pulled back. She tilted her head to the side and stared at me and bit her bottom lip with so much lust in her eyes. I licked my lips, picked her up putting her back against the wall, and went back in for a kiss.

"I love you so much Mick," I said between kisses I'm sorry." I placed her feet back on the floor then pulled the t-shirt she was wearing over her head, ripping off the black lace boy shorts she had on. Picking her up again, I walked over to the couch and laid her down then started to unbuckle my pants.

I slowly spread her legs then slid my dick in her aggressively while I used my thumb to massage her swollen pearl, causing her to grip my shirt and moan loudly. I had to bite my lip to keep myself from screaming out like a little bitch and bustin' early. Mickey felt good as fuck; tight, wet as hell, and warm just like I remember.

"Come back to me Mick," I kissed her neck. "Bring this pussy back to daddy," I was looking her dead in the eyes with a serious look. She didn't say anything so I pulled out.

"Tone stop playing!" she whined and hit my arm. "Put it back."

"Nah I don't think you want it, do you?" I teased her opening with the tip of my dick and that shit had her squirming like crazy.

"Yes baby I want, give it to me." Chuckling I gripped her thighs, slamming back into her.

"Antonio!" she moaned.

Stepping back, I got her off the couch and turned her around so I could enter her from the back. I felt her pussy muscles tighten up and her legs starting to shake so I pulled out again. A few seconds later I slammed my dick back in her, this time she arched her back deeper just like I wanted her to. Within minutes we were both cumming. "Shit girl," I grunted before smacking her on the ass.

"Fuck!" Mickey groaned loudly. "That shit was crazy."

"But you didn't miss a nigga? Oh please," I laughed.

"Shut the fuck up," she chuckled. "Help me up, I can't move." I picked her up off the couch and she wrapped her legs around my waist on instinct. "I want to sleep now."

"Oh, you got me fucked up. You finally giving some pussy up, I'm getting all this shit. This is an all-night thing baby girl."

"Nooooo," she whined making me laugh while I carried her upstairs. She doesn't even know I'm dead ass serious.

TOI

I tore open the envelope and pulled the paper out. "Y'all ready?" I asked Kayla and Jayla. We were sitting in Kayla's room so I could read them the results of this damn DNA test.

"Yeah just tell us what it says," Kayla answered me.

"Alright," I read the paper then looked up at them. "Well, he's your father."

"For real?" Jayla asked snatching the paper from my hands and reading it herself. "That's crazy, he's our father Kayla."

"Okay," Kayla shrugged.

"That's all you have to say? Kay we finally know who our father is and it's Saint Santana. Do you know how big of a deal that is?"

"We're sixteen Jayla, in two more years we'll be legal. We're damn near grown, what can he do for us now?"

"A lot," I told her. "You two need a father figure so you can realize these little boys out here aint shit. You don't listen when I say it; maybe talking to him will change things."

"Yeah right, it's too late for a father."

"No it's not, like you said you're sixteen not fifty. You can use a father, why are you so upset about this Kayla I don't get it."

"What do you expect me to be? You want me jumping up and down excited about a nigga I don't even know. Who's to say he's going to step up and be in our lives, then on top of that his wife doesn't like our mother.

If she says one thing about my mother while I can hear her I'm throwing something at her head and that's real talk."

"She's not going to say anything about your mother. Stop being so damn scary, Saint is not a deadbeat. You're his daughters, he's going to be there, alright?"

"If you say so," she shrugged. "I'll give it a shot, but he has one time to mess up and he can kick rocks."

"Mean ass," I chuckled. "Come on Jayla." We both got up and walked out of Kayla's room. I walked Jayla down to her room then went downstairs just as Que was coming in the door.

"Hey baby," he said when he saw me.

"Hi," I walked over to him and kissed his lips. "So, you know they're his daughters, right?"

"Yeah I know. I was there when he read the results. He wants them to come by this weekend, I told him I would bring them. Speaking of that, I need to talk to you."

"Talk to me about what?"

"About my family."

"What about them, Que?"

"I need you to tell your mother to cool out when it comes to the hostility with my aunt and before you say anything Saint already said he was going to talk to Beautii."

"What exactly do you want me to tell my mother?"

"I can't have y'all at each other's throats. The situation with Mia and my mother is enough."

"I can't do anything about your mother she doesn't like me over a dumb ass reason. Your sister sent some niggas at me to jump my ass, how does she still have an issue with me? Baby, she's going to take Mia's side regardless and I don't kiss ass. I'm not going to start any drama and I'll try to stay out the issues but that's all I can do," I shrugged my shoulders then made my way to the kitchen with him right behind me.

"That's good enough; I'm going to talk to my mother too. I just don't need y'all going at it."

"We won't go at it. Now please change the subject. What are you doing tonight?"

"Besides you? I don't have anything planned." He laughed.

"You're so damn nasty. You don't have any work to do?"

"Not tonight so you have me all to yourself. What do you want to do?"

"I want to eat, and watch movies. I want it to be just us two, no distractions or disruptions."

"We can do that. I'll get the movies and you get the food together." He kissed my cheek before making his way out the kitchen. I grabbed my phone so I could order all the food and shit we would need for tonight.

"How did you get a bootleg of *Us* so damn fast?" I asked Que once we were settled in the movie room. We had pizza, hot wings, popcorn, candy, soda, and juice. Anything you can get in the movie theater we had here.

"It's not bootleg, it's an exclusive copy. I know people so don't even worry about it."

"What people do you know?"

"You don't need to know all of that. Just know I got connections. Let me put this shit on though." He got up and went to go put the movie on while I started pigging out. I wasn't about to wait for his ass.

"What made you get a theatre in your house?"

"It was big enough plus I don't have to go to the movies I can just come down here. I was looking into some shit and I might just get a multiplex."

"You want to do a movie theatre?"

"Hell yeah, they make a grip and I'm thinking about just buying one. When I figure it out I'll let you know."

"Alright boss man make your moves," I chuckled.

"I'm trying to build some shit I can leave my kids so forth and so on."

"That's understandable. Real question though, do you think it's going to work out between the twins and Saint?"

"I don't know I'm hoping it does."

Kayla

Looking around the living room I was trying to figure out how the hell only two people lived in this big ass house. What was all this space for? I'm convinced rich people just don't know what to do with their money because all of this looked like a waste.

"Do you like the house?" Saint asked Jayla and I after he took us on a tour of his house. I guess it was supposed to be an icebreaker or whatever.

"It's nice, but why do you need so much space if it's just you two? Why not buy a condo or something?" I questioned.

"When we got this house we planned on having a bunch of kids but it didn't work out that way. Beautii can't have any kids," he said.

"That's messed up," Jayla said. "How many kids did you want?"

"I have five older sisters, so I wanted a big family just like I had."

"Well you have two, four are missing," I shrugged. "I'm going to be honest because I really want to know. What was the deal between you and our mother?"

"What do you mean?"

"Were you two in a relationship; was she just something to do? Did she mean anything to you? What was the situation? I'm trying to understand why she wouldn't tell you we were your kids."

"You want the whole story?"

"If you can give us that yeah, it's not like we remember too much about her. We were what, two years old when she died."

"Alright sit down." We all sat on the couch then I turned all of my attention to him.

"I met your mother in high school. All of us went to high school together."

"All of who?"

"It was me, your mother, Geneva, Toi's dad and Beautii. Your mother and I were like two years ahead of your aunt."

"You know Toi's father?" I asked shocked a little bit. Talk about somebody whose unspoken, I've never heard anything about Toi's dad at all.

"Of course I know him, I haven't seen him since he left town but I do know him."

"Alright so what type of person was our mother?" Jayla polled.

"She was funny; she could make anybody laugh doing the goofiest shit. She made straight A's in school; she was doing the damn thing. Your grandparents were real religious and they were a little strict so anytime she got the chance to do something she wasn't supposed to she took it."

"How did she get on drugs?"

"Well we all smoked weed, that wasn't a big deal. It's still not that big of a deal but then for whatever reason she started chasing a bigger high. She went from weed, to coke, and then she ended up on heroin. I don't know who got her on that shit but once she started she didn't stop. The thing about it was she was a functioning addict, you wouldn't know she was on drugs just by looking at her."

"If you cared about her why didn't you try and stop her?"

"The only time I would see Grace is when she needed some money from me then she would just disappear. It was only so much I could do. Your grandparents put her in a program with Geneva but she checked herself out. I put her in a program and actually paid for her to go. When she got out we spent a full two weeks together then she was supposed to go to the doctor or at least that's what she told me. She left to go to the appointment and never came back to me. A couple of months went by then I started hearing rumors about her being pregnant and Beautii automatically assumed she was pregnant by me. I didn't deny you two and I wasn't going to until I spoke to Grace. The next time I saw her she was about eight months pregnant with you two."

Really?"

"Yeah, I asked her if she was pregnant by me and she said no. She said if you were my kids she would've told me. Obviously she was lying to me because you two are mine. From what Geneva told me she never said anything because even though she didn't like Beautii she knew it would kill her to know she couldn't give me a baby, but Grace could."

"So how did you end up figuring out we were yours?" Jayla asked him.

"She ran into Geneva at the store and saw you two. It didn't take too long for her to put everything together and she told me about it, now here we are."

"I have one more question," I said. "Obviously you were the big man around. I know my mother wasn't the only woman you cheated on your wife with right?"

"You're right it was a lot of women."

"Alright so why is it that she's so damn bitter with our mother but not bitter with you? What was it about my mother that she's so bothered by if she didn't let any other chick get to her?"

"That's a difficult question." He shook his head.

"Is it because deep down she knows if my mother wasn't on drugs you would be with her or were y'all not that serious?"

"Nah we were serious but I couldn't really make your mother a permanent fixture in my life. She was on drugs and she wasn't trying to get better."

"So to put it simple what you're saying is you couldn't turn a junkie into a housewife so you picked Beautii because she had her shit together and not because you love her."

"Kayla!" Jayla snapped at me.

"What? I'm trying to understand what the problem is? If we're going to be around him we have to be around her too. I'll be damned if she treats me any kind of way just because she's still jealous of our mother. She died fourteen fucking years ago it's time to get over it."

"Calm down alright," Saint chuckled. "You really are your mother's child you sound just like her. It's kind of scary."

"I'll take that as a compliment."

"You should. Let me tell you something, I love my wife. I do, I love her with all my heart, but I would be lying sitting here telling you I didn't love your mother too. I'm sorry shit had to go the way that it did but there is nothing I can do about it now. The only thing I can do is be a father to you now. As far as Beautii goes I'm going to make sure she doesn't treat you any kind of way."

"How can you be so sure?"

"I know my wife and we've talked about this. Once all the awkwardness is gone I think you'll get along with her. I need you two to be nice too, no attitude…Kayla."

"Why is it me?" I asked him.

"I can tell you're just like your mother so I feel like you're the one to really watch out for. I'm trying to make this work so just give it a shot."

"Fine, I'll be nice to her as long as she's nice to me."

"That's all I'm asking. Well, now that you've seen the house I want you two to feel like y'all can come over here anytime you want. So how about I take you shopping so that you have clothes here."

"Really?" Jayla and I said at the same time.

"Yes really," he chuckled. "Come on." We all got up off the couch then made our way to the garage.

I don't know how this having a father shit works but I'm willing to at least try it out. Hopefully him and his wife don't fuck it up for me. I'm not really the forgiving type.

LEGEND

"So how is the baby supposed to come out?" Diamond asked Toi while we were in the car. We went to Toi's check-up and because I had Diamond for the weekend we decided to bring her with us. From the time we told her Toi was having a baby she's been hitting us with question after question.

"The doctor has to get the baby out," Toi answered. "But the baby has to be in my belly for a little while."

"How long?"

"Almost six months and they'll be here."

"I hope it's a girl, I want a sister daddy." Diamond told me.

"I hear you baby girl," I chuckled. "Baby, you want to go home or are you riding with me to drop her off to my mother?"

"I'll ride with you. I'm not getting out the car though." She shrugged then looked out the window.

"Que."

"What?"

"What is this black truck following us?"

"What are you talking about?"

"It's a black truck following us." Looking into my rearview mirror I sucked my teeth. "Who is that?"

"Does Diamond have her headphones and stuff on?" She looked in the backseat.

"Yeah she has her iPad on. Now who is that?"

"Feds."

"Feds? Why the fuck are the Feds following you?"

"Is that a serious question?"

"Oh my God, Que are you going to jail?"

"Shut up," I glared at her. I could tell by the look on her face she was irritated, hell I was irritated too but right now wasn't the time to discuss this shit. I wouldn't be surprised if these niggas put a bug in my car.

When we pulled up in front of my mother's house I parked and looked at her. "We'll talk about it later alright, you know we can't discuss too much. I don't know if they got a bug in my car or not."

"So we'll talk when we get in the house."

"We can't talk there either."

"What the fuck?" She shook her head. "You know what Que? Just go do you so we can get the fuck out of here."

"Diamond baby girl come on," I looked at the backseat at her.

"Okay, bye Toi see you next week."

"It's see you later baby D, but okay." Diamond leaned up front and kissed Toi on the cheek. "Be good."

"I am."

"I'll be right back."

After getting Diamond inside my mother's house Toi and I left. Since I didn't want to talk in the house I decided we would stop and get something to eat. As soon as we got out of the car she leaned up against the door with her arms crossed and face frowned up. Here we fuckin go.

TOI

"Stop looking at me like that, fix your face," Que said in a stern tone that let me know he was dead serious, so I let some of the anger out of my face just a little bit. "What do you want to know?"

"Why the feds are all of a sudden following you, why they would bug your damn car and our house. What the fuck is going on?"

"Alright, do you remember Mickey's birthday?"

"Yeah I remember so what about it?"

"Alright so you know what happened to Brick and Kareem that night. Somebody obviously cares about and loves those niggas because it was missing person reports put on both of them."

"What does that have to do with you? You didn't do anything to either of them."

"The police got told that they went missing after attending my club so now they think I have something to do with it."

"Why? That's too big of an assumption."

"It was known whose party was being thrown at my club. Being that they know Brick is Mickey's baby father, and Kareem was already wanted for killing Mickey's cousin they questioned her about them two going missing but she told them she didn't know anything. You would think they would just leave it alone right? No, they connected Mickey to you and you to me so they're trying to put that shit on me."

"So because Mickey is my friend they think you got rid of those niggas as a favor to her?"

"Exactly, but they can't put that shit on me because there are no bodies left. So they're following me and keeping tabs on my ass waiting to get something they can take me down for."

I ran my hand down my face then sighed looking at him. "Why didn't you tell me this before?"

"You're pregnant and I don't want you worrying about that dumb shit. I'm good I just have to be on my shit at all times like I've been doing for years. Don't even stress about this shit I'm fine."

"Yes you're fine now but what if they find some shit on you or something? What about us?"

"They would still need someone to testify against me and nobody is dumb enough to do that, alright?" He grabbed my arm and pulled me into his chest. "I'm not leaving you or being taken away from you or my kids."

"Promise me right now you're not going anywhere."

"I promise." Que kissed me on the forehead then hugged me tight.

I didn't bother to say anything else; I'm just going to trust him on this shit even though I had this nervous feeling in the pit of my stomach. Usually when Que promises me something I'm good and let whatever the issue is go, but something about that promise didn't seem too secure to me.

EPILOGUE

One Year Later
Legend

"You're the reason she's spoiled as hell. Put her down that's why we have a swing smart one." Toi came over to me and took my baby girl from my arms.

"You need to stop interrupting my bonding time with my daughter," I told her while she put the baby in her swing.

"Bond while she's in that swing. I don't need a baby that will never want to walk or sit down without somebody holding her. Not happening. Why aren't you dressed? We have to go in a little bit. Diamond is already dressed and in her room, we're waiting on you."

"I don't see how you don't have separation anxiety, aren't all first mothers supposed to be attached to their child?"

"Yes and I am attached to her but I need to get out of this house before I lose my damn mind. My life has revolved around her for the last six months, I need a small break. Now go finish getting dressed. My mama is coming to get her so she can baby sit." Toi pushed me out of the living room.

Shaking my head I went upstairs so I could finish getting ready. Today we were finally getting out of this house. It was a nine year olds birthday party but hell it's better than nothing. For the past six months our lives have been all about our newest edition to the family.

Jurnee Anais Montega was born on March 2, 2019 at 3: 42 A.M. A time and date I will never forget in my damn life. Toi was in labor for 23 hours and she was evil as fuck the whole damn time. Her tough ass turned down the epidural talking about she didn't want the baby to come in the world high, she thought she would be able to take the pain but boy was she wrong.

By the time she wanted them to give it to her it was too late so she ended up feeling everything her whole labor and that's what she gets for thinking she could handle the shit. I told her to get the epidural, I got told to shut the fuck up. Her mother, Mickey and Taj told her ass to get the epidural but she still didn't want to listen.

Even though she was mean as hell to me the entire time she was in labor, watching her give birth to my daughter made me love her ass even more. My respect for Isyss even went up some; even though she's an asshole and barely knows how to act she still gave me my first child. The only thing I regret is missing Diamond being born; I have a whole new respect for women after seeing that shit up close and in person.

"Quentin! Let's go!" Toi shouted from downstairs just as I was putting my sweatshirt over my head. When I was done getting ready she and Diamond were waiting. "Ma we're leaving!" She shouted again and Geneva came walking out of the living room holding Jurnee. "Mama, put her down why do you and this ding bat keep picking her up every five minutes?"

"She's my grand baby and I will pick her up as much as I want. When is Frik and Frak coming home?" she asked referring to Kayla and Jayla.

"They're with Saint all weekend so they won't be back until tomorrow night. You're by yourself, are you good with that?"

"Yeah I'll be fine. Tell Myles I said happy birthday."

"I will, I'll call you when we get there."

"Alright I know, go ahead." When she walked back in the living room all three of us went outside and got in the car.

"Look at the picture I posted of Jurnee." Toi gave me her phone with her Instagram app open. I looked at the picture and laughed. Jurnee has the same pretty brown complexion Toi has along with a head full of jet-black hair. I already know she's going to look just like her mama when she gets older.

"Why you got her hair looking like a pixie cut?"

She laughed. "Man I had to brush it somewhere she has a lot of it. I'm glad my baby isn't bald-headed but damn that's going to be annoying in a few years."

"You'll be alright. Toi, you know your mother needs some friends, right?" I told her after I pulled out of the driveway.

"No she doesn't. My mama is fine."

"Do you think she wants to sit in the house all damn day? No she wants to go out and have a good time."

"Well who is she supposed to hang out with? Any friends she had are still in the streets so that's not happening and I don't know any women her age besides your aunts and they don't like my mother because of Beautii. Hell they don't even like me."

"Wrong, nobody has an issue with you besides my mother and that's because of Mia."

"Which is stupid; it's been too damn long. Mia's dumb ass doesn't even live up here anymore, she's down in Atlanta giving other people hell and your mother still has a problem."

"I know but it's whatever. My aunt Stacy asks about you all the time."

"She's the youngest one right?"

"Yeah, she's around the same age as your mother. This is what we can do, they all want to see Jurnee so we can have dinner at the house and invite them over."

"I don't know about all of that."

"Why not?"

"Your mother does not like me, hell we just discussed this."

"Y'all need to talk and get that shit straightened out anyway. We should invite Beautii and Saint too."

"I don't have a problem with Saint but Beautii? Nah," she shook her head.

Despite the good relationship the twins built with Beautii and Saint, there's still tension between her, Toi, and Geneva. I've tried to get it straight, but it doesn't work. Thankfully Beautii treats Kayla and Jayla like she has some sense or shit would be way worse.

Laughing I shook my head. "I say we go for it, what's the worst that can happen?"

"Somebody can get beat the fuck up and have their tracks on the floor. I don't feel like doing that, I don't want that negativity in our house."

"Toi," I glanced her way.

"What?" She sucked her teeth. "Fine we can have this damn dinner."

"Alright, next weekend it's on."

EPILOGUE

MICKEY

"Ma," Myles called for me when he came downstairs to the living room where I was packaging some makeup orders. After thinking it over and going back to change some ideas I decided to start my online business selling makeup first and business was booming for me.

My makeup line Material Girl, was doing very well and we were only in our first five months. My matte lipsticks and lip-glosses that came in a bunch of different colors were a hit with the people. It kept me busy as hell but I'm paid like shit so I'm grateful.

"What Myles?" I looked at him.

"Can I go play with Marcus?" he asked referring to the little boy that lived in the house next door.

"Go ahead, and you better not act up over there. I'll be asking Sheila what you two are doing." As soon as I said that he grabbed his hoodie and ran out the front door.

"Aye Mick," Tone called my name while he was coming downstairs.

"What?"

"Are you cooking tonight?"

"Nope, I really wasn't planning on it."

"Alright so we're going out tonight then. I just needed to know that. You want to call your girls to come too or nah?"

"I spoke to both of them earlier. Taj said Mecca and Naima both have a cold so she's taking care of them and Toi has that dinner shit at her house tonight with her mother or whatever."

"Oh yeah I forgot about that shit. We need to go over there, that's going to be some good drama."

"No nosey ass, let them handle their business."

"Fine," he chuckled. "You see yourself where Toi is?"

"What do you mean?"

"I mean she has her business, they have their baby, the house and all of that."

"We have a house Tone, look around you."

"This is your house and we don't own this shit," he countered back. Nine months ago Tone moved in with me and Myles and it's been great having him here. Myles loves him and as far as their both concerned, they're father and son.

"You know what I mean babe but to answer your question I don't want what Toi has. I want my own life but I get what you're saying though. Do you want kids?"

"I mean, at some point yeah. I'm not getting any younger so if I have some I want them when I can actually deal with them."

"Does that mean it has to be now? I'm just now starting my business and to be honest I want you in some legit shit before I even think about giving you a kid."

"What do you mean by that?"

"You need to clean your money up."

"Who said my money wasn't clean?" he laughed. "Let me let you in on something ma, I'm not stupid. I have enough common sense to know that I need to have legit businesses. I own three car washes, two apartment buildings, four gas stations, and two supermarkets in Jersey. Trust me when I say my money is definitely clean. I don't plan on doing this shit forever. I got about another year in this shit then I'm done."

"Well damn why didn't you ever tell me?"

"You never asked," Tone continued. "Besides I plan on being with you for the rest of my life so you were going to find out anyway."

"Damn," I shook my head. I was surprised at all the things Tone said he had in place just because the nigga never opened his mouth and said anything about it. At least I know I'm not with a dummy. "I have another question though."

"What's up?"

"If you plan on spending the rest of your life with me, where is my ring?"

"I didn't get that yet but you'll be seeing that shit soon. I already know what's happening with us, you're going to be my wife. You're going to give me a child and you're never getting away from me again."

"Oh so you're just so damn sure huh?"

"Hell yeah, and you need to make up your mind about where you want to live. I told you once this lease is up we're out of here. I've seen a few nice houses in Scarsdale, you know Barry up that way."

"New York?"

"Yeah, why not?"

"I'm a Jersey girl, I don't know plus I'll feel bad leaving Taj in Jersey by herself."

"From what Yung told me he wanted to get them a house out there too but she doesn't want to leave her parents' house. She'll probably change her mind though; I know she doesn't want to raise Mecca around that shit."

"You're probably right but I say we go wherever the best house is," I shrugged.

"We have time to figure it out but you need to get over this not leaving Jersey shit. Fuck that though, back to tonight. We're going to go eat, might even see a movie. Be on some family shit tonight for real." He joked.

"Yeah alright," I laughed.

I was glad to have Tone back in my life and on a good note again. When he first broke up with me I was really on some fuck him shit, just because of the way we ended. He dumped me and it really got to me because I didn't think the shit was fair. I'm usually not into relationship remixes. You become my ex for a reason but with Tone it was different. I love him more than I've ever loved any other man, my son loves him and he loves the both of us so why shouldn't I do what's not only best for Myles but what's best for myself and give a good man a second chance?

He came over to me and kissed me on the cheek. "You know I love you right?"

"Yes I know," I smiled.

"Good," he kissed me on the lips and just as he was about to put his arms around me his phone started going off. "Hold up." Reaching into his pocket, he pulled his phone out and answered it. "What's up? Wait what the fuck you just say?" His face went serious. "Are you sure? Fuck man, alright I'm on my way down there right now. Tell that nigga do not spazz the fuck out and give those niggas a reason to do some bullshit. Alright," he hung up the phone then grabbed his keys off the coffee table.

"What happened? What's wrong?"

"Some shit is going down with Que. I'll be back after I try and handle this shit."

"What went down with him? What's going on Tone?"

"I don't know exactly but when I figure it out I'll call you. You might need to call Toi in a few is all I'm saying. I'll be right back." He kissed me on the cheek again then left out the front door.

What the fuck is going on?

EPILOGUE

TOI

"I can't believe you're about to have me in here with these people. Toi, I understand wanting peace and all of that, but this is not a good idea," my mother said while we put the finishing touches on the food. Que's family already showed up and were in the dining room waiting to eat dinner.

"I don't like the idea too much either but it's already done, they're coming over. Just ignore anything ignorant that might come out of their mouths. I don't want you fighting anybody, and no offense but you're a little bit too old for that."

"I'm not going to fight those hookers. I just don't feel like being bothered, but I love Que, so I'll at least try to deal with them the right way."

"Thank you very much. I gotta go get Jurnee, I'll be right back down so we can go in there with the evil ones," I went upstairs and got Jurnee ready to be around the other side of her family before heading back downstairs. I went into the dining room and put Jurnee in her high chair then sat next to my mother.

"Where is my son?" Maria asked and I shrugged my shoulders.

"I don't know, he said he was on his way when I talked to him. That was like twenty minutes ago. He should be here soon," I answered her.

"Toi she is so beautiful," Stacy said to me.

"Thank you," I smiled.

"She is very beautiful. She doesn't really look like us too much. Toi you have some very strong genes," Maria said. "Diamond looks like our family."

"Your family doesn't look all that much alike. Your sisters are all brown skin; you're the only light one. What's your point?" I noted.

"My father was their complexion if you must know. I look like my mother."

"Alright then and my daughter looks like me, again what is your point?" I was trying to keep calm with this woman but right now she is trying it. Que needs to hurry up so he can come get his damn mother.

"Um, this food is really good. You two did a good job," Saint said in an attempt to ease the tension.

"Thanks Saint," I said to him. We all ate in silence for a few minutes before Beautii finally decided to speak up.

"Toi, you know the twins have been spending a lot of time at our house. They're adjusting well."

"They told me, it's good y'all are all getting along. That makes things a whole lot easier. Why didn't y'all bring them back? They were supposed to come back today."

"Oh yeah they wanted to stay another night. We thought it would be alright since school is closed Monday."

"It's fine with me, next time they do that tell them to call and let me know though."

"Right," she nodded. "Well I think that Saint has been doing very well with them. He's talking to them about boys and all of that. They need that father figure in their lives. I know the three of you were raised by your grandmother right?"

"Yeah," I looked at her to see where she was going with this conversation.

"I think the right guidance is necessary for them right now."

"You're right about that."

"I'm glad you agree because Saint and I were talking about it and I think they should stay with us for good."

I stopped eating then looked at my mother who was chuckling and shaking her head. I then turned my attention back to Beautii. "You mean as in move in and live with you? Like they would be living at your house?"

"That's exactly what I mean. I think it would be best for them."

"Hold up," I laughed. "Let me make sure I understand. You want them to move away from me, the person who's taken care of them for the last almost ten years to move in with you. Some people they've only known for a year?"

"Just met or not he's their father Toi," Beautii argued back.

"I know he's their father but so the fuck what."

"What do you mean so what? They need their father."

"Need him for what? They're 17 years old not five, they're damn near grown." Now I was getting heated. She's really lost her damn mind.

"Listen Toi," Saint interrupted Beautii. "I'm not trying to take them from you. It was just something we talked about. If you're not okay with it, we'll keep the arrangement we have now. It's not even deep, alright?"

"No Saint," Beautii told him. "You want your daughters to come live with us and that's the best decision for them. They need stable people around them. Not a drug addict."

"Alright I knew that shit was coming." My mother put her fork down. "You really want to go there with me Beautii?"

"What did I say that was wrong? Are you not a drug addict?"

"I was a drug addict bitch yes, what the fuck does that have to do with you or the twins?"

"You're not the kind of example they need. They need stability, they need solid parents."

"Excuse me Beautii but you're not their parent so what the fuck are you talking about? I agree they need a father figure, Saint is it. He's their father and he's been doing great with them so far but let's not get ahead of ourselves here. You're not their mother they have one already," my mother argued back.

"Alright! Alright! Calm down, mama stop please," I told her then looked at Beautii. "My cousins are not moving away from me until they go off to college. They're 17 years old and they'll be graduating in June. I'm sorry you didn't know about them but they're damn near grown now. What kind of stability can you give them that I haven't? They were in church every single fucking Sunday up until my grandmother passed.

They do some out of the way shit but they've never earned less than a B and that's because I was up with them helping with their homework whenever they needed it. They can cook because of me and my grandmother, they know how to clean up after themselves because of us and despite the fact that they're a little boy crazy, they know how to value and respect themselves because I taught them how to keep their fucking legs closed."

"Toi I'm not trying to insult you."

"You just did though; don't ever talk about taking my family away from me, alright? That's the quickest way to get your ass told the fuck off. Beautii I've always respected you, even when you flipped on me I didn't come at your neck but my family comes before any and everybody. I don't play when it comes to my blood. Instead of judging my household you need to figure out a way to get your business back on track. The last time I checked, Taj has most of your old staff working for her and 95% of the clientele your stank ass attitude ran off. I know hearing the word Beauty Boss pisses you off to your core, focus on that shit and not me."

"I'm trying to figure out why you're so angry," Maria said, and I looked at her like she was stupid. "She's ready to give your cousins a solid family unit and you're trying to block that. Why? Are you jealous that it's something you never had?"

"You know what," I chuckled while sitting back in my chair. "I'm sick of your wanna be bougie ass."

"Excuse me?"

"You can be excused after I read your ass. Let me tell you something, I'm not jealous of anything. I don't have anything to be jealous first of all. A solid family unit? Two teenage girls living with the father they never knew and a step mother that hates their biological mother is a solid family unit? No it's not, so shut the fuck up with that."

"I know you're not talking to me like that."

"I am and what? What are you going to do? Tell Que? Or are you going to tell your daughter to plot with his baby mother again and get me jumped? I don't give a fuck what you do. I'll tell you what I'm going to do. I'm going to take my daughter upstairs then show you the front fucking door so you can get the fuck out and you won't be welcomed or allowed back until you learn how to stop being disrespectful to me."

"Hold on, I think we all need to calm down. This is getting to be too much," Stacy said.

"No I'm tired of trying with people. I'm not about to bend over backwards for your family to like or accept me. I really couldn't give a fuck about if you do or don't. I have twenty four fucking years of me. I'm not about to sit here and let a bitch that barely knows my ass be disrespectful while she's at my damn table. The only reason you don't like me is because of that hoe ass bitch you raise, and she can't stand me because she can't beat or be me the bitch is bitter tell her I said kiss my ass too," I stood up from the table.

"Toi calm down," my mother told me.

"Nah fuck this and fuck her too she can get the fuck out my house. The only reason it's words being exchanged and not blows is because that's my niggas mother and I will never put my hands on my elders. Plus, I don't trust these bitches to not jump me her daughter learned the punk ass shit from somewhere."

"I'm gone, she can get the fuck outta here, you're not about to cuss me out like I'm your age. Little girl you remember this shit when you need something," Maria said while getting up from the table.

"I won't ever need anything from you. My grandmother will rise from her grave before I ask your ass for anything ma believe that! Get the fuck out my house!"

We basically exchanged words and argued the whole time she was leaving my house along with Beautii's ass. It's sad because I respected Beautii so much but she's tried it one too many times I don't play this disrespectful shit. I don't give a fuck who you are.

I was so caught up in getting these muthafuckas out of my house I didn't even realize my mother was pushing the phone in my face. I took it from her then went in the kitchen.

"Who the fuck is this?" I asked. I know it was rude the person on the phone didn't do shit to deserve that rudeness but fuck it I was pissed off.

"Is this La'Toia Henderson?" a deep voiced asked me.

"Yes this is her, who is this?"

"This is Terry Bailey; I'm Mr. Santana's lawyer."

"Okay, why are you calling me? He's not here."

"No I know he's not and I know why he's not. Mr. Santana asked a Mr. Montega to tell me to call you."

"Antonio Montega?"

"Yes."

"Alright, what's going on? Why couldn't he call me?'"

"Mr. Santana was arrested earlier this evening."

"Arrested? The fuck for what? What happened?" I could hear my voice go up an octave when I spoke. Right now, my heart was starting to race, and the craziest thoughts were running through my head. I couldn't be hearing this shit right now.

"I can't discuss all the details over the phone, all I can say it involves two guns he had on his person and right now I'm trying to see if I can get a bail but Ms. Henderson these are charges that can put him away for a lot of years."

"Years? What exactly are you talking about right now?"

"He can be looking at ten years or more if they convict him of these charges. Now-" As soon as he said ten plus years, I didn't hear anything else because the phone immediately dropped from my hands and onto the kitchen floor.

"Toi?" My mother came into the kitchen and looked at me. "What's wrong with you? What happened? Who was that?"

"Que," my voice cracked.

"Que what? Is he alright what happened?" I couldn't tell her what his lawyer just told me because I started blubbering and crying like a damn baby. I could see the confused look on her face but she just hugged me while I continued to act like a damn child.

Ten years or more just kept replaying in my head over and over again. We just had a baby six months ago. What am I supposed to do without him for ten years or more?

To Be Continued in My Love His Loyalty

UNEDITED SNEAK PEEK!

MY LOVE HIS LOYALTY

Under the impression she was trying to make a better life for her children, Chanel let her fiancé convince her that living in Miami was the best decision for their family. Ten years later, she's tired of raising her kids by herself so she decides to relocate back to New Jersey so they can finally have a complete family. When Chanel finds out making money wasn't Barry's only reason for keeping her in another city, she begins to realize her love runs deeper than his loyalty.

With a brand new baby and a legal case pending Toi and Quentin's relationship is put to the test. She's prepared to hold him down but when she realizes what that entails, she learns that being the wife of a street legend isn't all it's cracked up to be,

INTRODUCTION

CHANEL SAMUELS

Walking down the hallway I checked in both BJ and Cayden's bedrooms making sure they were asleep. Lord knows I was grateful to have a little time to myself. Most of my day consists of running behind those two like a mad woman.

Making my way downstairs I made sure all my doors were locked then got myself a glass of wine. I went back upstairs to my bedroom, grabbed the blunt I already had rolled and went out on my balcony taking a seat. My eyes scanned over my luxurious backyard as I lit the end of my blunt.

I love my house; it's five thousand square feet of beauty and I'm going to miss it. As much as I don't want to leave my home, I have to so my family can be together in the right way.

Here I am in Miami, Florida living in a $900,000 home, three cars in the garage, a closet full of top of the line designer clothes and money at my fingertips. You would think I would be happier than hell but I'm not. The only thing that puts a smile on my face is my kids. I'm grateful that we are well taken care of but I'm tired of doing everything by myself.

Somehow I let my fiancé, if you can call him that, Brandon convince me to move down here from New Jersey. Our oldest son BJ was two years old at the time and he hit me with, it's a risk to be in the city while he was still coming up in the game.

INTRODUCTION

He comes down here for a couple of days every month and we talk most days but that's not enough for me anymore. I'm not about to keep living in a different state than the man I'm supposed to be marrying. He can miss me with all that it's dangerous bullshit. At this point the nigga could hire security if he wants to, it's not like he can't afford that shit.

Brandon used to sell weed here and there when we were in high school, but he wasn't really in the streets like that to my knowledge. It wasn't until I got pregnant when we were 18 that he got deeper into it. He was already friends with Legend Santana in high school and once they started running the streets together shit got real.

He felt like at that point he had a family to take care and getting that money was his only way of making it happen. Over the years he worked he continued to work with Legend and now they're all on top of the world. Since he was working his ass off to provide for us I didn't complain about our living arrangements. I kept quiet on that particular issue because I didn't want for anything.

Now ten years and another son later nothing but our bank accounts have changed. I'm down here with two kids while he's up in Jersey doing only God know what. Brandon comes down for a few days every month and we talk most days but that's a wrap. I can't keep doing everything by my damn self.

BJ is 12 and feeling himself. He's at that age where he thinks he's grown enough to start talking back and shit. Cayden is 8 years old, and he's constantly asking for his father so that's what he's about to get on the daily basis. I didn't lie down and get myself pregnant so I'm done raising them like I did.

Of course Brandon doesn't want me to come back. He claims shit is too crazy but I know that's complete bullshit. He just wants to keep doing him without hearing my mouth about it. I'm not stupid, I'm far from it; I know he's up there living like he's single. That's what niggas do when they have the freedom to live a lie but it's a wrap once I get back. I'll be damned if he does anything scandalous when I'm close enough to shoot his ass.

Playtime is over.

My name is Mollysha Johnson and I'm from Jersey City, New Jersey. Growing up language arts/english has always been my best subject. I've always loved reading and writing. Once I got my hands on my first urban fiction novel I was hooked to the genre. I admire and look up to authors like Wahida Clark, Keisha Ervin, Danielle Santiago and many more.

Writing is how I express my creativity and I love putting my all into it.

STAY CONNECTED:

Email: mollyshaj92@gmail.com

facebook.com/MollyshaJohnson

instagram.com/mollysha92

CPSIA information can be obtained
at www.ICGtesting.com
Printed in the USA
LVHW031823230419
615253LV00003B/483

9 781093 234701